FAB

LORDS OF THE RISING SUN

Dave Morris and Jamie Thomson

Illustrated by Russ Nicholson
Cover painting by Kevin Jenkins

Fabled Lands Publishing

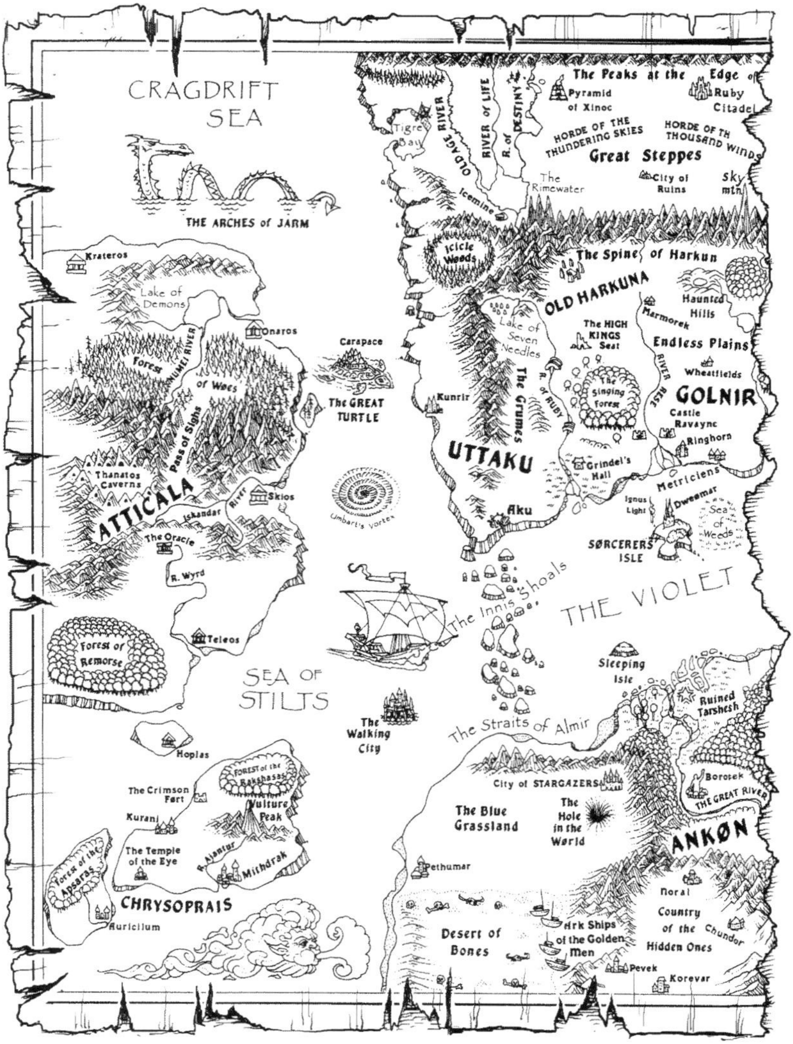

CRAGDRIFT SEA
THE ARCHES of JARM
Tigre Bay
OLD AGE RIVER
RIVER of LIFE
R. of DESTINY
The Peaks at the Edge of
Pyramid of Xinoc
Ruby Citadel
HORDE OF THE THUNDERING SKIES
HORDE OF THE THOUSAND WINDS
Great Steppes
The Rimewater
City of Ruins
Sky mtn.
Icemine
Icicle Woods
The Spine of Harkun
OLD HARKUNA
Haunted Hills
Marmorek
Lake of Seven Needles
The HIGH KINGS Seat
Endless Plains
Wheatfields
The Singing Forest
R. of RUBY
The Grumes
RIVER RESE
GOLNIR
Castle Ravayne
Ringhorn
Krateros
Lake of Demons
Onaros
NUMEI RIVER
Forest of Woes
Carapace
The GREAT TURTLE
Kunrir
Pass of Sighs
Thanatos Caverns
ATTICALA
Iskandar River
Skios
Umbart's Vortex
UTTAKU
Grindel's Hall
Metriciens
Aku
Ignus Light
Dweomar
Sea of Weeds
SØRCERERS ISLE
The Oracle
R. Wyrd
The Innis Shoals
THE VIOLET
Teleos
Forest of Remorse
SEA OF STILTS
Sleeping Isle
Ruined Tarshesh
The Walking City
The Straits of Almir
Hoplas
FOREST of the Rakshasas
The Crimson Fort
Kurani
Vulture Peak
City of STARGAZERS
Borotek
THE GREAT RIVER
The Blue Grassland
The Hole in the World
ANKØN
The Temple of the Eye
R. Ajantur
Mithdrak
Forest of the Apsaras
Pethumar
Noral
CHRYSOPRAIS
Auricilum
Desert of Bones
Ark Ships of the Golden Men
Country of the Hidden Ones
Chundor
Pevek
Korevar

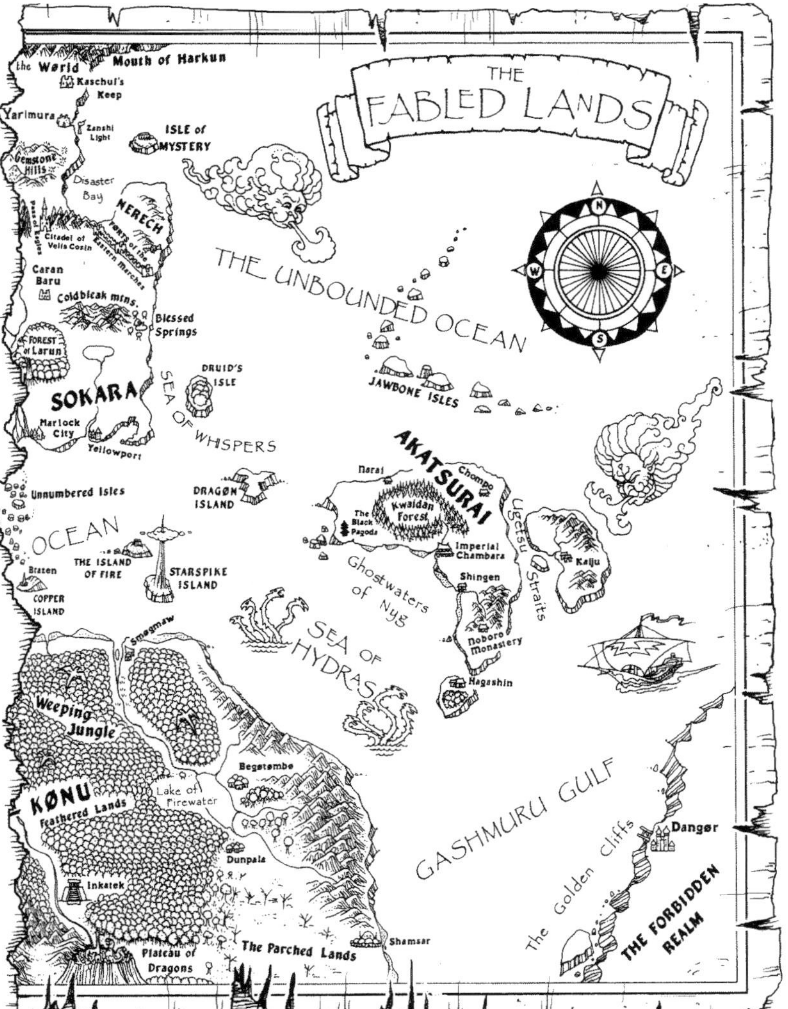
THE FABLED LANDS
the World
Mouth of Harkun
Kaschul's Keep
Yarimura
Zanshi Light
ISLE of MYSTERY
Gemstone Hills
Disaster Bay
NERECH
Pass of Eagles
Citadel of Velis Corin
Forts of the Eastern Marches
Caran Baru
Coldbleak mtns.
Blessed Springs
FOREST of Larun
SOKARA
Marlock City
Yellowport
DRUID'S ISLE
SEA OF WHISPERS
THE UNBOUNDED OCEAN
JAWBONE ISLES
AKATSURAI
Narai
Chompo
Kwaidan Forest
The Black Pagoda
Imperial Chambara
Shingen
Ugetsu Straits
Kaiju
Unnumbered Isles
DRAGON ISLAND
OCEAN
THE ISLAND OF FIRE
STARSPIKE ISLAND
Brazen
COPPER ISLAND
Ghostwaters of Nyg
SEA OF HYDRAS
Noboro Monastery
Hagashin
Smogmaw
Weeping Jungle
Begotombo
KONU
Feathered Lands
Lake of Firewater
Dunpala
Inkatek
GASHMURU GULF
The Golden Cliffs
Dangor
THE FORBIDDEN REALM
Shamsar
Plateau of Dragons
The Parched Lands

First published 1996 by Macmillan Publishers Ltd

[FL logo]

This edition published 2012 by Fabled Lands Publishing,
an imprint of Fabled Lands LLP

ISBN 13: 978-1478377108

Text copyright © 1996, 2012 Dave Morris and Jamie Thomson
Illustrations copyright © 1996 Russ Nicholson
Cover painting copyright © 1996 Kevin Jenkins

The right of Dave Morris and Jamie Thomson to be identified as the authors of this work has been asserted by them in accordance with the Copyright, Designs and Patents Act 1988.

All rights reserved. No reproduction, copy, adaptation or transmission of this work may be made in any form without the written permission of the publisher. Any person who violates the Copyright Act in regard to this publication may be liable to criminal prosecution and civil claims for damages.

Adventuring in the
Fabled Lands

Fabled Lands is unlike any other gamebook series. The reason is that you can play the books in any order, coming back to earlier books whenever you wish. You need only one book to start, but by collecting other books in the series you can explore more of this rich fantasy world. Instead of just one single storyline, there are virtually unlimited adventures to be had in the Fabled Lands. All you need is two dice, an eraser and a pencil.

If you have already adventured using other books in the series, you will know your entry point into this book. Turn to that section now.

If this is your first Fabled Lands book, read the rest of the rules before starting at section 1. You will keep the same adventuring persona throughout the books – starting out at 6th Rank in *Lords of the Rising Sun*, and gaining in power, wealth and experience throughout the series.

ABILITIES

You have six abilities. Your initial score in each ability ranges from 1 (low ability) to 8 (a high level of ability). Ability scores will change during your adventure but can never be lower than 1 or higher than 12.

CHARISMA	the knack of befriending people
COMBAT	the skill of fighting
MAGIC	the art of casting spells
SANCTITY	the gift of divine power and wisdom
SCOUTING	the techniques of tracking and wilderness lore
THIEVERY	the talent for stealth and lock picking

PROFESSIONS

Not all adventurers are good at everything. Everyone has some strengths and some weaknesses. Your choice of profession determines your initial scores in the six abilities.

- **Priest:**
  Charisma 6, Combat 4, Magic 5,
  Sanctity 8, Scouting 6, Thievery 2
- **Mage:**
  Charisma 4, Combat 4, Magic 8,
  Sanctity 1, Scouting 7, Thievery 5
- **Rogue:**
  Charisma 7, Combat 6, Magic 6,
  Sanctity 2, Scouting 4, Thievery 8
- **Troubadour:**
  Charisma 8, Combat 5, Magic 5,
  Sanctity 5, Scouting 4, Thievery 6
- **Warrior:**
  Charisma 5, Combat 8, Magic 3,
  Sanctity 6, Scouting 5, Thievery 3
- **Wayfarer:**
  Charisma 4, Combat 7, Magic 4,
  Sanctity 4, Scouting 8, Thievery 6

Fill in the Adventure Sheet at the back of the book with your choice of profession and the ability scores given for that profession.

STAMINA

Stamina is lost when you get hurt. Keep track of your Stamina score throughout your travels and adventures. You must guard against your Stamina score dropping to zero, because if it does you are dead.

Lost Stamina can be recovered by various means, but your Stamina cannot go above its initial score until you advance in Rank.

You start with 27 Stamina points. Record your Stamina in pencil on the Adventure Sheet.

RANK

You start at 5th Rank, so note this on the Adventure Sheet now. By completing quests and overcoming enemies, you will have the chance to go up in Rank.

You will be told during the course of your adventures when you are entitled to advance in Rank. Characters of higher Rank are tougher, luckier and generally better able to deal with trouble.

Rank	Title
1st	Outcast
2nd	Commoner
3rd	Guildmember
4th	Master/Mistress
5th	Gentleman/Lady
6th	Baron/Baroness
7th	Count/Countess
8th	Earl/Viscountess
9th	Marquis/Marchioness
10th	Duke/Duchess

POSSESSIONS

You can carry up to 12 possessions on your person. All characters begin with 65 Shards in cash and the following possessions, which you can record on your Adventure Sheet: **sword** and **chain mail (Defence +3)**.

Possessions are always marked in bold text, like this: **gold compass**. Anything marked in this way is an item which can be picked up and added to your list of possessions.

Remember that you are limited to carrying a total of 12 items, so if you get more than this you'll have to cross something off your Adventure Sheet or find somewhere to store extra items. You can carry unlimited sums of money.

DEFENCE

Your Defence score is equal to:
  your COMBAT score
  plus your Rank
  plus the bonus for the armour you're wearing (if any).

Every suit of armour you find will have a Defence bonus listed for it. The higher the bonus, the better the armour. You can carry several suits of armour if you wish – but because you can wear only one at a time, you only get the Defence bonus of the best armour you are carrying.

Write your Defence score on the Adventure Sheet now. To start with it is just your COMBAT score plus 6 (because you are 6th Rank and have no armour). Remember to update it if you get some armour or increase in Rank or COMBAT ability.

FIGHTING

When fighting an enemy, roll two dice and add your COMBAT score. You need to roll higher than the enemy's Defence. The amount you roll above the enemy's Defence is the number of Stamina he loses.

If the enemy is now down to zero Stamina then he is defeated. Otherwise he will strike back at you, using the same procedure. If you survive, you then get a chance to attack again, and the battle goes on until one of you is victorious.

Example:

You are a 3rd Rank character with a COMBAT score of 4, and you have to fight a goblin (COMBAT 5, Defence 7, Stamina 6). The fight begins with your attack (you always get first blow unless told otherwise). Suppose you roll 8 on two dice. Adding your COMBAT score gives a total of 12. This is 5 more than the goblin's Defence, so it loses 5 Stamina.

The goblin still has 1 Stamina point left, so it gets to strike back. It rolls 6 on the dice which, added to its Combat of 5, gives a total attack score of 11. Suppose you have a chain mail tabard (Defence +2). Your Defence is therefore 9 (=4+3+2), so you lose 2 Stamina and can then attack again.

USING ABILITIES

Fighting is often not the easiest or safest way to tackle a situation. When you get a chance to use one of your other abilities, you will be told the Difficulty of the task. You roll two dice and add your score in the ability, and to succeed in the task you must get higher than the Difficulty.

Example:

You are at the bottom of a cliff. You can use THIEVERY to climb it, and the climb is Difficulty 9. Suppose your THIEVERY score is 4. This means you must roll at least 6 on the dice to make the climb.

CODEWORDS

There is a list of codewords at the back of the book. Sometimes you will be told you have acquired a codeword. When this happens, put a tick in the box next to that codeword. If you later lose the codeword, erase the tick.

The codewords are arranged alphabetically for each book in the series. In this book, for example, all codewords begin with F. This makes it easy to check if you picked up a codeword from a book you played previously. For instance, you might be asked if you have picked up a codeword in a book you have already adventured in. The letter of that codeword will tell you which book to check (e.g. if it begins with C, it is from Book 3: *Over the Blood-Dark Sea*).

SOME QUESTIONS ANSWERED

How long will my adventures last?
As long as you like! There are many plot strands to follow in the Fabled Lands. Explore wherever you want. Gain wealth, power and prestige. Make friends and foes. Just think of it as real life in a fantasy world. When you need to stop playing, make a note of the entry you are at and later you can just resume at that point.

What happens if I'm killed?
If you had the foresight to arrange a resurrection deal (you'll learn about them later), death might not be the end of your career. Otherwise, you

can always start adventuring again with a new persona. If you do, you'll first have to erase all codewords, ticks and money recorded in the book.

What do the maps show?
The map at the back of the book shows the country of Akatsurai covered by this adventure. The map at the front shows the whole extent of the known Fabled Lands.

Are some regions of the world more dangerous than others?
Yes. Generally, the closer you are to civilization (the area of Sokara and Golnir covered in the first two books) the easier your adventures will be.

Where can I travel in the Fabled Lands?
Anywhere. If you journey to the edge of the map in this adventure, you will be guided to another adventure in the series. (*The War-Torn Kingdom* deals with Sokara, *Cities of Gold and Glory* deals with Golnir, *Over the Blood-Dark Sea* deals with the southern seas and so on.) For example, if you are enslaved by the Uttakin, you will be guided to *The Court of Hidden Faces* **321**, which refers to entry **321** in Book Five.

What if I don't have the next book?
Just turn back. When you do get that book, you can always return and venture onwards.

What should I do when travelling on from one book to the next?
It's very simple. Make a note of the entry you'll be turning to in the new adventure. Then copy all the information from your Adventure Sheet and Ship's Manifest into the new adventure. Lastly, erase the Adventure Sheet and Ship's Manifest data in the old adventure so they will be blank when you return there.

What about codewords?
Codewords report important events in your adventuring life. They 'remember' the places you've been and the people you've met. Do NOT erase codewords when you are passing from one book to another.

Are there any limits on abilities?
Your abilities (COMBAT, etc) can increase up to a maximum of 12. They can never go lower than 1. If you are told to lose a point off an ability which is already at 1, it stays as it is.

Are there any limits on Stamina?
There is no upper limit. Stamina increases each time you go up in Rank. Wounds will reduce your current Stamina, but not your potential (unwounded) score. If Stamina ever goes to zero, you are killed.

Does it matter what type of weapon I have?
When you buy a weapon in a market, you can choose what type of weapon it is (i.e. a sword, spear, etc). The type of weapon is up to you. Price is not affected by the weapon's type, but only by whether it has a COMBAT bonus or not.

Some items give ability bonuses. Are these cumulative?
No. If you already have a set of **lockpicks (THIEVERY +1)** and then acquire **magic lockpicks (THIEVERY +2)**, you don't get a +3 bonus, only +2. Count only the bonus given by your best item for each ability.

Why do I keep going back to entries I've been to?
Many entries describe locations such as a city or castle, so whenever you go back there, you go to the paragraph that corresponds to that place.

How many blessings can I have?
As many as you can get, but never more than one of the same type. You can't have several COMBAT blessings, for instance, but you could have one COMBAT, one THIEVERY and one CHARISMA blessing.

QUICK RULES

To use an ability (COMBAT, THIEVERY, etc), roll two dice and add your score in the ability. To succeed you must roll higher than the Difficulty of the task.

Example: You want to calm down an angry innkeeper. This requires a CHARISMA roll at a Difficulty of 10. Say you have a CHARISMA score of 6. This means that you would have to roll 5 or more on two dice to succeed.

Fighting involves a series of COMBAT rolls. The Difficulty of the roll is equal to the opponent's Defence score. (Your Defence score is equal to your **Rank** + your **armour bonus** + your **COMBAT score**.) The amount you beat the Difficulty by is the number of Stamina points that your opponent loses.

That's pretty much all you need to know. If you have any detailed queries, consult the detailed rules in the preceding pages.

A selection of pre-generated characters, colour maps of the Fabled Lands world and other bonus material are available on the website:

www.fabledlands.com

1

'Wait a minute, I can feel a pulse.'

Slowly the world seeps back. First sounds: the dull roar and mutter of words, the creak of timbers, the fluttering of canvas in the breeze. Then the hard wooden planking under your back and the smell of the rope on which your head is resting. A salty taste in your mouth, mingled with bile –

You sit up suddenly, coughing sea water out of your lungs. A circle of sailors are standing looking at you. One of their number, a man in finer clothes who seems to be a merchant captain, steps forward and helps you to your feet. Your clothes are wet through. You feel as weak as a kitten.

'We fished you out of the sea,' says the captain. 'You were clinging to a broken spar. We thought you were dead.'

You can only nod, still too dazed to string a sentence together.

'Who are you?' asks one of the men. 'Where are you from?'

You press your fingers to your head. Your hair is matted with blood and brine. 'I don't know...'

The captain looks at his crew. 'That's enough gawping. Back to work, the lot of you.'

Your only belongings are the clothes on your back and a **platinum earring**. Everything else was lost in the shipwreck – including all memories of your life until this moment. You must begin afresh.

Make a CHARISMA roll at a Difficulty of 11. If you succeed, turn to **370**. If you fail, turn to **389**.

2

There is not much traffic on the Northern Coastal Road, but occasionally you pass a group of merchants with their packs, or a dignitary being bounced about inside his sedan chair as his bearers carry him swiftly by.

Roll two dice.

Score 2-8	No significant encounters	turn to **671**
Score 9-12	The victim of a mugging	turn to **346**

3

You are in the uplands that separate the east and west coastal regions. This is as much a political barrier as a geographic one. The west is under the dominance of the imperial court; in the east, the great lords of the military families hold sway.

Go east	turn to **495**
Go west	turn to **672**
Go south	turn to **552**
Go north	turn to **336**

4

One of the guards catches up with you a few streets away from the palace. 'You are a merchant?' he demands in an imperious voice. 'I am interested in western styles of armour and would like to purchase any stock you might have.'

It is beneath his dignity to haggle, so you are able to strike a good bargain.

Armour	*To sell*
Leather (Defence +1)	60 Shards
Ring mail (Defence +2)	140 Shards
Chain mail (Defence +3)	270 Shards
Splint armour (Defence +4)	450 Shards
Plate armour (Defence +5)	950 Shards
Heavy plate (Defence +6)	2000 Shards

The only drawback is that he insists on buying all the armour you have on you – including any you happen to be wearing! If you sell him all your suits of armour, add the money to your Adventure Sheet and turn to **79**. If you refuse to sell him everything, turn to **55**.

5

You are on the lower slopes of the massive Kenen range. Even here there is a dusting of snow on the pine trees. Further up you can see long valleys stretching up the mountainsides, like wounds gouged into the rock, where the wind whips up an eternal mist of ice.

Descend	turn to **137**
Ascend	turn to **185**

6

At last the storm abates. The navigator has no idea of the ship's current position. After makeshift repairs, you limp towards the coast to try to get your bearings.

Roll one die.

Score 1-2	turn to **184**
Score 3	turn to **662**
Score 4-5	turn to **471**
Score 6	turn to **543**

7

The Chu River is spanned by a wooden bridge. It creaks slightly as you set out across it. At the mid-point you are stopped by a female warrior who wears maroon armour over a tunic of black and scarlet silk. She tells you she belongs to the extensive Black Swan family, whose members are famous for their martial prowess.

'If you wish to cross the bridge you must face me in a duel,' she says.

Accept her challenge	turn to **614**
Show her an **agate swan** if you have one	turn to **485**
Turn back	turn to **568**

8

The main streets of the outer town are channels of churned-up mud and dung. It is best to keep to the boardwalks on either side.

Visit the market	turn to **313**
Seek admittance to the inner keep	turn to **613**
Find a temple	turn to **607**
Look for a tavern	turn to **628**
Leave the city	turn to **634**

9

Storm clouds swell like black mushrooms above a churning sea. If you have a blessing of Safety from Storms, cross it off and turn to **247**. Otherwise turn to **222**.

10

Why has your god not returned you to life? The little priest has no idea. 'The Sage of Peace promises resurrection in the life to come,' he says, 'but his teaching advises us to forget our attachment to worldly things.'

'Mere philosophy!' you cry. 'We're talking about my life!'

'I'm sorry. What can I say?'

Turn to **322**.

11

If you have a ship in the harbour you can travel on by sea. Otherwise you must brave the lonely countryside of Akatsurai's north coast – or the perils of Kwaidan Forest.

Go east along the highway	turn to **2**
Go west over open country	turn to **493**
Enter the forest	turn to **398**
Set sail (if ship docked here)	turn to **224**

12

You manage to persuade Kokoro to return with you despite her misgivings. Takakura is overjoyed. He presents you with a **sword (COMBAT +1)** and you are given the title Junior Court Rank, entitling you to enter the palace precincts whenever you like. After noting that on your Adventure Sheet, turn to **79**.

13

A guard summons the Lord Chancellor's steward, the redoubtable Tadachika, who comes to meet you in the reception hall. He is a man with a heavy bald brow, sparkling eyes and thick arms that barely seem to reach across his vast chest.

'Begone!' he booms. 'Lord Kiyomori is enjoying a few days' peace and quiet. He does not wish to be bothered with affairs of state. If you have something to say, present yourself at his residence in Chambara later in the month.'

Turn and leave	turn to **362**
Attack Tadachika	turn to **680**

14

The bosun points out a bay fringed with white sand and palm trees. Above, on a wooded hillside overlooking the sea, there is a country inn amid a blaze of irises.

'Let's stop over for a few days, skipper!' the crew urge you.

Put into the bay	turn to **556**
Sail on	turn to **524**

15

The monk tells you that he acquired marvellous powers after mastering the Pure Land sutra. This enabled him to travel to a fabulous realm in the night sky where he learned many arcane secrets.

'I can help you to do the same,' he says, 'as long as you are genuinely pious.'

Ask for his help	turn to **525**
Attack him	turn to **425**
Bid him goodnight	turn to **610**

16

'Did you pass on my letter to Baroness Ravayne?' asks Kiyomori with a frown. 'I cannot understand why she has not shown any interest in marrying my son.'

It is hardly a mystery to you. Young Lord Shigemori is a fat waddling fellow with personal habits that would do no credit to a hyena. You don't mention this to Kiyomori. Turn to **289**.

17

Acknowledging defeat, Mister Dragon offers to teach you the basics of his fighting style.

Roll two dice. If you get higher than your current COMBAT score, increase it by 1. But if you roll exactly equal to your COMBAT score you are badly injured in sparring and permanently lose 1-3 points (roll one die and halve it, rounding up) from your unwounded Stamina score. If you roll less than your COMBAT score there is no effect.

Now turn to **297**.

18

The commanding officer stops his horse beside you and unfurls a scroll. After comparing one of the faces drawn there with your own, he snaps his fingers and says, 'Arrest this outlaw.'

Four soldiers come forward at a trot. To avoid capture you must make either a COMBAT or a THIEVERY roll (your choice) at a Difficulty of 14.

Successful roll	turn to **729**
Failed roll	turn to **452**

19

You and he recognize each other at the same instant.

'Talanexor the Fire Weaver...'

He nods, not exactly smiling. 'We meet again. For the last time, I suspect.'

A scythe of red fire sweeps from his hand towards you. You have just a split second in which to act.

Jump out of the basket	turn to **140**

Deflect the spell   turn to **663**
Cut the balloon loose   turn to **685**

20

You are at the mouth of the Gai River. If your ship is docked here, turn to **429**. If not, decide whether to go east (turn to **568**) or west (turn to **356**).

21

'Go back out into the world,' advises the abbot. 'You are not yet ready for enlightenment.'

'What must I do?'

'The saint of Vulture Peak will advise you.'

'Where will I find him?'

The abbot smiles. 'That is something you must discover for yourself. Now go.'

Lose the codeword *Friz* if you had it.

Turn to **211**.

22

The tengu king tells you about a man calling himself Tatsu. 'I trained him in the secret art of Oak Limb boxing, which made him invincible to attack on all points of his body except the top of his head.'

'Sounds good. Will you teach me?'

He laughs a long dry creaking laugh. 'It would take too many years. But I will show you the rudiments of the art.'

Permanently increase your unwounded Stamina score by 1-6 points (the roll of one die). Then turn to **259**.

23

Morituri scratches your chest with one long sharp fingernail and laps up the blood that spills forth. He clings like a limpet until you begin to feel dizzy. You have to force his mouth away. For a moment he stares at you as though on the point of a murderous rage, but then rationality returns to his face.

'Your life force is strong, ' he says appreciatively, licking the gore off his lips.

Permanently reduce your unwounded Stamina score by 1-6 points (the roll of one die). You do get a **hyperium wand (MAGIC +6)**, however, to sweeten the pill. You tuck it into your belt (add it to your list of possessions) and then look around for Morituri, but he has already departed. Turn to **583**.

24

You are intrigued by a ledge jutting out over a sheer cliff. It looks as if there is a man-made doorway leading off it. You thoughtfully assess the climb, which will require a SCOUTING roll of Difficulty 16 – or Difficulty 15 if you have **climbing gear**.

Successful SCOUTING roll	turn to **701**
Failed SCOUTING roll	turn to **689**
Not attempting it	turn to **646**

25

Once you have your own ship you can go anywhere on the high seas, exploring or trading. The shipbuilders of Hagashin are renowned throughout the Orient and you can get a good vessel at a fair price.

Three ship types are available:

Ship type	Cost	Capacity
Barque	200 Shards	1 Cargo Unit
Brigantine	400 Shards	2 Cargo Units
Galleon	700 Shards	3 Cargo Units

If you already own a ship docked at Hagashin you can sell it for 20% less than these prices. If you do buy a ship, record its details on the Ship's Manifest. The crew quality is average.

When your business is complete, turn to **302**.

26

Get the codeword *Fuligin* if you didn't already have it.

You are given tea at the clanhouse of Hofuna, the principal merchant in the town.

'So,' he says, 'have you come to invest some money with me? I have some really profitable ventures on the go right now.'

Make an investment	turn to **440**
Check on investments	turn to **483**
Leave	turn to **8**

27

It is only once you're under way that the captain remembers to mention the dangers of travelling by sea: 'Pirates, waterspouts, hurricanes, shark men and giant squids…'

Roll one die.

Score 1	Sunk by a tidal wave	turn to **241**
Score 2	Plague: lose 2 Stamina points permanently unless you have Immunity to Disease/Poison	turn to **612**
Score 3-6	You reach Chambara safely	turn to **612**

28

Lord Shuriyoku and his men are here. You can tell from their angry looks that this is not a social call. Turn to **694**.

29

In a whimsical mood, you call the mate to your cabin and offer him a glass of brandy.

'Would you sooner sail in the deep north, where the sea flows sluggishly on the verge of freezing, or in the balmy south?' you ask him.

'The south,' he says at once. 'If one must drown, it is better to drown comfortably.' He sets down the glass. 'What course, captain?'

North	turn to **406**
South	turn to **309**
East	turn to **100**
West	turn to **90**

30

Not many travellers use the lonely Northern Coastal Road. For company you have the sea breeze and the song of skylarks in the trees.

Roll two dice.

Score 2-9	The days pass uneventfully	turn to **53**
Score 10-12	Unexpected hospitality	turn to **328**

31

You are crossing a high saddle of land between the eastern and western coastal plains.

Go east	turn to **178**
Go west	turn to **704**
Go north	turn to **552**
Go south	turn to **54**

32
Lord Shuriyoku is known as 'the Eyes of the Shogun' because of the diligence with which he ferrets out secrets for his master. His greatest concern is not the coming civil war with the Starburst Clan, but the ambitions of the White Spear Clan of Yarimura.

If you have the codeword *Dog*, lose it and turn to **358**.

Otherwise, turn to **96**.

33
You are in a rugged land of sharp dry grass and stunted trees where the only signs of life are foxfires in the night and the cawing of tengu's cousins somewhere off in the cold white haze of day.

Go up into the mountains	turn to **319**
Follow the coast south	turn to **706**
Go west	turn to **633**

34
If you have the codeword *Frame*, turn to **57**. If not, turn to **76**.

35
Note on the Ship's Manifest that your ship is now docked at Mukogawa, then turn to **695**.

36

She strips you of your best armour, your best weapon and any cash you are carrying, then sends you on your way with a jaunty kick. Her peals of scornful laughter follow you to the end of the bridge.

| If you have a **cursed sword** | turn to **448** |
| If not | turn to **58** |

37

Takakura turns out not to be very curious as to why you are prowling around his palace at night. He is too preoccupied by his own cares. You learn that the Lord Chancellor, angered by Takakura's affair with a girl who had also besotted the chancellor's own son-in-law, has sent the girl away and confined Takakura to the palace without servants to wait on him.

'But surely you're the Sovereign?'

He manages a bleak smile. 'It's not as simple as that.'

| Offer to find the girl | turn to **679** |
| Take your leave | turn to **79** |

38

Nothing you say will persuade Kokoro to come back with you. As you are leaving, she makes you a present of her finest **lady's court robe**, a valuable garment of brocaded silk with raised white butterflies on a field of blue-washed grey. It would be rude to refuse this; add it to your list of possessions even if it means you have to discard something else.

Bidding Kokoro farewell, you set out back to the city just as dawn begins to show as a cherry-blossom tinge over the eastern hills. How will Takakura react when you give him the bad tidings? Perhaps it would be better not to go back to the palace but just to slink off quietly.

| Return to the palace | turn to **131** |
| Lose yourself in the city | turn to **79** |

39

It is late afternoon when you arrive at the heavily fortified manse of Lord Kiyomori, Patriarch of the Starburst Clan and Chancellor of Akatsurai. Dozens of soldiers patrol the estate behind his white walls capped with iron spikes.

    Sneak inside   turn to **205**
    Go up to the gate   turn to **60**

40

The ghost raises its hands and you are outlined by a discharge of eldritch energy. Make a MAGIC roll of Difficulty 15 to bear the brunt of its blast.

    Successful MAGIC roll   turn to **158**
    Failed MAGIC roll   turn to **140**

41

'It is nothing to do with you,' says one of the youths.

'Help me!' pleads the old gentleman. 'I dared to speak out against the chancellor's dictatorial policies, and now his thugs are going to beat me up.'

If you have the codeword *Fleet*, turn to **62**. If not, decide whether to help the old man (turn to **660**) or to stay out of it (turn to **79**).

42

There is a scream of agony – from you, not from Mister Dragon. You hop back, clutching your toes which you are sure must be broken, and Mister Dragon takes your other leg out from under you with a graceful sweep. The whole fight took about three seconds.

    Turn to **63**.

43

If you bought the **dragon mask**, remember to add it to your list of possessions. Then, if you paid the actor more than 250 Shards, turn to **232**. Otherwise turn to **397**.

44

The countryside of Shaku is an emerald patchwork of rice terraces that climb towards forests of tall palm trees where orchids glitter like fabulous jewels.

On the north coast is the city of Hagashin – a place of curious contrasts, where dingy wooden shacks cluster right up to the walls of golden palaces and verdant parks, where beggars walk the same streets as mighty lords, and where the stench of refuse mingles on the breeze with temple incense and delicate perfumes. Turn to **226**.

45

The Sage of Peace bestows blessings on his initiates for free. Write Luck in the Blessings box on your Adventure Sheet. The blessing can be used once to allow you to reroll any dice result. After using the blessing, remember to cross it off your Adventure Sheet. You can have only one Luck blessing at a time.

When you are through at the temple, turn to **155**.

46

The vampires move with long powerful bounds, but their slow reactions make it easy for you to outmanoeuvre them. If you have a piece of **parchment**, turn to **66**. Otherwise turn to **116**.

47

You are standing in the weed-choked courtyard. Pampas grass stands all around to the level of your shoulders, dampening your clothes with dew as you press forward. Clouds of midges rise like smoke into the air to swirl about in the early sunlight.

On your right is the bell-tower. You can see that many of the roof-tiles are missing, the shutters hanging askew. The man on the porch of the main building has not noticed you.

Approach the main shrine	turn to **92**
Go to the bell-tower	turn to **67**
Leave right away	turn to **398**

48

During an afternoon nap you are visited by a deity who is wailing in anguish. He explains his plight: 'I angered the wizard Shugen, who imprisoned me under a boulder in the ravine nearby. Free me and I shall reward you.'

When you wake up you take a look in the ravine. Sure enough, there is a massive boulder at the bottom all overgrown with ivy. To break the wizard's spell and free the deity, you need to make a MAGIC

roll at a Difficulty of 18.
Successful MAGIC roll	turn to **355**
Failed MAGIC roll	turn to **394**
Not making the attempt	turn to **44**

49

Donations have been streaming into the shrine lately. As the overlord of the battlefield, Juntoku is very popular with soldiers – especially now, on the eve of civil war.

The courtyard of the shrine is fined with flocks of well-fed pigeons, the special messengers of the god. You look around for a priest, finally catching the eye of a slight youth in a long-sleeved white robe.

'Just leave a donation and tell the god what you want,' he says.

To obtain a blessing requires you to make a CHARISMA roll at a Difficulty of 15, or a Difficulty of 12 if you are an initiate of Juntoku. If you fail the CHARISMA roll you lose all your current blessings. On a successful roll Juntoku gives you a blessing: write COMBAT in the Blessings box on your Adventure Sheet. The blessing works by allowing you to try again when you fail a COMBAT roll. You can use the blessing only once; it is then used up and you should cross it off. Also, you can have only one COMBAT blessing at any one time.

To become an initiate you must pay a donation of 50 Shards, and you can then write Juntoku in the God box on your Adventure Sheet. You must not already be an initiate of another god. (If you were already an initiate of Juntoku and want to renounce that status now, pay compensation of 40 Shards to avoid the god's wrath.)

When you have finished your devotions, turn to **178**.

50

The thief says he win train you in stealth and lockpicking in return for the **dragon mask**.

'I'd make a lot more money if I wore that,' he says. 'People would be so frightened that I wouldn't even have to draw my sword.'

If you agree to the deal, cross off the **dragon mask** and roll two dice. If you get more than your current THIEVERY score then you can increase it by 1.

Now turn to **316**.

51

Hand over any **sealed letters** that you have.

Yoritomo reads quickly, a derisive smile playing on his lips. 'See this calligraphy?' he snorts. 'This is how I know that Kumonosu will never amount to anything. He writes with a barbarian's hand!'

Your reward is not in the form of cash, which would be an insult to any proud Akatsurese knight. Roll one die to see what your lord gives you.

Score 1-2	**Sword (COMBAT +1)**
Score 3-4	**Lotus talisman (SANCTITY +1)**
Score 5	**Splint armour (Defence +4)**
Score 6	**Spear (COMBAT +4)**

Note the item on your Adventure Sheet and turn to **553**.

52

The pirates strip you of everything you own and then jeeringly toss you into the sea. Cross off your ship and crew as well as your possessions and money – you'll never see them again, and it will be a miracle if you survive to see dry land.

Make a SCOUTING roll at a Difficulty of 15.

| Successful SCOUTING roll | turn to **241** |
| Failed SCOUTING roll | turn to **140** |

53

You are in the middle of the highway that runs from Chompo to Narai.

Follow the road east	turn to **98**
Go west	turn to **703**
Strike out to the south	turn to **336**

54

A long road stretches through gently rolling countryside. Few travellers take this route. Those who go east are thought of as effete courtiers; those who go west are considered uncouth provincials.

Go east into Mukogawa	turn to **178**
Go west towards Shingen	turn to **124**
Leave the road and go north	turn to **444**
Leave the road going south	turn to **220**

55

'Varlet!' he says darkly. 'I will teach you not to defy a knight of the Sovereign's court.'

With no further ado, he draws his sword and leaps at you while passers-by look on aghast.

Imperial Guard, COMBAT 7, Defence 11, Stamina 14

If you defeat him, get the codeword *Fracas*. You can also take his **sword** if you wish. Then turn to **79**.

56

Storm clouds swell like black mushrooms above a churning sea. If you have a blessing of Safety from Storms, cross it off and know that turn to **471**. Otherwise, turn to **222**.

57

The merchant asks if you would like to buy specific cargo for your ship, or do you want to make a general investment?

Buy cargo	turn to **127**
Make an investment	turn to **152**

58

At one end of the bridge are the huts of the rivermen who live on the outskirts of Sakkaku. The other opens on to level countryside with only a few distant farms in sight.

Go east to Sakkaku	turn to **522**
Go west	turn to **568**

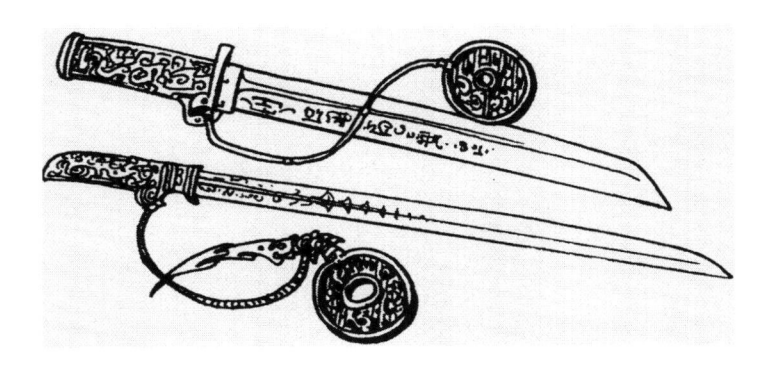

59

Chompo is the stronghold of the Northern Wistaria Clan, whose dominance of this region is so well-established that it is virtually the clan's private kingdom.

Unlike most of the southern cities, the central district of Chompo is enclosed by high fortifications built of round timbers. Within are the homes of the aristocrats: austere but imposing mansions that lie in a curve around the hillside. Outside this stockade are the humbler dwellings of merchants and craftsmen.

Enter the inner keep	turn to **613**
Remain in the outer town	turn to **8**

60

Turn to **109** if you have the codeword *Fleet*, otherwise turn to **132**.

61

You call on the gods to bear witness to this travesty of natural law: that a ghost should arise at once from the corpse of its former self and commence to wreak summary justice. The normal protocol allows for hauntings, nightmares and curses, but not this kind of brashness. Your prayer is that the gods will intervene to set matters aright.

Make a SANCTITY roll at a Difficulty of 13.

Successful SANCTITY roll	turn to **110**
Failed SANCTITY roll	turn to **133**

62

'I'll vouch for this man,' you tell the youths.

Grumbling, they slope off with sullen glances back at you. No doubt they'd like to beat you up as well, but they know you are a personal friend of the chancellor, Lord Kiyomori.

'This country's gone to the dogs, all right, when you get curs like that roaming the city in packs,' ventures the old man shakily. He is a lord of the Wistaria Clan. You have made a useful friend today.

Get the codeword *Fuchsia* and turn to **79**.

63

As winner of the bout, he lays claim to any money that you are carrying. If you have no money, he takes one of your possessions instead; roll one die to see which (e.g. if you roll a 4, he takes the fourth item listed on your Adventure Sheet). Turn to **297**.

64

South lie the quiet misty waters of the Ugetsu Straits. North, the sea is the colour of shattered tombstones under a sky sketched in charcoal and indigo ink.

Roll two dice.

Score 2-9	All is quiet	turn to **113**
Score 10-12	Pirates	turn to **145**

65

You keep up a vigil by Takakura's bedside. In the dark of the night an imposing figure enters the room. The other courtiers present take no notice as the newcomer sweeps up to where you are sitting.

'There is something of mine you have,' says a voice.

You look up, but cannot make out the details of his face in the dim candlelight. You know what he has come for: the **royal sceptre**. Cross it off your Adventure Sheet.

'This time he will live,' says the stranger. A breeze rustles his robes. Something flutters against your face and you awaken. It is dawn. Takakura looks up at you and smiles.

'A miracle!' cry the physicians. 'The sickness has gone!'

You know the truth, but who would believe you? Turn to **79**.

66

The vampires hiss, snap and claw as you dodge between them. Their clumsy reflexes give you an idea. Swiftly tearing the **parchment** into strips (cross it off your Adventure Sheet), you scribble mystic symbols and try to paste each strip on to a vampire's forehead. If your MAGIC works, the symbols will freeze the vampires' deathly spirit-essence, rendering them immobile.

Make a MAGIC roll at a Difficulty of 14 to see if you write the symbols correctly.

Successful MAGIC roll	turn to **91**
Failed MAGIC roll	turn to **116**

67

As you approach the tower there is a frantic skittering sound from above and a couple of roof tiles come crashing down. You glance up in time to see a couple of hunched figures scrambling out of sight inside the belfry. From the brief glimpse it looked as if they might be giant crows.

Ring the bell	turn to **141**
Call up to them	turn to **117**
Go to the shrine building	turn to **92**
Leave and resume your journey	turn to **398**

68 ☐

If the box above is empty, put a tick in it and turn to **118**. If it was already ticked, turn to **142**.

69

Nai is the awesome god of earthquakes, which are a constant danger in this part of the world. His statue shows him as an armoured warrior with a terrible rictus of glee on his scarlet face.

Become an initiate	turn to **119**
Renounce the worship of Nai	turn to **143**
Acquire a blessing	turn to **94**
Leave the shrine	turn to **323**

70

If you have the codeword *Frog*, turn to **120**. If not, turn to **95**.

71

Yoritomo is as busy as ever, but he has time to greet you. 'I am concerned that Lord Kumonosu of Yarimura should not intervene in our struggle against the Starburst Clan,' he confides to you. 'Go to Yarimura as my emissary and advise him to stay neutral.'

You bow and withdraw. Turn to **553**.

72

You steer a course between Dragon Island and the strange empire of Akatsurai, where knights would sooner cut themselves open like melons than suffer the slightest shame.

Roll two dice.

Score 2-9	Plain sailing	turn to **29**
Score 10-12	In shallow water	turn to **588**

73

The Eastern Coastal Road is busy with traders and messengers passing between the great cities of Chompo and Mukogawa.

Roll two dice.

Score 2-8	An untroubled journey	turn to **396**
Score 9-12	A talkative youth	turn to **70**

74

Palm trees line the paths between the rice paddies. Off to the north, a vast mountain as insubstantial as a shadow at dawn lazily trails a plume of dark smoke across the blue sky. 'That is Lord Thunder,' a peasant tells you. He is referring to the god of the volcano.

Roll two dice.

| Score 2-8 | A quiet journey | turn to **632** |
| Score 9-12 | A near disaster | turn to **231** |

75

You emerge at the top of a well.

Dusk is falling over a strange city, igniting stellar baubles in a sky of limpid violet. You look around in surprise at the low wooden buildings with their curved roofs and austere design.

A man in colourful robes comes out on to the porch of a nearby house, affecting to ignore you until you pester him with questions.

'This is Chambara, imperial capital of Akatsurai,' he says. 'How is it possible you don't know that? Are you deranged?'

'I came here by magic, out of that well.'

'Ah.' He nods. 'It is just as the geomancer said.' He disappears back into his house.

| Go back down the well | turn to **538** |
| Explore the city | turn to **79** |

76

The captain of a Sokaran vessel gives you a friendly word of advice: 'The Akatsurese have old-fashioned ideas about trade.'

'Old-fashioned in what sense?'

'They don't think it's at all respectable. Once they've got you pegged as a merchant, you'll find it devilish hard to break into high society.'

Think about it. If it matters to you that you are regarded as a member of the nobility, you'd better give up any idea of making trade deals here in Chambara. But if you're not bothered about that, the Sokaran captain can put you in touch with the local merchants.

| Decide against trading here | turn to **79** |
| Ask him to introduce you | turn to **104** |

77

The harbour mouth is surmounted by a ceremonial arch similar to the up curving gates that stand at the entrance of Akatsurese shrines. Note on the Ship's Manifest that your ship is now docked at Kaiju, then turn to **105**.

78

Get the codeword *Face*.

Your blank features will startle and horrify anyone you meet. The only remedy is to wear a **mask** if you have one. Any sort of mask will do: a **courtier's mask**, **dragon mask**, etc. People might think it odd that you go about masked, but it is better than scaring them witless.

If you do not have a mask you will automatically fail any CHARISMA roll from now on. Put your CHARISMA score in brackets and make a note beside it that you cannot use CHARISMA as long as you have no mask.

Now turn to **357**.

79

Chambara, a city built on a grid pattern at the mouth of the Moku River, is the imperial capital of Akatsurai. It is here that the Sovereign has his palace, at the north end of Chrysanthemum Avenue.

You can buy a town house here for 350 Shards. If you do, cross off the money and put a tick in the box beside the town house option below.

Visit a temple	turn to **301**
Visit a shrine	turn to **246**
Explore the city	turn to **578**
Go to the palace	turn to **123**
Go to the chancellor's mansion	turn to **39**
Go to your town house ☐ (if box ticked)	turn to **284**
Enquire after trade goods	turn to **34**
Do some shopping	turn to **223**
Find a swordsmith	turn to **469**
Go to the harbour	turn to **612**
Leave the city	turn to **299**

80

The Ghostwaters of Nyg are a place of ill repute. Mist lies in a heavy blanket across the sea and sends white tendrils writhing against the sides of the ship. To the north-east is imperial Chambara, capital city of the exotic land of Akatsurai.

'My brother went there,' the ship's surgeon tells you.

'What was it like?'

'I don't know. The poor devil never returned.'

Set course for Chambara	turn to **150**
Steer due east	turn to **200**
Follow the coastline south	turn to **102**
Head for Ankon-Konu	*Over the Blood-Dark Sea* **98**
Go west	turn to **202**
Steer due north	turn to **300**

81

As dawn is breaking you finally have to admit defeat. There is no point in going back to the palace to tell the Sovereign you have failed. That would only make him more despondent. You slink off and lose yourself in the city streets.

Turn to **79**.

82

Kiyomori is pleased to see you. Away from the capital, he is briefly able to forget the demands of office. As you sit chatting, he soon returns to his favourite topic: 'When I came to power twenty years ago, the country was all but paralysed as a result of court intrigues. I had hopes then of putting things in order and then retiring to a monastery, but that has not been my destiny. The current Sovereign is well-meaning but inexperienced, and his father Shirakawa is a crafty sorcerer who would sacrifice anything for the sake of his unwholesome arts. And now we have those Moonrise rebels in the east to worry about, the damnable dogs!'

You spend a few days at the villa enjoying the sea air. If injured, you get back 1-6 Stamina points. Soon Kiyomori's duties call him back to Chambara. It is time to move on. You travel with him for part of the way; turn to **173**.

83

Get the codeword *Fracas*.

Armed now with Tadachika's **sword (COMBAT +3)**, which you can add to your list of possessions, you confront the Lord Chancellor's elite guards. You cannot possibly kill them all. Your only hope is to fight your way out of the villa and escape.

The two nearest guards see what you are planning and slash at you with their curved swords. Make a COMBAT roll at a Difficulty of 14 to avoid being cut down where you stand. If you fail the COMBAT roll, you are dead – turn to **140**. Even if you succeed in the COMBAT roll, you still take a nasty gash and must lose 1-6 Stamina.

If you survive, you can make a break for it: turn to **696**.

84

When you tell him about the ticket in his hat he gives you a look of steely-eyed outrage.

'It is my taboo label, you oaf! It signals to all and sundry that I am in ritual seclusion and should not be approached.'

Having broken the taboo, you can only try to set matters right with a benediction.

Make a SANCTITY roll at a Difficulty of 14.

Successful SANCTITY roll	turn to **714**
Failed SANCTITY roll	turn to **730**

85

'We were servants in a noble household,' says the older man, 'but because of the envy of others we were discredited and lost our position. You know the expression *shoja hissui*? Those who flourish are destined to fall.'

If you have either *Fleet*, *Fuchsia* or *Frog*, turn to **558**. If you don't have any of those codewords, turn to **504**.

86

The skeleton crumbles to leave a foul-smelling vapour that makes blisters appear on your skin. Unless you have a blessing of Immunity to Disease/Poison you soon succumb: turn to **140**. If you do have such a blessing, cross it off your Adventure Sheet and read on.

The burial mound contains a heap of gold and gems worth somewhere between 500 and 3000 Shards (roll one die and multiply by 500). There is also one antique of considerable value; roll two dice to see what it is:

Score 2-4 **Jade crown (CHARISMA +5)**
Score 5-9 **Stone arrowhead (SCOUTING +4)**
Score 10-12 **Vajra baton (SANCTITY +5)**

When you have added the loot to your Adventure Sheet, turn to **416**.

87

You are roughly on a latitude with Chompo, capital of the Wistaria Clan. 'Where now, skipper?' asks the helmsman.

Steer south	turn to **745**
Steer north	turn to **161**

88

You search for the rock face where you found silver on your last trip. It is not easy to find. The snow smothers most features, and one mountainside is much like another.

Make a SCOUTING roll at a Difficulty of 16.

Successful SCOUTING roll	turn to **257**
Failed SCOUTING roll	turn to **307**

89

You come across two knights in threadbare robes who are making a pilgrimage to the Clearwater Shrine. They invite you to travel with them.

If you have an **ivory-handled katana**, turn to **115**. If not, turn to **138**.

90

You have entered the coastal waters of Dragon Island.

'We must be careful, skipper,' cautions one of the deckhands. 'I hear this is the home of Ranryu, the Serpent of Chaos.'

Drop anchor and go ashore	turn to **418**
Sail away from the island	turn to **122**

91

You search the corpses and find a **sword (COMBAT +1)**, a **dragon mask** and a set of **silver chopsticks**. Take these if you want and then turn to **529**.

92 ☐

The man is standing stock-still with his back to you under the ivy-strewn eaves of the hall. He has adopted a curious pose, balanced on one leg with his left arm stretched out to the side and his right folded in front of him. The dawn light, slanting over his shoulder, picks out a glint of metal in the shadow filled interior of the hall.

If the box above is empty, put a tick in it and turn to **188**. If it was already ticked, turn to **213**.

93

The play is about a dragon, or *tatsu*, that threatens a land-holder as he is making his way across the mountains to visit his sick mother. The tatsu's gaze is deadly, but luckily the land-holder has been given an iron fan by his wife before setting out and he uses it to shield his eyes.

Turn to **226**.

94

To get Nai's blessing you must donate 50 Shards (25 Shards if you're an initiate of Nai) and make a CHARISMA roll of Difficulty 16. If successful, write Divine Wrath in the Blessings box. This blessing can be used once at the start of a fight to inflict 1-6 Stamina points of damage on your opponent. The blessing can be used once at the start of a fight to inflict 1-6 Stamina points of damage on your opponent. The blessing is then used up and you should cross it off. You can have only one Divine Wrath blessing at anyone time.

Now turn to **323**.

95

You encounter a young man who is beset by worries. He is glad to have someone to whom he can pour out his troubles. You learn he belongs to a warrior clan but is in disgrace because of cowardice. His family has told him not to come back until he has proved himself.

If you have a **dead head**, a **pirate captain's head** or a **ghoul's head** that you can and want to part with, turn to **144**. Otherwise you can only advise the young man to bear up, then turn to **396**.

96

'I require you to undertake a mission on our lord's behalf,' says Shuriyoku. 'Go you to Yarimura. The magnate of the White Spear Clan, that dog Kumonosu, has his eyes on our lord's domain. Find out if his army would be any threat to us.'

Get the codeword *Fog* and then turn to **553**.

97

Rice paddies climb in sculpted green terraces towards the north. This is the fertile country between the Gai and Chu Rivers.

Roll two dice.

| Score 2-8 | A peaceful journey | turn to **551** |
| Score 9-12 | A storm brewing | turn to **160** |

98

By the side of the road, a signpost has rotted and fallen in the long grass. You turn it over and read: *The House of the Ugly Women*. Three roads meet at this point, but you cannot be sure which route the signpost originally marked out.

Go south-east towards Chompo	turn to **194**
Head in the direction of Narai	turn to **30**
Take the third path	turn to **146**
Strike out cross-country	turn to **282**

99

You go ashore to discover a terrifying vista of wind-blasted crags and smoking vents. Sinuous grey dragons crawl along the high ridges, pelting each other with jets of fire and acid. Their ferocious screeches echo across the barren landscape.

Make a MAGIC roll at a Difficulty of 20.

| Successful MAGIC roll | turn to **466** |
| Failed MAGIC roll | turn to **468** |

100

You are in coastal waters off Oni Province, the north-western outpost of the Akatsurese empire.

'What course, captain?' asks the helmsman.

Make for Dragon Island	turn to **72**
Head for the Sea of Hydras	turn to **309**
Tack along the north coast	turn to **224**
Steer due south	turn to **250**

101

Do you have a **royal sceptre**? If so, turn now to **134**. If not, read on.

The serpent opens one eye, gives you a baleful look, and submerges. Once the ripples have vanished there is no sign to show it wasn't just a trick of your imagination.

You climb the side of the valley to where the stream gushes out from a cleft in the rocks, where you find a tiny shrine to the river god. If you succeed in a SANCTITY roll at Difficulty 14 you can gain a blessing of Immunity to Disease/Poison, as long as you didn't already have one.

Turn to **111**.

102

Akatsurai is an empire comprising three islands. You are sailing close to the straits that separate the southern island from the rest of the country.

Recover 1 Stamina point if injured, then roll two dice.

Score 2-10	Peace and quiet	turn to **443**
Score 11-12	Pirates	turn to **145**

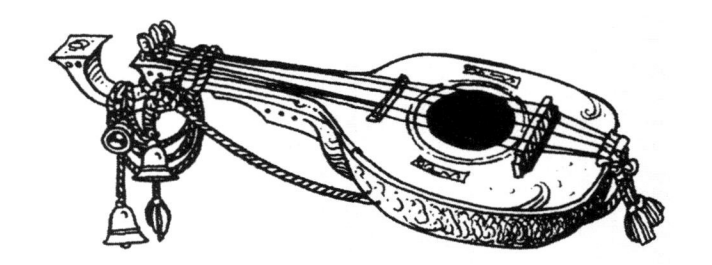

103

Shuriyoku presents you with your reward, a pouch containing 350 Shards.

'Well done,' he says. 'Espionage is never a pleasant business, I know, but this gold will sweeten the aftertaste of treachery.'

Make a note of the money and then turn to **553**.

104

You are taken to the household of the Autumn Moon family, who arrange all the commercial interests of the powerful Wistaria Clan.

'We will be happy to do much business with you,' says Koishi, the head of the household, proffering a cup of rice wine. 'May the gods see that our association brings mutual prosperity.'

Get the codeword *Frame* and then turn to **57**.

105

The mate reports that everything is ship-shape. 'We can sail as soon as the tide turns, if need be,' he says with a wary glance towards the town.

Put to sea	turn to **745**
Disembark	turn to **128**

106 ☐

If the box above is empty, put a tick in it and turn to **129**. If it was already ticked, turn to **154**.

107

Soldiers stand at the gate to the inner keep. They are wearing the grey-and-mauve livery of the House of Wistaria and each carries a spear whose blade shimmers like liquid fire in the sunlight. Recognizing you as a person of distinction, they stand aside to let you pass.

Turn to **572**.

108

You are skirting the coast roughly south of Sakkaku. From time to time you see scarlet-sailed warships from Chambara, but they are interested only in pirates.

Choose your next course.

West	turn to **250**
East	turn to **150**
South	turn to **80**

109 ☐

If the box above is empty, put a tick in it and turn to **157**. If it was already ticked, turn to **180**.

110

Your prayers are answered; Akugenda's vengeful ghost is snuffed out leaving only a wisp of brown smoke and the acrid smell of ozone.

Kiyomori looks at his men, most of whom are crouching back in terror, and then at you, standing boldly with your hand upraised to ward off evil.

'Come down to my villa,' he says. 'We'll have supper.'

You spend a pleasant evening dining on the veranda, which gives a majestic view out to sea. You have done well for yourself making friends with Kiyomori. He is the most powerful man in the country.

Get the codeword *Fleet* and turn to **362**.

111

You come to a shrine gateway that stands close to the outskirts of Kwaidan Forest. Dawn sunlight is turning the morning mist to gold dust and the trees to faded watercolours, but strangely there are no birds singing. You look in through the gate. The courtyard is filled with long grass and weeds. The shrine buildings look derelict and overgrown. Then you notice a man standing on the porch of the main shrine.

Go through the gate	turn to **47**
Continue on your way	turn to **398**

112

You may have found Mister Dragon's one weak spot – as long as you strike exactly right.

Ron two dice.

Score 2-8 turn to **17**
Score 9-12 turn to **454**

113

The navigator reports that he has found the passage that could take you to the Jawbone Isles. This news only makes your crew edgy; they fear to travel where no man has gone before.

Set course for the Jawbone Isles	turn to **239**
Make for the coast of Yodoshi	turn to **136**
Steer south into the straits	turn to **745**

114

Takakura weakens fast and before dawn he is dead. 'He was never strong, even as a child,' says Shirakawa, his father, before turning and sweeping out of the room.

Later a courtier comes to inform you that Shirakawa is making changes. You are no longer welcome at the palace. Lose the title Senior Court Rank (and also Junior Court Rank if you forgot to erase it earlier) and then turn to **79**.

115

The knights recognize the katana as having belonged to a clan cousin of theirs. 'He was murdered in Golnir,' says one of the knights darkly.

They both turn to face you, hands hovering over their sword-hilts. If you want to defuse the situation you will need to make a CHARISMA roll at a Difficulty of 14.

Successful CHARISMA roll	turn to **163**
Failed (or not attempted) roll	turn to **186**

116

The vampires lunge at you with outstretched arms like sleepwalkers in the throes of a homicidal nightmare. Fight them one at a time.

First Vampire, COMBAT 6, Defence 10, Stamina 14
Second Vampire, COMBAT 6, Defence 10, Stamina 14
Third Vampire, COMBAT 6, Defence 10, Stamina 14
Fourth Vampire, COMBAT 6, Defence 10, Stamina 14
Fifth Vampire, COMBAT 6, Defence 10, Stamina 14

If you defeat them all, turn to **91**.

117

Small glassy eyes peer back at you from the darkness above the rafters. Make a CHARISMA roll at a Difficulty of 17. You can add 1 to the dice roll for every 50 Shards you offer to tempt the creatures down (remember to cross the money off).

Successful CHARISMA roll	turn to **165**
Failed CHARISMA roll	turn to **141**

118

Oblivion engulfs your mind. You fall and lie in a dead faint for nine days and nights. You awaken to see the moon rising over the mountains. Finding a rock pool inside the cave, you study your reflection in amazement. Your skin is as hard and dark as lead and your eyes burn like silver coins.

Some of the dragon's essence has seeped into your own soul. Like a dragon, you have become tough, wily and unrelenting. Increase your COMBAT and MAGIC scores each by 2 but reduce CHARISMA by 2. You can also permanently increase your unwounded Stamina score by 1-6 points (roll one die).

Your dragon nature, however, disqualifies you from the priesthood. Reduce your SANCTITY score to 1. Cross the Gods Box off your Adventure Sheet entirely – you can never be an initiate of any deity from now on. If you are a Priest you must choose a new profession (Mage, Rogue, Troubadour, Warrior or Wayfarer) and alter your Adventure Sheet accordingly.

Remember to cross the **tatsu pearl** off your list of possessions before turning to **488**.

119

To become an initiate of Nai costs 75 Shards. You may not already be an initiate of another god. Write Nai in the God box on your Adventure Sheet, then turn to **69**.

120

'Have you heard?' says an excited youth as he goes by. 'The chancellor's men have caught that villainous wizard Akugenda the Unseen. They're going to try and execute him at Shingen, but I'll bet he's got a few tricks up his sleeve yet.'

'Shingen is a long way off,' you reply, unimpressed. 'The news might be out of date, and Akugenda already a year in his grave.'

He shrugs and walks off. Turn to **396**.

121

At dusk you come to a yawning hole in a hillside. It is overgrown with creepers and you would never have noticed it but for the glimmer of grey light corning from within.

Enter	turn to **169**
Walk on	turn to **31**

122

You are sailing out of the waters around Dragon Isle.

Go north	turn to **406**
Go south	turn to **309**
Go east	turn to **72**
Go west	*Over the Blood-Dark Sea* **55**

123 □

The palace is a complex of buildings set in ornamental gardens inside a low white wall. This is the home of the Sovereign, Takakura, who is supposedly a direct descendant of the Spirit of the Sun.

If the box above is empty, put a tick in it and turn to **172**. If it already has a tick, turn to **317**.

124

A shrine reveals itself as a splash of gold and red half-hidden in the trees beside a waterfall. As you stand watching, a group of white-clad women come out to dance for the local spirit.

Stop at the shrine	turn to **731**
Press on	turn to **147**

125

You are on the middle stretch of the Western Coastal Road, just south of the town of Shingen. Willows droop from the banks of earth on both sides, keeping the road in cool shade. Every so often the road opens out to give you a breathtaking view of the sea crashing against the base of the cliffs.

Go north	turn to **362**
Go south	turn to **733**
Leave the road	turn to **653**

126

Your ship goes down and is lost with all hands. Cross its details off the Ship's Manifest. You are cast into the sea clinging to a broken timber and it takes all your strength just to keep your head above water. Make a SCOUTING roll at a Difficulty of 14.

Successful SCOUTING roll	turn to **241**
Failed SCOUTING roll	turn to **140**

127

'No doubt you will buy the goods that are cheap and plentiful in Akatsurai and transport them to foreign lands where you can sell at an indecent profit!' says Ko-ishi with a broad grin.

The prices he quotes are for entire Cargo Units. Any cargo you buy will be delivered to your ship in the harbour, and you should therefore note it on the Ship's Manifest.

Cargo	*To buy*	*To sell*
Furs	250 Shards	160 Shards
Grain	80 Shards	60 Shards
Metals	700 Shards	550 Shards
Minerals	550 Shards	500 Shards
Spices	600 Shards	500 Shards
Textiles	180 Shards	150 Shards
Timber	200 Shards	150 Shards

When you have completed your business, turn to **79**.

128

Beyond the warehouses and shipyards lining the seafront, you can see the pretty blue-lacquered lodges of Kaiju rising up the high tree-lined slopes at the back of the bay.

Go into town	turn to **270**
Visit the warehouses	turn to **153**
Go aboard your ship (if docked here)	turn to **105**
Buy a ship	turn to **176**
Pay for passage on a ship	turn to **199**

129

As you get closer to the person walking ahead, you see it is a woman wrapped in a thin ragged tunic and carrying a sack. She must be very poor; her straw sandals are worn through and her feet are raw with blisters. Perhaps that is why she is sobbing quietly to herself.

Drawing level, you ask if she is all right but she turns away and buries her face in her sleeve. Her weeping is quite piteous. It is obvious she is very upset.

Offer to help	turn to **177**
Continue on your way	turn to **357**

130

Shingen lies on the Western Coastal Road from Chambara to Hidari. Pilgrims pass through here on their way up to Noboro Monastery.

Take the road north	turn to **173**
Take the road south	turn to **125**
Take the road east	turn to **195**
Follow the river	turn to **359**
Set sail (if ship docked here)	turn to **200**

131

Takakura takes the **lady's court robe** from you and holds it to his face, breathing in his lost love's perfume. 'I am sorry I couldn't persuade her to return,' you say, bowing.

Takakura heaves a deep sigh. 'It is not your fault. Secretary Masayori will see you are rewarded for your efforts on the way out.'

And so you are dismissed. Cross the **lady's court robe** off your Adventure Sheet. Masayori, a disdainful individual with a long thin neck and globular head, gives you a purse containing 150 Shards for your efforts.

'You won't come back here if you know what's good for you,' he says. 'We don't need foreign devils meddling in court affairs.'

Well, you've been told. Now turn to **79**.

132

The guards refuse to let you in. 'Lord Kiyomori is too important to be bothered with the likes of you,' says their captain.

Obviously you are not going to get anywhere by being direct.

Sneak in after dark	turn to **205**
Give up any hope of seeing Kiyomori	turn to **79**

133

A vaunting laugh issues from the heart of the ghostly image. 'Not all your piety nor wits will save you when this lightning hits!' it shrieks.

A web of dazzling blue fire leaps from its fingers, reducing your flesh to bubbling fat and ashes. Turn to **140**.

134

You blink and look again. What you took for a serpent's head really is just a large rock in the middle of the stream. A man in elegant black silk steps on to it.

'Excellent,' he says, 'you have brought my sceptre.'

Give it to him	turn to **159**
Keep it yourself	turn to **182**

135

Mister Dragon parries whatever weapon you are using by catching it between the palms of his hands. Then, with only a slight shrug of the shoulders, he snaps it in two. Remove that weapon from your list of possessions and turn to **719**.

136

The coastal cliffs form walls of rock on one side; walls of black storm-clouds tower on the other. 'Let's not get trapped between them,' cautions the helmsman.

Roll two dice.

Score 2-9	A safe journey	turn to **87**
Score 10-12	A blustery wind	turn to **447**

137

From this vantage point it is easy to spy out the paths leading back down. You take it slowly but surely, reaching the foothills after a couple of days.

Turn to **338**.

138

They belong to the Camellia Clan, a once-prosperous house that has fallen on hard times. 'But there is a new wind blowing from the east,' says the younger knight, 'and the fortunes of our family may rise again.'

They start to reminisce about past glories, entirely forgetting about you.

Turn to **243**.

139

The tengu pelt you with sticks and pine cones, flutter down to tear your clothes, and cavort about tormenting you on all sides. There are far too many of them to fight. You can only run for your life.

Lose 1-6 Stamina points, all your possessions and half of any money you're carrying. Assuming you survive, the tengu finally tire of their sport and let you go.

Turn to **603**.

140

You are dead. If you have a resurrection deal, turn to the section noted on your Adventure Sheet after first erasing your current possessions, money and any details on the Ship's Manifest.

If you don't have a resurrection arranged, this is the end and you can only start afresh with a new character. First make sure to erase all ticks, codewords and Adventure Sheet details in all your *Fabled Lands* books. You can begin again at **1** in any of the books in the series.

141

You only succeed in frightening the creatures away. With disgruntled squawks they fling themselves from the tower and go flapping heavily off into the woods.

Investigate the main building	turn to **92**
Leave the shrine	turn to **398**

142

This time you are completely transformed into a dragon. You become very powerful indeed, but the bad news is that you forget all about your previous life as a human being. Perhaps when you lie curled up in your cave you will sometimes dream of a time when you were human, but when you awaken to slay the adventurers who disturb you those memories will soon fade.

That is the end for you in your current persona. To start again, erase all the ticks, notes, codewords, etc, in all your *Fabled Lands* books and then start with a new persona at **1** in any of the books in the series.

143

You take a lighted taper to the altar and silently announce your decision to the god. As you depart, a slight tremor makes the ground shake under your feet. No one else seems to have noticed. Could it just be a message to you from Nai himself? And if so, what does it portend?

Turn to **323**.

144

Cross the **head** off your Adventure Sheet.

'This is excellent' says the youth, knotting the head's hair to his belt. 'It looks really fierce! I can go home now – everyone will think I've slain my first foe.'

He reveals that he is the nephew of Lord Yoritomo, self-styled Shogun of the realm. He promises to recommend you to his uncle. 'He's always on the lookout for new henchmen.'

You have made a useful friend. Get the codeword *Frog* and turn to **396**.

145

A tall-prowed vessel with triangular sails comes sweeping without warning from the east. Along her rail you see warriors of olive hue whose dark eyes gleam with avarice and bloodlust. There is no mistaking men of that stamp, whatever their race or flag - pirates!

It is too late to put about. The pirates pull alongside and come swarming aboard. Their leader issues a challenge to single combat. He is a huge insane-looking man with a wiry brush of hair sticking straight up from his scalp. You have to beat him in order to survive.

Wacko, COMBAT 12, Defence 22, Stamina 29

Surrender	turn to **52**
Fight on and win	turn to **218**

146

You are on a road that looks as if few people use it. Clumps of limp, grey grass protrude from mist-covered marshland on either side. The few trees look like broken bits of stone.

Go to the end of the road	*Into the Underworld* **633**

Go back to the lands of men — turn to **98**

147

Pulling yourself away from the serenity of Clearwater Shrine, you decide which way to go now.

Make for Shingen	turn to **195**
Take the road to Mukogawa	turn to **54**
Go north cross-country	turn to **444**
Go due south	turn to **220**

148

Much of the way simply consists of arduous climbs up steep mountain paths, but from time to time you have to scale a rock face.

Make a SCOUTING roll at Difficulty 12. You can add 1 to the dice roll if you have **climbing gear**.

Successful SCOUTING roll	turn to **5**
Failed SCOUTING roll	turn to **219**

149

Get the codeword *Frog* if you didn't have it already. Also, if you gave the priests at least 100 Shards, you receive a blessing of Safety from Storms. When you are ready to resume your voyage, turn to **745**.

150

'Ah, you can almost smell the rich spices of the Orient!' says the bosun as he stands at the rail and sucks in a deep breath.

'That's seaweed you're smelling, you lubber!' laughs the first mate. 'Either that or your own sweet grog-soaked breath.'

'Enough skylarking!' you call. 'Look lively now.'

Roll two dice.

Score 2	Pirates attack	turn to **145**
Score 3-10	Nothing untoward	turn to **381**
Score 11-12	Submerged rocks	turn to **588**

151

You are accosted by the side of the street by a blind man who stares at you with milky-white eyes. 'Travel straight to the woods from here,' he hisses in a tone of great urgency. 'Go upstream and look for a door under an old oak. Take the left-hand path.'

He veers off, tapping the boardwalk with his cane, and is lost in the crowd. A strange encounter.

Lose the codeword *Cenotaph* and turn to **8**.

152

'The Autumn Moon family has handled all the financial affairs of the Wistaria Clan for seven generations,' says Ko-ishi. 'Your money could not be in safer hands.'

Get the codeword *Fuligin* if you didn't have it already.

Make an investment	turn to **175**
Check on investments	turn to **198**
Bid him good-day	turn to **79**

153

You enter a whitewashed building at the back of the harbour. Apart from a few crates, the warehouse is almost bare. The merchants tell you most of their stock has been sold to the Moonrise Clan in Mukogawa. They quote the following prices:

Cargo	To buy	To sell
Furs	125 Shards	75 Shards
Grain	225 Shards	200 Shards
Metals	750 Shards	650 Shards
Minerals	500 Shards	450 Shards
Spices	—	600 Shards
Textiles	250 Shards	175 Shards
Timber	200 Shards	100 Shards

These prices are per Cargo Unit. Any Cargo Units you buy will be taken to your ship, so note them on the Ship's Manifest.

After you've completed your business, turn to **128**.

154

You catch up with a pilgrim on his way to the Wistaria Clan shrine in Chompo. 'Ordinary riff-raff aren't allowed into the shrine,' he tells you, 'but I'm assured of a welcome because I saved an old Wistaria lord from getting beaten up by skinheads in Chambara.' Turn to **357**.

155

Narai is a city of high wooden stave-halls and long bridges built between the many tranquil rock gardens. Seen in winter, with snow dusting the rooftops and smudging the contours of the landscape beyond, it is a place of almost ethereal beauty.

You can buy a town house here for 300 Shards. If you do, put a tick in the box beside the town house option below.

Visit your town house ☐ (if box ticked)	turn to **414**
Go to the harbour	turn to **433**
Go shopping	turn to **511**
Visit a temple	turn to **532**
Leave the city	turn to **11**

156

If you have the codeword *Flux*, turn to **204**. If not but you are a Troubadour, turn to **227**. Otherwise, turn to **251**.

157

Kiyomori is pleased to see you. 'I would have sent you an invitation to the banquet if I'd known you were going to be in town,' he says. 'You're just in time for the play. I've had a stage built in the garden and a theatrical troupe is going to give us a performance of a play called "No heads". Intriguing, eh?'

'It's a curious title, certainly,' you have to admit.

Stay and watch the play	turn to **557**
Sneak inside the house	turn to **205**
Make your excuses and leave	turn to **79**

158

The force of the ghost's attack staggers you, but you refuse to fall. Summoning all your occult skill, you divert the energy into two blistering white streams that spill off to either side, charring the grass but leaving you unscathed.

Luckily, Kiyomori is himself a priest, and your intervention has bought him the precious seconds he needed to chant the rite of exorcism. Akugenda's ghost gives a dismayed wail as it feels its power beginning to fade. Hastily you join your own prayers to those of the Lord Chancellor. Turn to **110**.

159

Cross off the **royal sceptre**.

The god of the valley rewards you with a blessing of Safety from Storms. However, unlike an ordinary blessing, this will never be used up; it is permanent. Note it on your Adventure Sheet (and remember to mark it as permanent).

The god waves his hand in front of your face. You wake to find yourself lying on the bank of the stream, although you cannot remember dozing off. The rock is again just that: a flat mossy boulder shaped vaguely like a serpent's head.

Turn to **111**.

160

The world flickers deathly white as though a god had opened his eyes, followed at once by a boom of thunder that shakes right through your body.

If you have a blessing of Safety from Storms or a **catastrophe certificate**, cross it off and turn to **551**. (In the event that you have both, you decide which to cross off.) If not, turn to **183**.

161

An overcast blurs the boundary between sea and sky. If not for the dark line of cliffs to the south you could imagine yourself suspended in a pale grey void. Roll two dice.

Score 2	Carried by a strong current	turn to **745**
Score 3-10	An uneventful day's sailing	turn to **184**
Score 12	Pirates	turn to **145**

162

A draught snuffs out your light. Or was it a draught? As the thick darkness closes around you there is a noise very like a chuckle might sound in a dead and desiccated throat.

| Run for your life | turn to **584** |
| Fight blind | turn to **563** |

163

You convince them that you slew their cousin in a fair fight.

'Tsebaka was like an unsheathed sword,' they say, nodding. 'He never could stay out of trouble.'

They advise you to give them the **ivory-handled katana** in case you run into other warriors of their clan who might not be so amenable. Cross it off your Adventure Sheet if you do, then turn to **243**.

164 ☐☐☐☐

You are taken to the tengu king, whose throne is a lightning-split cryptomeria tree swaddled in a century's growth of moss.

Put a tick in one of the boxes above.

If you have just ticked the first box   turn to **22**

If you have just ticked the second box	turn to **187**
If you have just ticked the third	turn to **212**
If you have just ticked the fourth	turn to **235**
If all the boxes were already ticked	turn to **259**

165

Down from the belfry come two tengu: scampering creatures with glossy black plumage and crow-like beaks. They tell you the shrine was abandoned because of a terrible massacre many years ago that caused it to become defiled.

'We used to roost in the main hall and store our loot on the altar, but we gave that up when a goblin spider took up residence.'

They soon lose interest in talking to you. 'Come to the heart of the wood if you dare,' says one, tilting its head to one side and giving you an inscrutable look. 'Our king likes mortals.'

They flit off into the brightening sky.

Go over to the main building	turn to **92**
Leave the shrine now	turn to **398**

166

Something catches your eye among the heaps of silver and gold. At first glance it is only a plain wooden baton, but you sense a powerful aura of magic. It is surely the **royal sceptre** you have been searching for. Add it to your list of possessions and lose the codeword *Fresco*, then turn to **646**.

167

You find an inn where you can stay for 1 Shard a day. For each day you spend at the inn, you can recuperate 1 lost Stamina point until your Stamina score is back to normal.

When you are ready to move on, turn to **323**.

168

If you possess a **dead head** or a **ghoul's head**, turn now to **191**. If not, read on.

You fall asleep under a tree and dream about huge black birds that live in the middle of the woods and teach tricks of magic and martial arts to a few favoured travellers. One of the birds offers to trade a magic lodestone that will help you find them.

When you wake up, you find that a **compass (SCOUTING +1)** has replaced one of the items in your knapsack. Roll one die and the result is the number of the item replaced, counting from the first (e.g. if you roll a 3, the third item listed on your Adventure Sheet is replaced). If you roll a number that does not correspond to an item on your Adventure Sheet then you get the compass without losing anything. Turn to **3**.

169

You enter a warren of enchanted tunnels that link places all across the world. From here you can travel to distant places, emerging by magic through a vent in empty space.

To Aku	*The Court of Hidden Faces* **444**
To Dweomer	*Over the Blood-Dark Sea* **571**
To the Great Steppes	*The Plains of Howling Darkness* **118**
To Yellowport	*The War-Torn Kingdom* **10**
To Erebus	*Into the Underworld* **689**
To Hagashin	turn to **226**

170

You are sailing in the Ghostwaters of Nyg. When you enquire the reason for this region's name, none aboard can enlighten you.

'Nyg was a wizard of old,' says the navigator with a shrug. 'I know no more than that.'

Go east	turn to **80**
Go north	turn to **309**
Go south	*Over the Blood-Dark Sea* **98**
Go west	*Over the Blood-Dark Sea* **136**
Head for land	turn to **250**

171

The priests can offer a range of blessings. Pay 35 Shards and roll randomly using one die, or choose the blessing you want for 60 Shards.

Score 1	CHARISMA blessing
Score 2	COMBAT blessing

Score 3   MAGIC blessing
Score 4   SANCTITY blessing
Score 5   SCOUTING blessing
Score 6   THIEVERY blessing

The blessing allows you to try again when you fail an ability roll. Blessings only work once and are then used up. You can have only one blessing of each type at a time, so if you rolled for a random blessing and got one you already had then you have wasted your money.

Turn to **79**.

172

A shopkeeper gives you directions, but you take a wrong turn and get lost in a derelict part of the city. There is no one to ask the way.

By the time you find your way to the palace gates it is nearly dark. Curiously, there are no guards on duty. Peering inside the gate, you see a garden filling with purple dusk and a solitary lamp burning in a gazebo surrounded by ivy-strung trellises. The main buildings of the palace are plunged in darkness.

Go across the garden	turn to **615**
Search the palace buildings	turn to **636**
Turn back	turn to **79**

173

The road runs from Chambara, the capital, to the town of Shingen where the Lord Chancellor has his private residence. It would be a daring highwayman indeed who tried to ply his trade along this heavily-patrolled route.

Roll two dice.

Score 2-8	A quiet journey	turn to **196**
Score 9-12	A military patrol	turn to **505**

174 ☐

The wind races across rolling grassy hillsides, swiftly driving the shadows of clouds ahead of it, and for a time you feel as if you are the last person alive in the world.

If the box is empty, put a tick in it and turn to **570**. If it was already ticked, turn to **192**.

175

If you have any of these codewords, delete them now: *Almanac*, *Bastion*, *Catalyst* or *Eldritch*.

You can invest money in multiples of 100 Shards. Ko-ishi will use this money to buy and sell commodities on your behalf while you are away from the city.

Write the sum you are investing in the box below – or withdraw a sum you invested previously. When you have completed the transaction, turn to **79**.

```
┌─────────────────────────────────────────────────────────┐
│ MONEY INVESTED                                          │
│                                                         │
│                                                         │
│                                                         │
│                                                         │
│                                                         │
└─────────────────────────────────────────────────────────┘
```

176

You are shown a couple of vessels. When you sourly remark that you are hardly spoiled for choice, the owner of the ships remarks that the Moonrise Clan has bought up the best vessels for its navy. Choose a ship if you still want one and copy her details on to the Ship's Manifest. (Don't forget to cross off the money.)

Ship type	Cost	Capacity
Barque	250 Shards	1 Cargo Unit
Brigantine	550 Shards	2 Cargo Units

You can sell a ship for 10% less than these prices. If you buy a ship, the crew quality is average. Note that the ship is docked at Kaiju and then turn to **128**.

177

No sooner have you spoken than the woman drops her sleeve and rounds on you. Your heart freezes when you see that she has no eyes or nose or mouth – there is only a featureless blank where her face should be. A ghastly moan splits the air as she reaches out to touch you. Her fingers brush your lips. There is an instant of blind panic, then you pass out.

You recover at dusk to find yourself lying half in the ditch beside the path. An old farmer with a lantern is hobbling through the fields towards you.

'Are you hurt?' he starts to ask. Then, as he sees you look up, he gives a frightened whimper and runs off. You put a hand up to feel, and your worst fears are confirmed. You no longer have a face.

Turn to **78**.

178

Mukogawa is a city of strong gleaming ramparts built on cliffs overlooking the sea. White banners flutter and snap in the breeze and soldiers in white surcoats patrol the streets. This is the stronghold of the Moonrise Clan, whose ancestral shrine is just across the straits on Udai Island.

Leave the city on foot	turn to **203**
Visit the Moonrise Clan manor	turn to **726**
Go to the harbour	turn to **281**
Visit the shrine of Juntoku	turn to **49**
Get lodging at an inn	turn to **717**
Go to the armoury	turn to **744**

179

The courtiers look at you in shock. The frown on Takakura's face tells you that he is not pleased by your reply. 'What are you saying?' he mutters darkly. 'Is it not true that the Sovereign's wish is second only to the decrees of heaven?'

This is a sticky situation. You will need a CHARISMA roll at a Difficulty of 15 to wriggle out of it.

Successful CHARISMA roll	turn to **271**
Failed CHARISMA roll	turn to **286**

180

If you have the title Paladin of Ravayne, turn to **345**. Otherwise, turn to **289**.

181

Wrapping a fur rug around your shoulders, you sit out on the veranda with a cup of hot rice wine and watch the moon rise above the pines.

Roll two dice.

Score 2-8	A holy visitor	turn to **366**
Score 9-12	An uneventful night	turn to **610**

182

'Such temerity,' says the god, compressing his lips.

He turns his back on you, steps off the rock and vanishes in a fount of black water. You feel a sudden baleful influence.

Make a MAGIC roll at a Difficulty of 25.

Successful MAGIC roll	turn to **207**
Failed MAGIC roll	turn to **230**

183

With a terrifying screech, a blazing creature drops directly out of the sky. It collides with a tree, throwing up a fountain of white sparks, and rebounds towards you. You catch a fleeting glimpse of a slavering muzzle, muscular body, and wet fur engulfed in dazzling light. Then it strikes.

If you are a Priest, turn immediately to **208**. Otherwise you must fight this creature.

Thunder Beast, COMBAT 15, Defence 20, Stamina 20

When it hits you, reduce the damage inflicted by 1 for every 1000 Shards you are carrying. (This is because its electrical attacks are dissipated by strings of cash.)

If you kill the thunder beast, it vanishes in a mass of hissing sparks; turn to **551**.

184

'The cliffs of Kito Province,' says Mister Stone, the senior midshipman, with a sigh. 'My wife's family hails from there.'

'Wives are for landlubbers,' growls the bosun. 'A mariner's ship is all the mistress he needs.'

'And his captain the only master,' you remind him. 'Look alive, mister; I'm setting a new course.'

Go south	turn to **136**
Go west	turn to **684**

185

From here on the climbing gets much harder. Ice-laden wind off the peaks makes your fingers numb, and though you cling to the mountainside it returns a rough embrace.

Make a SCOUTING roll at Difficulty 14; you can add 1 to the dice roll if you have **climbing gear**.

Successful SCOUTING roll	turn to **233**
Failed SCOUTING roll	turn to **210**

186

The knights demand satisfaction. One of them stands back as his cousin advances with drawn sword. At least it looks like you will get a fair fight, since they are not both attacking you at once. Fight them one at a time.

First Knight, COMBAT 7, Defence 13, Stamina 14

Second Knight, COMBAT 8, Defence 14, Stamina 17

If you defeat them you can have their two sets of **ring mail (Defence +2)** and their **swords**. There is also a pouch containing 9 Shards.

After looting the bodies, turn to **243**.

187

The tengu king throws aside dignity to teach you the art of concealment.

'You must become a shadow,' he says. 'Slide across the ground without weight and you will make no sound. Press yourself down until you have no thickness. Melt into the background until you scarcely exist.'

It sounds esoteric, but it seems to work. Increase your THIEVERY score by 1, then turn to **259**.

188

The long grass rustles as you walk up to the main shrine building, but the man on the veranda apparently hasn't heard you.

Go up and touch him on the shoulder	turn to **432**
Advance with caution	turn to **510**
Turn and leave	turn to **398**

189

You stumble on a region of broken decayed rock overgrown with stunted trees and rank grass. Deep channels form a dank, low-lying grotto where the walls are spattered with patches of lichen.

If you have the codeword *Fist*, turn to **214**. If not, turn to **237**.

190

There is a ship bound for Hagashin, on the south island. The captain wants 10 Shards to take you along.

Pay for passage to Hagashin	turn to **302**
Stay in Hidari after all	turn to **323**

191

You get lost in a sudden fog that rises without warning off the waterlogged rice paddies. Suddenly you hear a champing noise and you pull off your haversack to find that the head has gnashed its way out. The head gives you a painful bite before you manage to throw it away into the fog.

Lose 2-12 Stamina points and also reduce your unwounded Stamina score by 1 point permanently if you don't have a blessing of Immunity to Disease/Poison. Almost as bad, half your money has fallen out of the pack and you have no hope of finding it now, so cross it off your Adventure Sheet. Also remember to cross off the **head**.

Turn to **3**.

192

You are suddenly beset on all sides by huge spidery things that dart up out of hidden burrows. Fight them all at once: each time that you strike at one of them, they all get to strike back at you.

First Spider, COMBAT 8, Defence 12, Stamina 17

Second Spider, COMBAT 8, Defence 12, Stamina 13
Third Spider, COMBAT 12, Defence 12, Stamina 12

You cannot escape from them. If you win, turn to **280**.

193

'In Chambara,' says one of the sailors, 'I once saw a knight cut a man down and walk away, with no better excuse than to test the edge of his sword.'

'The Akatsurese are bloodthirsty fiends,' says the ship's carpenter. 'And yet, do you know what they call us? Whitefaced devils! They are irredeemable!'

Where will you set your course?

To the north	turn to **72**
South to the Sea of Hydras	*Over the Blood-Dark Sea* **136**
East to Akatsurai	turn to **250**
West	*Over the Blood-Dark Sea* **172**

194

The road curves down towards Chompo with farmland to either side. Where now?

To Chompo	turn to **59**
To the coast	turn to **98**
Due east	turn to **242**
Due west	turn to **282**

195

Apart from pilgrims seeking the Clearwater Shrine, few people use this road. There is little contact between the chancellor's court at Shingen and the rebel military government of the east.

Go south-west to Shingen	turn to **362**
Go north over open country	turn to **704**
Strike out to the south	turn to **220**
Visit the shrine	turn to **124**

196

Bees hum in the blossom-laden branches overhanging the road. Some way ahead, a pedlar's cart creaks lopsidedly along, followed by a gaggle of laughing children. From this idyllic scene you would never guess that Akatsurai is a country poised on the brink of civil war.

Go up the coast to Chambara	turn to **79**
Go south to Shingen	turn to **362**
Go east over open country	turn to **704**

197

You jump lightly on to the serpent's head just as its eyes snap open. You feel as though your heart skipped a beat. Without waiting for it to attack, you hurry on up the valley towards the trees.

There is a flicker in the corner of your eye. It felt as if a cold wind blew past you, ruffling your clothes. You look back towards the stream, but there is now no sign of the serpent.

'Hallo,' says an imperious voice.

You jump back a pace. A tall man in long robes of dark green silk is standing under the trees just in front of you. Where did he come from?

'I am the god of the valley,' he says. 'Since you were brave enough to cross the river by stepping on my head, I know you will not shrink from undertaking a dangerous task. Go now to the Yasai Mountains and retrieve my royal sceptre and you will be richly rewarded.' With those words he departs.

Get the codeword *Fresco* and turn to **111**.

198

To find out how well your investments have done, roll two dice. Add 1 to the score if you are an initiate of the Three Fortunes. Also add 1 for each of the following codewords that you have: *Almanac*, *Bastion*, *Catalyst* and *Eldritch*.

Score 2-3	Lose entire sum invested
Score 4-5	Loss of 50%
Score 6-7	Loss of 100%
Score 8-9	Investment remains unchanged
Score 10-11	Profit of 10%
Score 12-13	Profit of 25%
Score 14-15	Profit of 50%
Score 16-17	Profit of 100%

Now turn to **175**, where you can withdraw the sum recorded in the box there after adjusting it according to the result you have just rolled.

199

There are two ships leaving Kaiju harbour within the next week. You can travel aboard the *Divine Wind*, bound for Chambara, for 15 Shards; or you can hire passage on the *Majesty*, returning to Metriciens, for 35 Shards. (Bear in mind that if you wish to carry on your adventures in Metriciens you will need *Cities of Gold and Glory* and *Over the Blood-Dark Sea*.)

Chambara, cost 15 Shards	turn to **27**
Metriciens, cost 35 Shards	*Over the Blood-Dark Sea* **260**
Stay in Kaiju	turn to **128**

200

Here the waters are pale as moonstone and there is the scent of luxuriant blossoms on the breeze. Viewed from here, the coast of Akatsurai resembles a delightful tapestry in soft green and blue dyes. Recover 1 Stamina point if injured.

'Our current position is just off the west coast of Yodoshi, the main island,' reports the navigator. 'Where now, captain?'

Tie up at Shingen wharf	turn to **470**
Steer south	turn to **350**
Steer north	turn to **150**
Head out to sea	turn to **80**

201

In a remote village where you are invited to spend the night, at dusk a traveller arrives with a haversack of odds and ends. To help sell his wares he gathers the villagers around and starts to spin a yarn.

If you possess a **mask** of any sort, turn to **248**. If not, turn to **225**.

202

Flying fish patterned like jewel-coloured dragonflies go skimming across the azure water.

'Many are the marvels of the sea,' says the bosun with a sigh. 'If I live to be a hundred I could never hope to see a tenth part of them.'

Recover 1 Stamina point if injured, then roll two dice.

Score 2-4	Attacked at sea	turn to **145**
Score 5-10	All's quiet	turn to **170**
Score 11-12	Blown off-course	turn to **309**

203

Three great roads converge on Mukogawa, but the two leading west are seldom travelled these days because of the hostility that exists between the lords of the Moonrise Clan and the official government of Lord Kiyomori. The third road goes north to Chompo, where the Wistaria Clan rules in ancient splendour.

Take the road to Chompo	turn to **495**
Go west to Chambara	turn to **552**
Go south-west towards Shingen	turn to **54**
Go south along the coast	turn to **438**

204

Forewarned by the cautionary tale of the hermit Jobutsu, you make sure to blow the dust out of the flute before starting to play.

If you have the codeword *Cerumen*, turn to **324**. Otherwise, turn to **343**.

205

You walk around the corner out of sight, melt into the shadows and double-back into the mansion. But Kiyomori has not risen to be dictator of Akatsurai by being careless, and there are guards at the end of every corridor.

Make a THIEVERY roll at a Difficulty of 16.

Successful THIEVERY roll	turn to **670**
Failed THIEVERY roll	turn to **693**

206

You can hire a local guide for 10 Shards or go hunting on your own.

Take the guide	turn to **229**
Go alone	turn to **253**

207

Unseen hands try to remove the sceptre from your belt but you drive them off with a protective spell. Leaning down over the stream, you catch a glimpse of the god's face shimmering there in the dark depths. He draws away, frightened by your power, and you are left with only your own reflection.

At last you understand the powers of the **royal sceptre**. It can be used as a weapon with a COMBAT bonus of +5 and also gives +5 to your other abilities (CHARISMA, MAGIC, SANCTITY, SCOUTING and THIEVERY) — but remember that ability bonuses from two different items cannot be added together.

Note the sceptre's powers on your Adventure Sheet and then turn to **111**.

208

The thunder beast cannot abide the scent of holy incense on your robes. With a roar like a cannon-shot, it leaps back up into the clouds.

Turn to **551**.

209

At the back of a cliff-lined bay on Udai Island stands a shrine dedicated to the worship of the Moonrise Clan's ancestral spirits.

Priests in white robes come down to the beach to meet you. They are armed with moon spades – poles with a shovel-shaped blade on one end, a scythe on the other. Their vows are supposed to prohibit them from shedding blood, but they will fight to defend the shrine.

Attack the priests	turn to **291**
Make an offering to the spirits	turn to **496**
Embark and set sail	turn to **745**

210

You lose your grip while negotiating an overhang, plunging down a sheer precipice. If you are lucky, the tree branches below might just save your life. Lose 4-24 Stamina points (roll four dice) unless you have **rope** or **climbing gear**, in which case lose only 1-6 Stamina.

If you survive the fall, turn to **5**.

211

The time you have spent traversing the mountains has left you invigorated. Regain 1 Stamina point if injured. Now, however, it is time to go back down to the world of men.

Go west	turn to **653**
Go east	turn to **535**
Go south	turn to **74**
Go north	turn to **220**

212

'Pay attention,' says the tengu king, sailing high over your head with an effortless leap. 'This is a tricky technique to master, and if you get it wrong in a fight it'll prove worse than useless.'

Roll two dice.

Score 2-6 Reduce your COMBAT score by 1
Score 7 The lesson teaches you nothing
Score 8-12 Increase your COMBAT score by 1

After your lesson is over, turn to **259**.

213

You move closer through the long grass, but still he has not noticed you.

Announce your presence	turn to **236**
Sneak up on him	turn to **260**
Turn and depart	turn to **398**

214

You take a nap in a moss-lined cleft of rock. When you wake, you notice a young woman burying something under a tree nearby. Her long hair hangs down around her face as she digs, obscuring her vision so that she hasn't noticed you.

Go over to her	turn to **311**
Stay hidden until she's gone	turn to **261**

215

Sanobu's shrine is built on a wide shelf of rock overlooking the waterfall. There is no effigy of the god, just a dim chamber at the back of the shrine where you can view the exposed mark in the rock which is supposedly Sanobu's footprint.

To obtain a blessing you must pay 35 Shards and make a CHARISMA roll at a Difficulty of 15 (Difficulty 12 if you are an initiate of Sanobu). On a successful roll you get a blessing of Safety from Storms which you can write in the Blessings box on your Adventure Sheet. This blessing may help you at sea, but it works only once and is then used up. You can have only one Safety from Storms blessing at a time.

To become an initiate you must pay a donation of 50 Shards, and you can then write Sanobu in the God box on your Adventure Sheet. You must not already be an initiate of another god. (If you were already an initiate of Sanobu and want to renounce that status now, you must pay 30 Shards by way of compensation.)

When you have finished your devotions, turn to **270**.

216

The music of the flute is so beautiful that you are inspired to join in with a song. Roll two dice and add your CHARISMA. (You can use the bonus of any one item you possess that augments your CHARISMA, just like making a normal CHARISMA roll.)

Score 2-10	Your hideous racket offends the gods; lose any blessings.
Score 11-20	Your song pleases the gods; gain a point of CHARISMA.
Score 21+	Your singing makes the gods jealous; lose a point of CHARISMA.

After amending your Adventure Sheet, turn to **732**.

217

The occupant of the sedan chair is none other than Lord Yoritomo of the Moonrise Clan – the self-proclaimed Shogun, or First General of Akatsurai. He is not shaken by the close call he has just had, just annoyed with himself for getting careless.

If you have the codeword *Frog*, turn to **294**. If not, turn to **375**.

218

The pirates obey their own warped code of honour, surrendering now that you've slain their leader. You can take his **sword (COMBAT +1)** and **splint armour (Defence +4)**. The new pirate leader also presents you with the **pirate captain's head**; if you want it. He agrees to take you to their lair in a secluded cove midway between Shingen and Hidari, where they hand over their loot.

Roll one die to see what you get:

Score 1-2	1000 Shards and **lockpicks (THIEVERY +1)**
Score 3-4	750 Shards and a **silver nugget**
Score 5	550 Shards and an **iron fan**
Score 6	350 Shards and a **bag of pearls**

Record the loot on your Adventure Sheet and turn to **556**.

219

You slip, grab a handful of weathered rock that crumbles under your fingers, and slide back down the ravine. Sharp rocks tear at your clothing and batter your tumbling body. Lose 3-18 Stamina points (roll three dice) unless you have **rope** or **climbing gear**, in which case lose only 1-6 Stamina. If you are still alive, turn to **319**.

220

In the uplands, night brings moonlight as dazzling as polished silver. With the sunrise, morning mist unveils pretty meadows and meandering flower-lined paths.

Roll two dice.

| Score 2-7 | You see no one | turn to **243** |
| Score 8-12 | Two poor knights | turn to **89** |

221

You are on the road running west from the capital towards Oni Province, a place of sinister renown. Pine trees throw stripes of shade across a dusty road washed with sunlight, so that it seems a giant tiger lies lazily across the landscape.

Follow the road west	turn to **500**
Travel to the capital	turn to **79**
Strike out due north	turn to **337**

222

The storm keeps up for days. Your only recourse is to strike the sails and let the ship run before the wind until it blows itself out.

Roll one die if your ship is a barque, two dice if it's a brigantine, three if it's a galleon. Add 1 to the roll if you have a good crew; add 2 if you have an excellent crew.

| Score 1-3 | The ship founders | turn to **126** |
| Score 4-20 | You weather the storm | turn to **6** |

223

The Akatsurese do not have much use for currency, preferring a system of gift-giving and favours, but by a long process of bartering around the city you are able to buy or sell any of the following:

Items	*To buy*	*To sell*
Compass (SCOUTING +1)	400 Shards	350 Shards
Cross-staff (SCOUTING +2)	900 Shards	650 Shards
Sextant (SCOUTING +3)	1500 Shards	900 Shards
Lantern	90 Shards	80 Shards
Parchment	5 Shards	3 Shards
Tatsu pearl	2500 Shards	1000 Shards
Platinum earring	—	750 Shards

When you have completed your business, turn to **79**.

224

These are rough waters. You brace yourself against the rail of the bridge and listen to the mariner's constant lullaby: the roar of the waves, the scream of the wind, the dour muttering of the sails, and the soft reassuring creak as the ship flexes her timbers.

Roll two dice.

| Score 2-9 | An uneventful voyage | turn to **247** |
| Score 10-12 | The wind gets up | turn to **9** |

225

He tells a story about a poor knight whose wife became inexplicably ill. He roamed far and wide searching for a cure and finally encountered an old hermit who told him that he should search for a dragon, because all dragons have a magical pearl in the roof of their mouth. The hermit claimed that such a pearl was the only thing that could heal the knight's wife.

Eventually, after many adventures, the knight encountered the dragon and slew it. He then discovered that the hermit had been the dragon in human form. It had cursed the knight's wife because of an old feud with her family. After the dragon's death the curse was lifted, the wife recovered, and they lived happily ever after on the fortune they got for selling the magic pearl.

Get the codeword *Farm* and turn to **611**.

226

Built over a network of canals, Hagashin presents a very different appearance from the cities of the north. Tall conical towers rear above the rooftops, clad in gold leaf and adorned with sweeping spikes and long bronze bells, making the skyline seem ablaze in the sunlight. The bridges that span the canals are supported by fierce statues of demons that stand waist-deep in the green water. Tall porticoes enclosed by filigree screens front each building, so that as you walk along a street you catch glimpses of silhouettes watching from the verandas on either side.

You can buy a town house here for 200 Shards. If you do, put a tick in the box next to the town house option below.

Lodge at an inn	turn to **667**
Visit the theatre (at a cost of 5 Shards)	turn to **256**
Go to your town house ☐ (if box ticked)	turn to **238**
Browse around the market	turn to **262**
Find a temple	turn to **690**
Go to the docks	turn to **302**
Leave the city	turn to **249**

227

You examine the flute. Sometimes these old heirlooms lie untended in a drawer for years. You are careful to blow all the dust out of it before starting to play. Turn to **324**.

228

If you have a **lacquer box**, turn to **748**. Otherwise read on.

Dusk is lost in a swirl of cold grey clouds when a woman stops you on a lonely moorland path and asks if you will do something for her.

'Please deliver this to my sister on Toho Island,' she says, proffering a **lacquer box**. 'But on no account should you open it.'

Agree to deliver it	turn to **252**
Decline to help	turn to **376**

229

The guide's name is Akoboshi. Cross off his fee of 10 Shards if you haven't already done so. When you ask him what game there is hereabouts, he replies: 'Well, there are foxes, badgers and wild boar, but it's risky to bother creatures like those. They often live to a ripe old age, you see, and learn many magical tricks. It's safer if we just hunt deer.'

At the end of a long day you return to the lodge weary and footsore. Lose 1 Stamina point. You never got a glimpse of a deer, but Akoboshi has given you a few hunter's tips. Roll one die, and if you get more than your SCOUTING score you can increase it by 1.

Turn to **610**.

230

The **royal sceptre** has gone, whisked away from you by magic. Cross it off your Adventure Sheet. Also lose any resurrection deal as well as any blessings you may have had arranged, as the god has exerted his power to cancel them.

Turn to **111**.

231

You notice a distant plume of smoke rise off the cone of the volcano. At this distance it is like a puff of incense from an altar lamp. The distant whip crack of an explosion follows several seconds later, just loud enough to draw your attention to the huge boulder that is hurtling through the air straight towards you.

To dodge the boulder, roll two dice and try to score less than or equal to your Rank. Reduce the dice roll by 1 if you are a Rogue, and 2 if you are an initiate of the Three Fortunes.

Dodge the boulder   turn to **632**
Fail to dodge   turn to **255**

232

Overwhelmed by such kindness, he assures you he will tell all his friends about you. 'In these sinful days it is so rare to find a person of honour and charity,' he says. 'I think you are destined to be a great saint.'

An exaggeration? Who can tell? Get the codeword *Foment* and turn to **397**.

233 □

It is with a feeling of exhilaration that you stride the snow-clad slopes just below the highest peaks. Blazing white snow makes the clear backdrop of the sky seem as dark as ink.

If the box above is empty, put a tick in it now and turn to **257**. If it was already ticked, turn to **88**.

234

If you have the title Enlightened One, turn now to **508**. Otherwise, read on.

The abbot explains that this is not a decision to be taken lightly. 'Achieving enlightenment requires strenuous effort,' he says. 'Are you prepared to withdraw from the world for months or even years? And have you the strength to prevail against the demons that will beset you?'

'Demons?'

He nods. 'The demons of your own unconscious mind.'

Begin your training	turn to **258**
Leave the monastery	turn to **211**

235

The tengu king demonstrates some esoteric finger exercises that can be used to augment your magical strength. Roll two dice, and if you get higher than your MAGIC score then increase it by 1.

Turn to **259**.

236

The man turns and looks at you, still keeping his odd stance. He has eyes of such startling intensity that you hardly take in the details of his face. He could be thirty years old, or seventy.

'Have you no manners,' he says, 'that you interrupt a Master of the Way while he is practising *qi gong*?'

Apologize and leave	turn to **398**
Ask him to teach you	turn to **310**
Ignore him and go into the shrine	turn to **352**

237

A grey fungus as big as a football explodes without warning, scattering a cinnabar-coloured cloud of spores into the air. You breathe in a lungful of them. They later germinate, causing a bronchial disease. Unless you have a blessing of Immunity to Disease/Poison you must lose 1 Stamina point permanently - i.e. reduce your unwounded Stamina score by 1. (If you do have a blessing, remember to cross it off.) Turn to **529**.

238

You can leave possessions and money here at your town house. Record anything you leave in the box. Each time you return, roll two dice to see what has happened in your absence:

| Score 2-9 | Your belongings are safe |
| Score 10-12 | Earthquake; the town house and its contents have been destroyed unless you are an initiate of Nai |

If your town house has been destroyed, turn to **226** and erase the tick beside the town house option there. Otherwise read on.

ITEMS AT TOWN HOUSE

The town house is a good place to relax after your travels. If injured, restore your Stamina to its normal score. When you are ready to leave, turn to **226**.

239

Surges of white foam warn of hidden reefs ahead. If you want to proceed you must make a SCOUTING roll at a Difficulty of 13 to steer a safe course.

Successful SCOUTING roll	turn to **650**
Failed SCOUTING roll	turn to **588**
Turn back	turn to **64**

240

You race down the side of the hill and launch yourself into the fray. Even with you on their side, the knights are still outnumbered. You will need to make a COMBAT roll at Difficulty 14 to turn the tide of battle.

| Successful COMBAT roll | turn to **217** |
| Failed COMBAT roll | turn to **140** |

241

Somehow you manage to keep your head above water. You swim until you have no strength left and it is only determination that keeps you going.

A ship heaves into view. You raise your arm and give a feeble cry. By some miracle you are spotted. You are hauled aboard, wrapped in blankets and given a bowl of hot soup. You have been rescued by merchants from Metriciens who will drop you at their next port of call. Roll one die.

Score 1-2	The capital	turn to **612**
Score 3	Hidari	turn to **323**
Score 4	Mukogawa	turn to **281**
Score 5	Narai	turn to **433**
Score 6	Kaiju	turn to **128**

242

You pass through fields of wheat where peasants' huts stand amid islands of white poppy flowers.

Roll two dice.

| Score 2-8 | Nothing of note | turn to **266** |
| Score 9-12 | A flying lantern? | turn to **560** |

243

You are in Banshu District, the heart of Akatsurai, where the land climbs slowly towards the great Urushi Range.

Join the road to the north	turn to **195**
Venture into the mountains	turn to **359**
Visit the Clearwater Shrine	turn to **124**
Go east	turn to **438**

244 ☐

You are admitted to the palace without delay. If the box above is empty, put a tick in it and turn to **574**. If it was already ticked, turn to **595**.

245

You are travelling in the foothills of the Yasai Mountains. Pockets of mist lie deep in the valleys, making the crags seem to be icebergs adrift in an arctic sea.

Make a SCOUTING roll at a Difficulty of 13. You can add 1 to the dice roll if you have **climbing gear**.

Successful SCOUTING roll	turn to **626**
Failed SCOUTING roll	turn to **283**

246

Akatsurai is known as the Land of a Thousand Gods. The people revere a vast pantheon that ranges from the great celestial spirits such as Juntoku, Lord of War, down to little hearth gods and deities of the rocks and streams. On almost every street corner there is a shrine. You go into one and the priest asks how he can be of service.

Make an offering	turn to **171**
Buy or sell a wand	turn to **267**
Leave the shrine	turn to **79**

247

You are sailing along the north coast of Yodoshi, largest of the Akatsurese islands. 'Where shall I set our course?' asks the first mate.

Put into Narai harbour	turn to **268**
Head west	turn to **100**
Head east	turn to **684**

248

He tells a story about the mujina; a creature that lurks on lonely backroads at dusk. 'Its face is completely blank, and that's quite a shock when it just spins round to you and goes BOO!' he says, specifically addressing the smallest children sitting in front of him. They look as if they'd like to run and hide under the bedclothes but are now so scared they can only huddle together.

'But that's not the worst bit,' he goes on. 'Oh no. You see, the mujina is envious of people's faces so it just rips them off and keeps them in a sack on its back. Think of all those stolen faces, wriggling and squirming and muttering to themselves in the dark. Creepy, eh?'

One of the children starts to cry. As he is taken off to bed, you put some questions to the storyteller. 'Is it true? Where does the mujina live?'

'As to where it lives: in Kwaidan Forest, I'm told. But is it true? That I cannot say.'

Get the codeword *Fist* and turn to **611**.

249

'There is not much these days to be seen in the countryside hereabouts,' says a voice.

You look round. Beyond a fretwork screen hovers an indistinct shadow.

'How did you know I was thinking of travelling on?'

The shadow gives a thin old laugh. 'Your eyes. They have a gleam of wanderlust.'

Set out into the countryside	turn to **457**
Go to the harbour	turn to **302**

250

The sea tosses fretfully, the sky is thick with muttering clouds. 'Storms or dark sorcery,' remarks the bosun in a doomful voice.

Roll two dice.

Score 2-9	The portents come to nothing	turn to **471**
Score 10-12	The fury of heaven	turn to **56**

251

You put the flute to your lips – and immediately start coughing and spluttering as though your lungs are about to split. You failed to realize that an ancient heirloom like this is often left unused for years, gathering a lot of dust in that time. As you collapse helplessly, gasping for a cup of water, the other courtiers look down their noses at you.

Masayori leads you outside on to the veranda, where you slowly recover. 'Bad luck,' he says. 'I'd say your career as a courtier is pretty much over. No one ever recovered from a public disgrace like that.'

Sure enough, you later hear that your Junior Court Rank title has been revoked. Cross it off your Adventure Sheet and then turn to **79**.

252

Record the **lacquer box** on your list of possessions, and next to it write '*Lords of the Rising Sun* **272**'. If you look into the box at any time, turn to **272** in this book to find what is inside. (You will have to remember the number of the entry you are reading at the time because **272** will not guide you back there.)

Turn to **376**.

253

Taking your weapons, you set off through the woods in search of game. Around midday, just as you are thinking of taking a break, a shaft of sunlight picks out a badger in the gloom under the trees. It lumbers off into the undergrowth as you approach. It seemed to be limping – an injury might explain why it is out and about in the middle of the day. To track the badger to its set you will need to make a SCOUTING roll of Difficulty 14.

Successful SCOUTING roll	turn to **305**
Failed SCOUTING roll	turn to **288**

254

'You must communicate my good wishes to your mistress,' says Kiyomori. 'Assure her that both our houses would be enriched by stronger links. Indeed, I am told she is a comely wench – and my son Shigemori is yet unmarried.'

He hands you a **diplomatic letter**. Add it to your list of possessions before turning to **289**.

255

You trip and go sprawling. The boulder comes down like a giant's foot about to stamp out your life, but at the last instant it changes course and crunches into the earth a few paces away. A few small fragments break off and go whizzing in all directions, one scratching your face for 1 Stamina point.

'Sorry,' says a voice. 'My mistake. Your time wasn't up yet.'

You look around but can see no one. A scroll is pressed into your hands. 'This will ensure the same sort of thing doesn't happen again,' says the voice.

You now have a **catastrophe certificate**. Add it to your possessions and turn to **632**.

256

If you have the codeword *Foment*, turn to **274**. Otherwise read on.

You spend an evening at the theatre watching the usual entertainment: roistering heroes foiling the schemes of skulking wizards, sly silver-tongued witches and bumbling animal spirits. The Akatsurese audiences lap up this kind of thing. Afterwards you take a stroll by the canals and watch the moonlight dance on the water.

Turn to **226**.

257

You find a cliff where the crevices give off metallic glints. You can gather as many **silver nuggets** as you can carry (a maximum of twelve, if you have no other possessions).

When you are ready to descend the mountain, turn to **275**.

258 ☐

If the box above is empty, put a tick in it and turn to **276**. If it was already ticked, turn to **292**.

259

The tengu king cannot teach you anything more at this time. He gives orders for his elite guard, the Leaflet Knights, to escort you safely to the edge of his domain. Though reaching the centre of the forest took days, the return journey is completed in the space of seven wingbeats. As you turn to thank your escort, you see only seven big black crows flapping off into the woods.

Turn to **420**.

260

The man seems to be a Taoist recluse. He is intent on some sort of balancing exercise, so you might be able to get past without him noticing. Make a THIEVERY roll at a Difficulty of 16.

Successful THIEVERY roll	turn to **352**
Failed THIEVERY roll	turn to **373**

261

She puts a sack in the hole she has dug and quickly fills it in with loose soil. When she straightens up and sweeps back her hair you get a nasty shock – she has no face. Pressing back out of sight, you wait for her to leave and then go to see what she buried. Inside the sack you find dozens of peeled human faces. They look like rubber masks, but they are warm to the touch and make soft twittering noises when you touch them. These are real faces.

If you have the codeword *Face*, turn to **277**. If not then you hurry off before the woman comes back; turn to **529**.

262

The markets of Hagashin consist of many narrow shops jammed along a warren of back streets. You can buy or sell any of the following:

Armour	To buy	To sell
Leather (Defence +1)	50 Shards	45 Shards
Ring mail (Defence +2)	100 Shards	90 Shards
Chain mail (Defence +3)	200 Shards	180 Shards
Splint armour (Defence +4)	–	300 Shards

Weapons (sword, axe, etc)	To buy	To sell
Without COMBAT bonus	50 Shards	35 Shards
COMBAT bonus +1	250 Shards	180 Shards
COMBAT bonus +2	–	380 Shards

Other items	To buy	To sell
Compass (SCOUTING +1)	400 Shards	350 Shards
Lockpicks (THIEVERY +1)	–	300 Shards
Candle	2 Shards	1 Shard
Parchment	8 Shards	5 Shards
Platinum earring	–	810 Shards

Items with no purchase price are not available to buy, although if you have one you can sell it. When you have finished here, turn to **226**.

263 ☐

If the box above is empty, put a tick in it and turn to **48**. If it was already ticked, turn to **334**.

264

With your help the barbarians make short work of their foes. They leap joyfully about, cavorting over the bodies and grunting as they pat you on the back. When they start building a fire to roast the corpses, though, you think it may be time to get going.

You can salvage a **lady's court robe** and a **dagger (COMBAT +2)** from the wreckage of the sedan chair as it goes up in flames.

Lose the codeword *Frog* if you had it and turn to **280**.

265

You swim out through the breakers to where the boat is drifting. You can see the two children huddled miserably together in the stern as the current drags them steadily further out to sea. They are so frightened that they can only stare in silence when you pull yourself up over the side and start to raise the sail.

The wind is getting up. Make a SCOUTING roll at a Difficulty of 15 to sail the boat back to shore.

Successful SCOUTING roll	turn to **750**
Failed SCOUTING roll	turn to **318**

266

You are on the headland near to the city of Chompo. This region is known as Kito Province.

Join the road north of Chompo	turn to **194**
Join the road to the south	turn to **73**
Go into the city	turn to **59**

267

The priest shows you a selection of wands. The shape is different from the wands of the west as they are wide and flat with rounded ends. The glyphs inscribed along the side are unfamiliar to you, but the priest assures you that the wands function perfectly well.

Magical Equipment	To buy	To sell
Amber wand (MAGIC +1)	500 Shards	250 Shards
Ebony wand (MAGIC +2)	1000 Shards	500 Shards
Cobalt wand (MAGIC +3)	2000 Shards	1000 Shards
Selenium wand (MAGIC +4)	4000 Shards	—
Celestium wand (MAGIC +5)	8000 Shards	—

After you have finished your business here, turn to **79**.

268

Dusk is falling as you come into the harbour and there is a nip of frost in the air. Lanterns hanging along the raised verandas of the city create splashes of glimmering amber light in the gloom.

Note that your ship is docked at Narai and then turn to **155**.

269

Overtaken by nightfall on a deserted hillside, you take shelter in a ramshackle barn. You are so weary after your travels that the straw feels as comfortable as a feather bed, and in spite of the raw wind outside you are soon fast asleep.

You wake in pitch darkness. The sound of bells and hushed voices is what must have woken you. Crawling to the door of the barn, you look out on a sombre moonlit scene. A group of mourners in ceremonial white stoles have set down a coffin right outside. 'We'll just rest a bit before going on,' you overhear someone say.

Show yourself	turn to **303**
Watch from hiding	turn to **401**
Go back to bed	turn to **521**

270

Kaiju is a charming fishing town of smart villas with low-pitched roof climbing a hillside tufted with feathery pine trees. The Shi River cascades down through the town in a spectacular waterfall where, according to legend, the god Sanobu paused to wash his feet after traversing the lost lands of the east. Kaiju is the town of which a

famous poet wrote:
> *'Blue like smoke under rails of spring rain,*
> *The town where my heart dwells*
> *Is surely half in the next world.'*

Decide what you will do now.

Go to the seafront	turn to **128**
Find an inn	turn to **702**
Go to pray at the shrine	turn to **215**
Do some shopping	turn to **354**
Leave town	turn to **285**

271

'Your majesty, I meant only that I would be ashamed to display my meagre ability in the presence of a true master.'

'A true master?' Takakura is intrigued. 'Whoever can you be referring to?'

The sick look on Masayori's face shows that he can see what's coming, but it is too late for him to slip away. 'Lord Masayori taught me all I know,' you announce for everyone to hear.

Takakura turns with a smile to the trembling Masayori. 'Aha, my esteemed Secretary of the Left! So it is you who we sometimes hear playing so melodiously in the middle of the night. Take the flute and entertain us now, then.'

There is no way to back out. Masayori takes the flute from you with a distraught look and plays it as best he can. The Sovereign is not fooled. He knows now that Masayori was trying to embarrass you in front of the whole court. You later hear that he has been dismissed from his post and sent to be governor of Oni Province.

Turn to **595**.

272

Make sure you know the number of the entry you were just reading; this entry will not guide you back there.

To your horror the box turns out to be full of gouged-out human eyes! What a gruesome gift. For breaking your word not to look inside the box, you are cursed and must permanently lose 1 point from each of your abilities (CHARISMA, etc). When you have amended your ability scores, turn back to the entry you were reading previously.

273

All three heads attack you at once. This means that they will all get a die roll to try to injure you while you are striking back at just one of them. Also, you do not get the benefit of your armour because you won't have gone to sleep wearing it.

First Flying Head, COMBAT 8, Defence 18, Stamina 5
Second Flying Head, COMBAT 8, Defence 18, Stamina 5
Third Flying Head, COMBAT 8, Defence 18, Stamina 5

If you manage to kill all three, turn to **661**.

274

You are well-known to the actors of Hagashin, who respect your reputation for generosity. They steer you away from the humdrum plays performed at the canalside theatres.

'Those are just for the punters,' says one, slipping his arm into yours. 'We'll show you something better.'

You are taken to an open-air theatre built high up on the hillside, where the audience sits on stone benches above the performers so that the sea and sky form a spectacular backdrop.

Roll two dice to see which play is being performed today.

| Score 2-8 | The yeoman and the dragon | turn to **93** |
| Score 9-12 | The artful frog | turn to **708** |

275

The high wind has blasted grotesque shapes in the rock, like distorted gargoyles hewn by a mad sculptor. They crouch above the chasms and leer blindly at you as you descend.

Make a SCOUTING roll at a Difficulty of 14; you can add 1 to the roll if you have **rope** and 1 if you have **climbing gear**.

| Successful SCOUTING roll | turn to **5** |
| Failed SCOUTING roll | turn to **210** |

276

If you have the codeword *Friz* you can retrieve any items you left here previously and must then turn to **21**. If you don't have the codeword *Friz* then read on.

You enter the great hall at the centre of the monastery complex. A vast statue of the Sage of Peace towers up to the rafters. Incense rises from smouldering sticks set around its feet and runs in thin white rivulets across the smooth contours of stone.

Initiates who are attempting to achieve enlightenment cannot take any belongings beyond this point. Success or failure depends solely on the initiate himself. If you are about to start your training, you can leave your possessions here by writing them in the box. If you have just finished the test, transfer possessions left here back to your Adventure Sheet.

Commence your training	turn to **349**
Leave the monastery	turn to **211**

WORLDLY GOODS

277

You are relieved to find your own face among the ones the woman buried. Just as you are about to put it back on, you notice a particularly beautiful face that stands out among the rest. It has a smooth complexion, clear grey eyes, strong countenance and hair the colour of honey. It is the face of a prince or an angel.

Put on your original face	turn to **353**
Take the other face instead	turn to **332**

278

The innkeeper's wife bustles about getting a room ready for you. It proves to be quite comfortable if you ignore the Spartan furnishings and the slightly musty smell.

'We get so few travellers passing through these days,' says the innkeeper's wife in a tone so apologetic it sounds as if she might burst into tears.

Each day spent at the inn costs 1 Shard and allows you to recuperate 1 Stamina point, up to the limit of your unwounded Stamina score. When you are ready to move on, pay your bill and turn to **522**.

279

Beside a lake stands a mansion with ornamental dragons carved from blocks of blue jade on either side of the entrance. The roof rises in sweeping tiers resembling the high prow of a ship, and the whole edifice is decorated with sinuous silver spikes that look like icicles pointing up at the sun.

If you have the codeword *Faded*, turn to **44**. Otherwise turn to **435**.

280

You are in the desolate countryside of Kumo Province, home only to wild savages and hairy spider-goblins.

Head towards Kaiju	turn to **592**
Go up into the hills	turn to **245**
Follow the east coast	turn to **706**

281

The quayside is bustling with activity as ships unload supplies in preparation for the civil war which everyone expects within a few months. If you have a ship here you could easily sell it, as the Moonrise Clan is only too eager to expand its fleet.

Sell a ship	turn to **315**
Buy a ship	turn to **655**
Get passage on a ship	turn to **462**
Trade at the warehouses	turn to **676**
Go aboard your ship (if docked here)	turn to **695**
Hire crewmen for your ship	turn to **724**
Go to the city centre	turn to **178**

282

You pass through fields dotted with villages, listening to the haunting cry of wild deer off in the woodlands.

Roll two dice.

Score 2-8	A peaceful journey	turn to **316**
Score 9-12	A rogue in a thicket	turn to **727**

283

You stumble while climbing, twisting your ankle painfully. Lose 1 Stamina point, then (if still alive) turn to **245**.

284

If you have the codeword *Fruit*, turn to **453** now. If not, read on.

Your town house is a single-storey villa on Plum Blossom Street. You can leave possessions and money here to save having to carry them around with you. Record anything you leave in the box below. Each time you return, roll two dice to see what has happened in your absence.

Score 2-8	Your belongings are safe
Score 9-10	Theft; all the money you left here is gone
Score 11-12	Fire; the town house and its contents have been destroyed

If your town house has burned down, turn to **79** and erase the tick beside the town house option there. Otherwise read on.

```
ITEMS AT TOWN HOUSE



```

The town house has an ornamental garden overlooked by a simple but delightful veranda. Here you can rest and recuperate from your travels. If injured, restore your Stamina to its normal score. When you are ready to leave, turn to **79**.

285

There are no proper roads out of Kaiju. Most of the citizens have no desire to venture into the barbaric hinterlands of Toho island. If you wish to travel on from here by sea you should go down to the harbour.

Go west over the fields	turn to **554**
Travel east out of the city	turn to **592**
Go to the harbour	turn to **128**

286

You try to extricate yourself but succeed only in sounding obstreperous — much to the delight of the scheming Masayori, who planned this to disgrace you in front of the court.

Finally Takakura dismisses you with a bad-tempered gesture. 'Go, then! If your music is so precious that it cannot be wasted on mortal ears, take yourself to the mountains and play instead for the entertainment of the celestial powers.'

You are ushered out and your title of Junior Court Rank is revoked. Cross it off, then turn to **79**.

287

You have the misfortune to encounter a spectral lady at twilight. Reaching towards you with dead white hands, she implores you to give her news of her dear sister in the west.

If you have a **lacquer box** , turn to **304**. If not, turn to **325**.

288

Get the codeword *Fusty*.

You scour the woods without success until finally it begins to get dark and you have to make your way back to the hunting lodge. The proprietor greets you cheerily. 'A good day's sport?' he enquires.

Turn to **181**.

289

Kiyomori calls for music, wine and dancers. The two of you sit long into the night discussing all sorts of things, from weighty affairs of state to the ideal time to view the cherry blossom.

Roll two dice.

| Score 2-4 | A quarrel | turn to **327** |
| Score 5-12 | A pleasant evening | turn to **79** |

290

You come across an old burial mound from the time when people used to bury their dead rather them cremate them, as is the custom in Akatsurai nowadays. A recent shower has washed away part of the earth covering the mound to reveal a patch of bare white stone.

Tunnel into the mound	turn to **306**
Continue on your way	turn to **416**

291

The crewmen who came ashore with you are too superstitious to join in the fight. You have to fight the priests alone. Each time you hit one of them, all three will get to strike back at you.

   First Shrine Warden, COMBAT 9, Defence 15, Stamina 22
   Second Shrine Warden, COMBAT 9, Defence 15, Stamina 21
   Third Shrine Warden, COMBAT 9, Defence 15, Stamina 20

If you flee back to your ship and sail off, turn to **745**. If you defeat the three priests, turn to **499**.

292

Do you have the codeword *Ink*? If so, turn to **308**. If not, turn to **21**.

293

Sakkaku is famous for being the home of the god Dosojin, overseer of the many roads and remote trails. He is the patron god of travellers. His shrine is an imposing structure of black wood decorated with polished silver plaques.

To obtain a blessing you must pay 45 Shards and make a CHARISMA roll at a Difficulty of 14 (or Difficulty 10 if you're a Wayfarer). On a successful roll you get a blessing of Safe Travel which you can write in the Blessings box on your Adventure Sheet. This blessing allows you to reroll the dice once when travelling to a new region, so as to avoid an encounter. You can only have one Safe Travel blessing at a time. When it is used, cross it off your Adventure Sheet. You will then need to come back here to get another one.

Now turn to **522**.

294

Yoritomo clasps you by the hand – a signal honour from a lord of such exalted rank. In front of his surviving guards he gives you the title Hatamoto. Note this on your Adventure Sheet. It means that you have the right to wear the Moonrise Clan's livery and to act as the Shogun's emissary.

'Come to visit me soon in Mukogawa,' says Yoritomo as he sets off. Turn to **280**.

295

You must pay 2 Shards a day to stay at the inn. Each day you rest here you can recover 1 lost Stamina point. Remember that your Stamina will not increase above its normal unwounded score, though.

When you are ready to leave, turn to **573**.

296

You stand on an outcrop of rock and survey the majestically inhospitable moorland that stretches to the horizon in all directions. In the north hovers a smudge of violet shadow that marks the high expanse of the Kwaidan Forest.

Westwards, by your reckoning, the Moku River flows down into Kotobuki Bay. Far to the south runs the Great Saddle Road, while the east is open country as far as the sea.

Go west across the Moku River	turn to **337**
Go north to the Kwaidan Forest	turn to **398**
Go south and join the road	turn to **631**
Go further east	turn to **515**
Travel to Chambara	turn to **79**

297

You are travelling over open country between the Chiku and the Hitsu. The sun rises over mountain peaks and sets in deep ocean.

Join the road	turn to **125**
Travel north to Shingen	turn to **362**
Travel south to Hidari	turn to **323**
Go up into the mountains	turn to **359**

298

You are at the north-western tip of Toho Island, in desolate territory where no sane man would make his home. Choose your next move:

South	turn to **554**
East	turn to **446**
South-east	turn to **319**

299

Many routes converge at Chambara. If you do not wish to travel by road, you could strike out over open country or take passage on a barge going upriver. Alternatively, you could put to sea.

Go to the harbour	turn to **612**
Take the road to Sakkaku	turn to **221**
Take the road to Mukogawa	turn to **631**
Take the road to Shingen	turn to **173**
Go upriver	turn to **593**
Head north-west	turn to **337**
Head north-east	turn to **672**

300

Occasionally the bosun surprises you with a profound thought. Today it is this: 'We are nearer to the next life by sea than by land.'

Perhaps he is right.

Roll two dice.

Score 2-8	A voyage without incident	turn to **108**
Score 9-12	An enemy vessel	turn to **145**

301

There are numerous temples in the suburbs of Chambara, all dedicated to the Sage of Peace whose example guides men towards enlightenment. Here the clerics can live a life of monastic contemplation and lay worshippers can come for healing, blessings and advice.

Buy a talisman	turn to **421**
Ask for healing	turn to **399**
Seek a blessing (if an initiate)	turn to **380**
Become an initiate	turn to **320**

302

The canals of Hagashin debouch into a lagoon sheltered by a low headland of piled stones. Several ships ride at anchor, their sails furled like curling autumn leaves.

Buy or sell a ship	turn to **25**
Go aboard your ship (if docked here)	turn to **321**
Hire new crew members	turn to **586**
Pay for passage to another port	turn to **647**
Buy cargo for your ship	turn to **606**
Go into the city	turn to **226**

303

The mourners take no notice when you step out among them. At first you think they are overwhelmed by grief; but then it dawns on you that they really can't see you. You reach out to touch one, but your hand passes straight through him.

'I'm afraid they can't see you because you're dead,' says a voice. You turn to see a little fat priest standing there. 'You died of exposure seven nights ago,' he says, 'and since you're a stranger in the district we've had to go to the expense of burying you.'

If you have a resurrection deal	turn to **10**
If not	turn to **322**

304

She receives the **lacquer box** with the almost witlessly pleased expression of a small child being given a bag of candy. 'Good, good, good,' she says in her reedy voice. 'Your reward is to be fearless from now until your dying day.'

Gain 1 point on your COMBAT score up to the maximum possible score of 12, but lose 2 points from SANCTITY. Whether you realize it or not, you have run a wicked errand for these two witches.

Now turn to **298**.

305

The badger has taken refuge in a hole in a bank. As you stoop to peer inside, two long thin hairy arms suddenly sprout out of the hole and seize you by the throat. You must fight for your life.

Hairy arms, COMBAT 9, Defence 18, Stamina 12

You can break free and run off, but the arms will rake at your retreating back for a final 1-6 Stamina points if you do.

Flee back to the lodge	turn to **181**
Fight on and win	turn to **326**

306

There seems to be a large chalk boulder plugging the tomb entrance. As you clear away the earth it dawns on you that the boulder looks very like a gigantic skull. You are chuckling at your own overwrought imagination when the boulder opens its jaws with a gleeful clacking sound and sits up, shrugging the soil off ancient white limbs. You have unearthed the monstrous skeleton of an ancient giant.

Skeleton Spectre, COMBAT 13, Defence 20, Stamina 21

If you turn and flee, it will get a final free blow at your retreating back doing 2-12 Stamina points less the Defence bonus of your armour.

Fight on and win	turn to **86**
Run away	turn to **416**

307

Instead of silver deposits, you stumble across a cave inhabited by a giant white tiger with an imperial glyph imprinted on its forehead. This is no ordinary beast.

If you have the **mirror of the Sun Goddess**, turn to **329**. If not, turn to **348**.

308

You hold out your hand to the abbot. Ever since you touched the saint, a fragrance like sandalwood has hung about your fingers.

The abbot nods and says, 'You have journeyed right across the world and returned to us. Has anything changed?' He gestures all around him at the ivy-clad buildings, the serenely smiling statues, and the mountain peaks above the treetops.

'I have changed.'

'A good answer. You may attempt the test again.'

Lose the codeword *Ink* and turn to **276**.

309

The sea heaves and swells. 'No sight of land,' calls down the sailor in the crow's nest.

Roll two dice.

Score 2-3	The ship runs aground	turn to **588**
Score 4-11	A peaceful voyage	turn to **193**
Score 12	Prey for pirates	turn to **145**

310

He strokes his beard and considers your request. At last he announces that he will train you in magic if you can give him 'a wand that wounds'.

Decide what item you are presenting to him (if any) and, after crossing it off your Adventure Sheet, turn to **392**.

311

The woman looks up, displaying a featureless blank where her face ought to be. If you have the codeword *Face*, turn to **374**. Otherwise read on.

Here in this desolate woodland spot, the sudden horror is more than you can take. You pass out, recovering much later to find that night has fallen. There is no sign of the faceless woman. She has left her sack, which is wriggling and squeaking as if filled with mice. You can't bring yourself to look inside it. Instead you creep off into the undergrowth before the woman comes back.

Turn to **529**.

312

The woodland is a tangled green web of roots and branches pinpricked with stray shafts of daylight. A stream runs down between banks of bare earth, wet stones glinting through the current like tarnished silver. Above the treetops nearby rises a spire of grey rock.

Go upstream	turn to **330**
Go towards the rock spire	turn to **351**

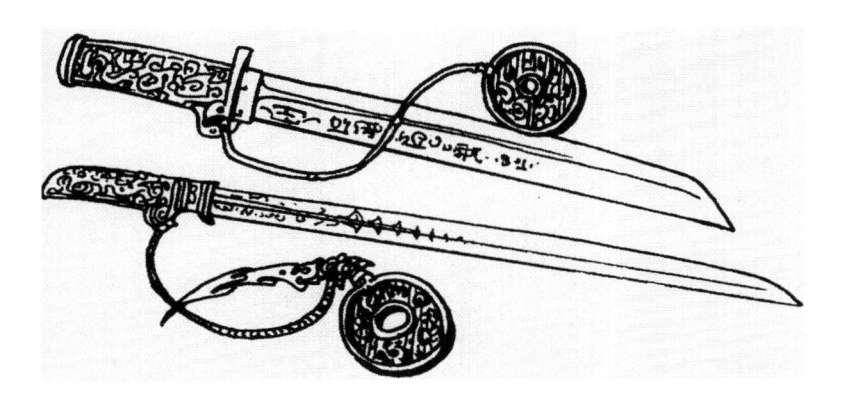

313

The market stalls are laid out under a long colonnade built up against the flanks of the inner stockade.

Item	To buy	To sell
Compass (SCOUTING +1)	400 Shards	350 Shards
Cross-staff (SCOUTING +2)	750 Shards	650 Shards
Lantern	80 Shards	60 Shards
Parchment	8 Shards	5 Shards
Platinum earring	–	525 Shards
Silver nugget	–	150 Shards
Bag of pearls	–	200 Shards

Items with no purchase price are not available locally. When you have finished, if you want to see the local merchants about investing some money, turn to **333**. If not, turn to **8**.

314

The animal bounds over your head, sweeping down with its incandescent wings as it flies through the air. The wingtips scorch the grass where they touch it and you are right in their path. 'Thus perish all evildoers!' booms the animal's voice.

Make a MAGIC roll at Difficulty 14 to protect yourself.

Successful MAGIC roll	turn to **492**
Failed MAGIC roll	turn to **140**

315

Lord Karamochi, the chief of naval strategy, offers the following prices for second-hand ships:

Ship type	*Sale Price*
Barque	240 Shards
Brigantine	500 Shards
Galleon	900 Shards

You cannot back out of the sale now that Karamochi has made an offer – you must sell him your ship. Cross it off the Ship's Manifest, add the money to your Adventure Sheet, and turn to **178**.

316

You are in the countryside not far from Chompo.

Go to the city	turn to **59**
Head west into the highlands	turn to **336**
Go south	turn to **515**
Join the Northern Coastal Road	turn to **98**

317

Guards in scarlet and grey surcoats stand at the gate ready to bar your path. Check the Titles & Honours box on your Adventure Sheet. If you have the tide Junior Court Rank, turn to **244**. If you have Senior Court Rank, turn to **539**. If you have neither, turn to **377**.

318

It starts to get dark. You soon lose sight of land in the gathering murk. The boat speeds on all night and all the next day with open sea on all sides, until finally you reach a verdant island where bubbling brooks pour through leafy glades. Slender men and women in gorgeous silks come down to the beach to offer you wine and crystallized fruits.

Restore your Stamina to its normal score if you were injured. After a couple of days, your hosts point you in the direction of the mainland. On the way back, the little girl announces that the island must have been Horai, the home of the sea elves. Whether this is so or not, the fisherman is delighted to have his children back safe and sound. He cannot thank you enough.

Get the codeword *Fire* and turn to **514**.

319

The rugged precipices of the Kenen range are enough to deter all but the most experienced mountaineer. Your gaze rises up, past huddled pines and cliffs of bare grey rock, towards the ice-covered peaks.

Press on into the mountains	turn to **148**
Turn back while you still can	turn to **338**

320

The abbot explains the sage's teaching. 'To achieve enlightenment you must free yourself from desire,' he says.

'Surely a person without desire is merely apathetic?'

He shakes his head. 'The force of your spirit is like a wild horse that pulls you headlong. You must tame this horse so that you can ride it. The essence of the sage's teaching is to make you a whole person.'

Make a SANCTITY roll at a Difficulty of 15.

Successful SANCTITY roll	turn to **339**
Failed SANCTITY roll	turn to **360**
Do not make the attempt	turn to **79**

321

The first mate reports that he can have the ship ready to sail whenever you give the word. You begin to think that perhaps the Akatsurese make him nervous.

Put to sea	turn to **450**
Leave the ship	turn to **302**

322

'How is it that you can see me?' you ask the priest.

'I have diligently chanted the Peacock Sutra every day for eighty-five years,' he says in a tone of quiet modesty. 'As a result of this I have magical powers.'

'Including resurrection?'

'Yes...' he says with reluctance. 'But I always advise souls to pass on to their next incarnation without regret.'

Insist that he resurrects you	turn to **341**
Accept your fate	turn to **559**

323

Hidari, at the mouth of the Hitsu River, is a town of closely packed dwellings situated in between the ivy-trailed rock walls of a narrow valley.

Continue your journey	turn to **342**
Take lodging at an inn	turn to **167**
Visit the shrine to Nai	turn to **69**
Pay for passage on a ship	turn to **190**

324

The entire court is entranced by your haunting melody. As you continue to play, the room fills up with nobles who heard the music outside and came in from the garden to see who could be playing so beautifully.

'It is the foreign devil!' you overhear someone say.

'Ssh! Do not speak thus of the Sovereign's favourite.'

After the recital is over, the Sovereign declares himself is so moved that you are immediately elevated to the highest position of privilege. Lose the title Junior Court Rank and get Senior Court Rank instead, then turn to **595**.

325

She rants and lays curses in a terrifying voice until you are forced to run off with your hands over your ears. The experience has unnerved you more than you might care to admit.

Reduce your COMBAT score by 1 and then turn to **298**.

326

Suddenly the struggling stops. You are astonished to see the long limbs have gone. There is only an old badger lying in front of you breathing its last. Perhaps the local folktales are right when they attribute strange powers to animals like badgers and foxes.

You return to the lodge with your kill. The proprietor cooks it but refuses to share in the meal out of fear. What about you?

Eat the badger	turn to **344**
Leave it	turn to **181**

327

Kiyomori tends to get short-tempered when he's drunk. Suddenly, for no reason at all, he is ranting at you with spittle on his lips and his eyes wide in a wine-flushed face.

If you have the codeword *Fossil*, turn now to **367**. If not you must make a CHARISMA roll at Difficulty 13 to calm Kiyomori down.

Successful CHARISMA roll	turn to **386**
Failed CHARISMA roll	turn to **407**

328 ☐

If the box above is empty, put a tick in it and turn to **347**. If it was already ticked, turn to **369**.

329

The tiger leads you to the back of its cave where there is a pile of gold and jewels. It allows you to stuff several handfuls of this treasure into your haversack in exchange for the mirror. Cross the **mirror of the Sun Goddess** off your Adventure Sheet and get 8000 Shards in its place.

The tiger watches to see that you leave its mountain forthwith. Turn to **275**.

330

The stream emerges from a cleft in the rocks ahead, forming a little waterfall that catches the green light like handfuls of scattered emeralds. Not far off stands a hollow oak whose twisted boughs are so swollen and heavy that they barely clear the ground.

Go towards the oak	turn to **509**
Climb the ridge above the waterfall	turn to **412**

331

Inside the shrine there are many white cocoons strung high up in the recesses above the rafters. Some are wrapped around nothing but desiccated bones, others contain dead bodies well-preserved by the venom that slew them. You also find a **warhammer (COMBAT +4)**, a suit of **splint armour (Defence +4)** and 660 Shards.

When you have taken whatever you want and perhaps said a quick prayer, you can leave: turn to **398**.

332

People cannot help but be impressed by your striking good looks. Increase your CHARISMA score to 12. You wonder who the face you now wear originally belonged to. Perhaps you will never know.

Lose the codeword *Face* and get *Feral* instead. Also lose the codewords *Bullion*, *Clanger* and *Fracas* if you had them. Then turn to **529**.

333

If you have the codeword *Frame*, turn to **26**. If not, turn to **434**.

334

A fox has its foot caught in a snare. Finally you cannot stand its cries of pain any longer. When you go to set it free, you find an item lying under the bushes nearby.

Roll one die.

Score 1	**Paper sword**
Score 2	**Silver chopsticks**
Score 3	**Lantern**
Score 4	**Rope**
Score 5	**Peacock feather**
Score 6	**Crimson arrow**

The fox limps off. Take the item if you want it and then turn to **44**.

335

The wind blows in icy gusts out of a coal-black sky. If you have a blessing of Safety from Storms, cross it off and turn to **713**. Otherwise, turn to **222**.

336

Beyond the wheat fields, the terrain rises into a desolate range of gently undulating moorland. Thickets of pampas grass stir fretfully in the breeze, as though spirits were passing just outside your range of vision.

Roll two dice.

Score 2-9	Not a soul in sight	turn to **357**
Score 10-12	A solitary traveller	turn to **106**

337

Caught in a sudden downpour, you find shelter under the eaves of a small shrine. When the sun emerges from behind the clouds at last, it floods the wet fields with dazzling golden light. It is a scene of breathtaking beauty. No wonder that the people of Akatsurai revere all the gods of nature that surround them.

Go north to the forest	turn to **398**
Go south to the coast	turn to **221**
Go west towards Sakkaku	turn to **378**
Go east over the Moku River	turn to **672**

338

The undulating foothills of the Kenen Mountains, with their many secluded valleys and dense pine groves, gradually give way to rolling moorland.

Head for Kaiju	turn to **592**
Go south	turn to **674**
Go north	turn to **633**
Go east to the sea	turn to **446**

339

You study hard and are soon an expert in the holy riddles that the Sage of Peace used to bring enlightenment to his followers. The abbot is pleased with your progress. 'You have mastered all I can teach,' he says. 'To progress further you must travel to one of the remote monasteries.'

Note that you are now an initiate of the Sage of Peace. (This does not prevent you from also being an initiate of another temple, because the sage is not a jealous god.) Now turn to **380**.

340

Note on the Ship's Manifest that your ship is now docked at Hagashin, then turn to **321**.

341

The priest can only bring you back to life if you agree to sacrifice some of your innate vital force – an energy he calls *ki*. This means you must lose 2 points off your MAGIC score.

You complain. 'The priests of the west do not deprive a person of their *ki* when bringing them back to life.'

'But they call upon the gods to restore life,' he points out. 'I must revivify you with nothing but my own skill.

Agree to the revivify spell	turn to **382**
Change your mind	turn to **559**

342

The imposing cliffs that enclose Hidari give a clue to the immensity of the great Urushi Mountains that lie inland.

Take the road to Shingen	turn to **673**
Travel up the east coast	turn to **74**
Go up into the mountains	turn to **359**
Set sail (if ship docked here)	turn to **450**

343

You play well enough not to become a laughing stock, but that is all. 'Hmm,' is the only remark the Sovereign makes after you have finished.

Masayori takes the flute from you. From the smug look on his little round face you suspect that somehow he has got one over on you.

Turn to **595**.

344

After the meal you sink into a deep sleep. Your dreams that night are strange and full of wonderment. Roll one die. If you roll higher than your MAGIC score, increase it by 1. Also, if the roll is higher than your COMBAT score, increase that by 1.

After making any necessary amendments to your Adventure Sheet, turn to **610**.

345 ☐

If the box above is empty, put a tick in it and turn to **254**. If it was already ticked, turn to **16**.

346

A man is lying in the roadway. For all you know he might be dead.

See if you can help	turn to **368**
Pass by on the other side	turn to **671**

347

At the end of a long day you are happy to be offered a bed by an old couple who live down on the beach below the road. They ply you with wine and food and insist on hearing you recount the stories of your many adventures.

If you are a Priest, turn to **388**. If not, turn to **409**.

348

The tiger resents your intrusion. It flexes claws as long as battlefield daggers and prepares to leap.

King Tiger, COMBAT 12, Defence 22, Stamina 44

There is no point in fleeing; you could never hope to outrun the tiger. If you defeat it you can take 12,000 Shards in treasure from its lair before setting off back down the mountain.

Turn to **275**.

349

The abbot searches you to verify that you are not carrying anything that could help you cheat in the tests. (If you have any possessions that you did not leave in the great hall, they are confiscated; cross them off your Adventure Sheet.) A stone plug is raised from the floor and the monks lower you on a rope into the catacombs below the monastery.

The first test requires you to find your way through a darkened maze. Make a SCOUTING roll at a Difficulty of 14.

Successful SCOUTING roll	turn to **390**
Failed SCOUTING roll	turn to **371**

350

You drift down the coast at a leisurely rate. The breeze is barely enough to rattle the canvas.

Roll two dice.

Score 2-5	A small bay	turn to **14**
Score 6-12	Nothing of note	turn to **524**

351

Dense thickets clog the ground in every clearing, so that even when you catch a glimpse of the sky it is difficult to make any real progress.

Press on the way you're going	turn to **372**
Turn back and try another path	turn to **529**

352

Spider silk hangs like wisps of mist over a mildewed altar. Among the decaying strands of webbing you find 5-30 Shards (roll one die and multiply by five).

When you are ready to resume your journey, turn to **398**.

353

Your first thought is that it feels good to have a nose again. Now you can use CHARISMA without having to wear a mask. Erase the brackets around your CHARISMA score and lose the codeword *Face*, then turn to **529**.

354

The merchants of Kaiju offer these goods for sale:

Item	*To buy*	*To sell*
Compass (SCOUTING +1)	380 Shards	360 Shards
Cross-staff (SCOUTING +2)	700 Shards	660 Shards
Lotus talisman (SANCTITY +1)	250 Shards	150 Shards
Paradise talisman (SANCTITY +2)	500 Shards	300 Shards
Parchment	8 Shards	5 Shards
Tatsu pearl	—	700 Shards
Climbing gear	65 Shards	40 Shards
Platinum earring	—	500 Shards
Silver nugget	—	170 Shards
Bag of pearls	—	120 Shards

When you have finished your shopping, turn to **270**.

355

A bolt of lightning splits the boulder in two and the deity leaps forth.

Dazzled by the blast, you cannot see him but you can hear his words: 'You have given me the greatest of gifts, which is freedom. If death should ensnare you, I in my turn will set you free.'

Write *Lords of the Rising Sun* **710** in the Resurrection Arrangements box on your Adventure Sheet. If and when you get killed, turn to **710** in this book. This is a special boon, which the deity grants even if you have another resurrection deal arranged. The deity departs.

Turn to **44**.

356

You are traversing wide, windswept heathland where it is possible to go from dawn to dusk without seeing a living soul.

Roll two dice.

Score 2-5	Asked to run an errand	turn to **228**
Score 6-12	Nothing untoward	turn to **376**

357

You are skirting the high, forested Kwaidan Mountains of central Akatsurai. The locals believe the forests are the abode of cantankerous spirits and, indeed, the very word kwaidan means a ghost story.

Enter the forest	turn to **312**
Go east	turn to **282**
Go north	turn to **30**
Go south	turn to **515**

358

Lord Shuriyoku is pleased to receive your report. 'The chancellor is a lion, but he is an old lion. Kumonosu is a rodent in his prime, hence he is more dangerous.'

Shuriyoku gestures for his guards to search you. 'Don't be offended. These are parlous times and we must be watchful in case of double agents.'

If you possess a **crimson arrow**, turn to **694**. If not, turn to **103**.

359

You ascend the Urushi Mountains through thick pine forests and alpine meadows where the air is clean and scented with heather.

Streams splash and gurgle down steep rocky slopes and, when you stop to drink, you find the water is ice cold.

Roll two dice.

Score 2-8	Alone in the mountains	turn to **379**
Score 9-12	A magnificent beast	turn to **415**

360

You try for several days to master the doctrine of the Sage of Peace, but it proves too much for you. In your despondency you succumb to material pleasures, seeking solace in wine and wild living. The abbot sees that you are not yet ready to achieve enlightenment, and tells you to come back when you have gained more wisdom.

Lose a point of SANCTITY and turn to **79**.

361

Note on the Ship's Manifest that you have docked at Hidari harbour, then turn to **323**.

362

Shingen is a quiet seaside town where the Lord Chancellor has his private residence. There is no mistaking the building: a sprawling mansion of polished cedarwood with scarlet gonfalons streaming from the eaves. It sits on a hillside, glaring down on the town like a tiger sunning itself on a rock.

Take lodging at an inn	turn to **393**
Call on the chancellor	turn to **523**
Travel on from here	turn to **130**

363

Noboro Monastery stands in a secluded valley. The buildings are made of unpainted wood and the green tiles of the roofs blend with the surrounding trees, making the monastery almost invisible at a distance.

Stop at the monastery	turn to **383**
Continue on your way	turn to **211**

364

While your men go off to replenish the water supplies and catch a few birds, you stretch out under a shelf of rock. The lulling sound of the waves makes you feel sleepy, but just when you're on the point of dozing off, a paladin in black and yellow livery appears and greets you in the name of his queen.

You look around for your men. They are not in sight. The paladin asks you to accompany him to see his queen.

Go with him	turn to **608**
Attack him	turn to **629**

365

Looking outside, you see three heads flying around in the moonlight. You remember seeing a play about these flying head goblins. The hero of the play destroyed them by attacking their bodies. You take a skewer from the wall and pierce the heart of each in turn. From outside come three terrible sighs and the heads drop to the ground, quite dead.

At dawn you continue on your way. You can take a **dead head** if you think it might be useful.

Turn to **296**.

366

A smiling monk approaches from the direction of the woods. What makes this odd is that he is sitting cross-legged in meditation and hovering through the air.

If you have the codeword *Fusty*, turn to **15**. If not, turn to **405**.

367

You divert Kiyomori's anger by mentioning the behaviour of the shaven-headed youths who comprise the secret police.

'Your town house was burned down? Kiyomori is taken aback. Suddenly his anger has a fresh target. 'Those wretched young thugs! Oh, you should have come to me at once, my dear old friend.'

Later, as you leave, Kiyomori gives you 400 Shards to buy a new town house. 'I'll deal with those kaburos, never fear,' he assures you. Lose the codeword *Fossil* and turn to **79**.

368

You kneel beside the body and feel for a pulse.

Roll two dice.

Score 2-5	turn to **387**
Score 6-7	turn to **408**
Score 8	turn to **427**
Score 9-12	turn to **477**

369

You come across an old couple who make a living selling clams. Since they rarely get to hear much news, they insist that you stop over for the night at their home and tell them of your travels.

Regain 1 Stamina point if injured and turn to **53**.

370

A tall intense man with a piercing gaze, Captain Numachino might seem intimidating to some but your natural charm soon wins him round. He invites you to his cabin where he tells you about Akatsurai over a cup or two of hot rice wine.

'We are living in interesting times,' he says. 'That is considered a curse among my people, though for an adventurer like yourself it opens up a world of opportunities.'

'Such as?'

'You might consider becoming a mercenary. Traditionally the country has been ruled by the Imperial Sovereign, usually with the guiding advice of the Wistaria Clan, but for the past twenty years real power has been in the hands of the Starburst Clan – specifically Lord Kiyomori. The Sovereign is a young man, not in the best of health, and as he weakens so does the legitimacy of the Starburst government. In the east a new power is ascending: the Moonrise Clan. Their leader, Yoritomo, has proclaimed himself Shogun and intends to sweep away the Starburst Clan by main force.'

You roll your eyes. 'Interesting times, you say? Confusing, certainly!'

He laughs. 'Well, if politics does not interest you, what about trade? It is easy to get rich when a country is making itself ready for war. But I must warn you there is a certain stigma attached to being a merchant, at least as far as the ruling classes are concerned.'

'Is there no career without such drawbacks?'

'The career of a wanderer. In that way you can win both riches and honour, for the wild places of Akatsurai abound with monsters, magic and ancient treasure.'

Turn to **389**.

371

A monk comes to wake you. You are lying on a prayer mat in front of the effigy of the Sage of Peace. The silvery glimmer of departing night filters into the incense-filled haze. 'What is happening?' you ask, confused. 'I can't remember leaving the catacombs.'

'You failed the tests,' replies the monk. 'Come with me.'

Get the codeword *Friz* and turn to **276**.

372

You are lost deep in the interior of the wood, a night country of whisperings and stygian murmurs.

Roll two dice.

Score 2-7	You find a game trail	turn to **412**
Score 8-12	Bitten by a snake	turn to **480**

373

The Tao master takes out a fan and waves it at you. 'You are beginning to irritate me,' he says. 'Get you gone.'

The first wave of the fan creates a breeze, the second brings a gale, and the third sends you sailing high into the air and over the treetops. Although you hold on tight to your possessions, 1-6 of them are torn away by the raging wind. (Roll one die; you decide which possessions to lose.)

At last the wind abates. Roll two dice to see where you land.

Score 2-5	The capital	turn to **79**
Score 6-7	Up in the mountains	turn to **275**
Score 8-9	Wild countryside	turn to **674**
Score 10-12	A lonely road	turn to **500**

374

The mujina greets you with a strange hollow sound – a sigh like wind under the eaves of a derelict house at midnight. You cannot read any emotion in the pale smooth blank of her face. Is she angry at being surprised? Delighted by the thought of fresh pickings? Either way, her embrace is deadly.

Mujina, COMBAT 8, Defence 13, Stamina 15

If you slay her you can unearth the sack she was burying. It is full of stolen faces, of course. Turn to **277**.

375

Yoritomo assures you there will always be a warm welcome for you at his clanhouse in Mukogawa. Gathering his surviving guards, he gets back in his sedan chair and continues on his way.

You loot the barbarians but find only two **axes** and a **spear**. Get the codeword *Frog* and then turn to **280**.

376

You are in the demon-haunted wilderness that is Oni Province. Clouds cast doleful shadows on the heath.

Head north	turn to **395**
Cross the Gai River to the east	turn to **568**
Make for the Black Pagoda	turn to **472**
Go down to the sea	turn to **20**

377

'Get you gone,' says the captain of the guards. 'This is the Sovereign's palace. You cannot simply wander in off the street.'

There is nothing you can do. You turn and walk away. If you have the codeword *Frame*, turn to **4**. If not, turn to **79**.

378

You make your way past fields where peasants stand knee-deep amid the flooded rice shoots. By day you listen to their songs, by night you sleep under a roof of leaves and stars.

Roll two dice.

Score 2-7	An uneventful journey	turn to **397**
Score 8-12	A penniless actor	turn to **455**

379

If you are an initiate of the Sage of Peace, turn to **363**. If not, turn to **211**.

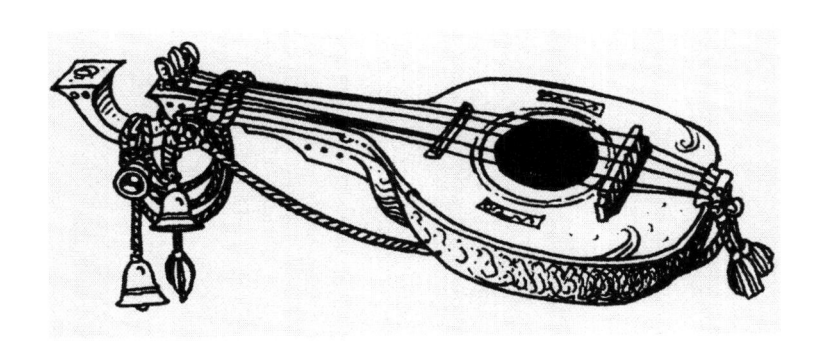

380

The Sage of Peace can be called on to help his followers at any time. Write Luck in the Blessings box on your Adventure Sheet. The blessing can be used once to allow you to reroll any dice result. After using the blessing, remember to cross it off your Adventure Sheet.

You can have only one Luck blessing at a time. Once it is used, you have only to return here to get a new one. Turn to **79**.

381

You are sailing in Kotobuki Bay, close to the mouth of the Moku River where stands Chambara, the imperial capital.

Make for Chambara harbour	turn to **400**
Steer south-east	turn to **200**
Steer west	turn to **300**
Head out to sea	turn to **80**

382

The priest pokes his finger in the middle of your forehead and you go as stiff as a board, falling back against the side of the barn where you remain immobile while the moon sets. At dawn you begin to get some feeling back in your limbs, which gradually thaw out so you can move. You know you must be alive because you are cold, tired, hungry and you ache all over.

Permanently reduce your MAGIC score by 2, then turn to **611**.

383

The monastery is a centre of learning dedicated to the arts and sciences. You can rest here for a while if you are in need of the monks' healing skills. Recover 1-6 Stamina points if injured.

Resume your travels	turn to **211**
Train as a monk	turn to **234**

384

The Sovereign is disappointed in you. 'What it is to be a prince,' he sighs, 'who can command duty but cannot even ask for loyalty!'

By way of chastisement he orders Masayori to revoke your title. Lose Senior Court Rank and get Junior Court Rank instead.

Turn to **79**.

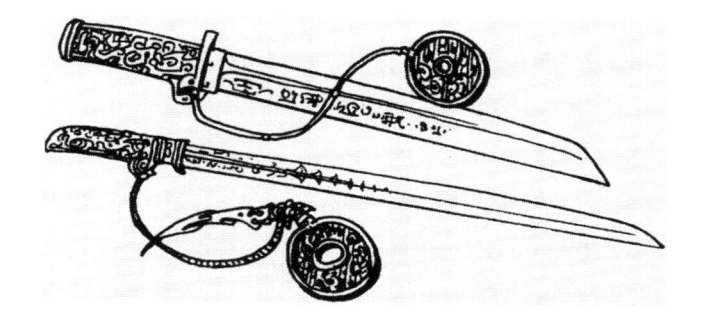

385

Not even the greatest knight in the world could fight ten well-trained opponents at the same time. Your sword pierces the stomach of the first man, but you are too slow to parry the attack of the guard right behind him. Lose 2-12 Stamina points (the roll of two dice).

Your only chance is to feign death. Make a MAGIC roll at a Difficulty of 15 to temporarily stop your own heart. If you don't manage to fool them, they will cut you to ribbons!

Successful MAGIC roll	turn to **404**
Failed MAGIC roll	turn to **140**

386

You readily admit to being an unworthy friend, thus appealing to Kiyomori's sentimental nature. His angry rant turns into a stern ticking-off, which soon gives way to a comradely hug and a fulsome apology for being so cantankerous.

'You really know how to handle Dad!' says his son Shigemori enviously as he sees you out.

Turn to **79**.

387

The man suddenly sits up and holds a knife to your throat while his accomplices emerge from the bushes. You are surrounded by spears and can only stand helpless while they relieve you of your money.

'Don't you want my belongings?' you ask sarcastically.

'Nah,' says the chief robber. 'Too hard to get rid of.'

Cross off all your money and turn to **671**.

388

The old couple tell you the tragic story of how their daughter drowned this very afternoon. It seems that a ghoul roams the district and unless a priest can be found to administer the last rites it will come in the night to devour the body.

You offer to perform the rites yourself. Make a SANCTITY roll at a Difficulty of 12 if you are an initiate of Tyrnai, Nagil, the Sage of Peace, Chthonios, Nergal or Gashimra; otherwise the SANCTITY roll is at a Difficulty of 18.

Successful SANCTITY roll	turn to **620**
Failed SANCTITY roll	turn to **478**

389

One of the crew is very taken with your **platinum earring** and offers you 75 Shards for it. If you agree to sell, cross the **platinum earring** off your Adventure Sheet and make a note of the money.

Captain Numachino cannot organize his voyage for your convenience. He says you will be put ashore at the next port.

Roll two dice to see where this is.

Score 2-4	Kaiju	turn to **270**
Score 5-6	Chambara	turn to **79**
Score 7	Hidari	turn to **323**
Score 8-9	Mukogawa	turn to **178**
Score 10-12	Narai	turn to **155**

390

You emerge from the maze into a passage that leads to a small funnel-shaped chamber. Peering out from behind a cleft in the rock, you see five grotesque warriors guarding a book that rests between them on a jewelled lectern. They are staring fiercely in all directions, alert and ready to deal with any interloper.

You know without being told that your task is to steal the book from their midst.

Make a THIEVERY roll at a Difficulty of 14.

Successful THIEVERY roll	turn to **411**
Failed THIEVERY roll	turn to **371**

391

The granite door is set straight into a bank of tumbled earth and stones. The trellis of withered ivy suggests it is very old indeed. It looks like a tomb entrance.

Enter the tomb	turn to **530**
Turn back while you still can	turn to **583**

392

If you gave him a weapon (a **sword**, for example) with a COMBAT bonus of at least +1, turn to **413**. If you gave anything else, turn to **373**.

393

The innkeeper charges 1 Shard a day. For each day you spend here you can recover 1 lost Stamina point, up to the limit of your unwounded Stamina score. When your injuries are fully healed (or when your money runs out), turn to **362**.

394

The wizard Shugen instantly appears in a gout of blue flame and deals you a crippling blow with his wand. Lose 2 from your MAGIC score. Weakened by your efforts to free the trapped god, your only option is to make a run for it.

Turn to **44**.

395

The landscape sweeps as far as you can see in all directions, a wuthering expanse of barren heath and grey swamps.

Roll two dice.

Score 2-7	Nothing of note	turn to **416**
Score 8-12	A burial mound	turn to **290**

396

You are on the great highway running down the east coast of Akatsurai.

Head north to Chompo	turn to **59**
Leave the road and go west	turn to **282**
Travel south to Mukogawa	turn to **417**

397

You are travelling through the rice paddies of Midwest Akatsurai. North of here lies the immense Kwaidan Forest.

Head west over the Chu River	turn to **707**
Go further east	turn to **337**
Make for Sakkaku	turn to **522**
Journey south	turn to **500**
Venture into the forest	turn to **398**

398

Steep hills whose flanks are thickly grown with hoary groves of pine trees comprise the sinister Kwaidan Forest.

Roll two dice.

Score 2-7	An eerie silence prevails	turn to **529**
Score 8-12	Footfalls in the gloom	turn to **741**

399

In return for treating your injuries, the clerics expect a small donation to the upkeep of the temple. They will heal 1-6 lost Stamina points for 3 Shards or 2-12 Stamina points (the score of two dice) for 5 Shards.

When you have taken your medicine and paid the priests their due, turn to **79**.

400

Hundreds of longboats are moored in the harbour. The sail-master points out the red-dyed canvasses and the monkey totem on top of each mainmast. 'This is the renowned war fleet of the Starburst Clan,' he avers.

Note on the Ship's Manifest that your ship is docked in Chambara harbour, then turn to **79**.

401

'Who was it?' one of the pallbearers asks.

'Just a vagabond,' replies another. 'They found the body in this very barn. Died of exposure. Apparently old Kitsuno owns the land hereabouts, so he got lumbered with the funeral costs.'

'Poor chap. Still, he can afford it.'

The lid of the coffin is open. You sneak a peek and then wish you hadn't. It is not a pleasant experience to see your own dead body.

Speak to the mourners	turn to **303**
Go back to sleep	turn to **521**

402

Gaman Monastery consists of dozens of small buildings with low-pitched roofs standing beside a grove of fir trees.

You are given a cell containing a bed mat, a book of sutras, and a pitcher of water. In common with the other monks, you eat only twice a day – a bowl of rice, a dish of pickled vegetables, and a mug of soup. All the same, you soon feel refreshed and alert. Your studies continue apace. Roll two dice, and if you get higher than your SANCTITY score then increase it by 1. However, if you roll exactly equal to your SANCTITY then you get bored with the rituals of devotion and must lose a point.

Turn to **422**.

403

You drive off the creature with a spell that causes strong winds to disperse the dark cloud. The next morning you report to the Sovereign: 'The creature will not trouble you again, your majesty. It was sent by an evil man who plots your destruction, but you are safe now because I have caused the curse to rebound on the one who sent it.'

A few days later, Lord Masayori is obliged to retire from court life because his skin has erupted in weeping sores that smell like rotten fish. Others say how awful it is, but you know Masayori has got his just deserts.

Turn to **423**.

404

You sink into a trance in which voices roar and blur.

'The assassin is dead, my lord.'

'Good. Throw the body into the sea.'

You are stripped of all your possessions and money (cross them off your Adventure Sheet) and then flung off the cliffs.

When the current has carried you up on to a stretch of shoreline safely out of sight of the villa, you cancel the trance spell. Turn to **362**.

405

The monk offers to preach the sermon of the Thunder Peak, which he says will give you protection from danger.

Listen to his sermon	turn to **619**
Attack him	turn to **639**
Go to bed	turn to **610**

406

The whole crew gathers at the rail to stare into the north east. There stretches the Unbounded Ocean, a stark wilderness of unending grey water. It is a daunting sight.

Roll two dice.

Score 2-9	A trouble-free voyage	turn to **465**
Score 10-12	On the rocks	turn to **588**

407

Nothing you say can patch up this argument. Kiyomori calls for his manservant and has you all but thrown into the street. Lose the codeword *Fleet* and turn to **79**.

408

It is a poor old friar who has been hit on the head and robbed. You help him up and see that he is well enough to continue on his way to Narai.

In return for your kindness he gives you a blessing. Write Luck in the Blessings box on your Adventure Sheet. The blessing can be used once to allow you to reroll any dice result. After using the blessing, remember to cross it off your Adventure Sheet. You can have only one Luck blessing at a time, so if you had one already the only thing the old friar can give you is his gratitude. Turn to **671**.

409

You get up in the night feeling thirsty. Stumbling out to the stream behind the cottage, you catch sight of a scraggly creature with luminous grey flesh and red eyes loping down the path from the cliff top.

'Take this stranger!' cries out a voice from behind you. 'Just leave our daughter's body untouched!'

It is the old man and his wife. They invited you to stay overnight so that the ghoul would devour you rather than the corpse of their daughter.

| Run off into the night | turn to **506** |
| Stand up to the ghoul | turn to **527** |

410

Note that your ship is now docked at the mouth of the Gai River. Your men are too fearful to come ashore with you.

'This is Oni Province, skipper,' says the mate. 'Don't you know what "oni" means? It's the Akatsurese word for devil.'

You disembark alone. Turn to **356**.

411

You distract the warriors with a pebble and, while they are searching in the tunnel, you slip out into the shadows and across the chamber to snatch the book.

Another passage lies ahead. You follow it to a grotto where a shaft of light pierces the gloom from a hole in the ceiling. The light glitters on the surface of an underground lake, throwing shifting patterns of blue-green light across the walls. A masked figure steps out of the shadows. He attacks without waiting to see why you have come.

The Enemy, COMBAT 12, Defence 22, Stamina 35

Turn and run	turn to **371**
Fight and win	turn to **430**
Fight and lose	turn to **479**

412

Vines as heavy as hawsers dangle from the sombre black branches clustered overhead. Is it day or night? You can hardly tell.

| Follow the rise of the land | turn to **372** |
| Look for a brook | turn to **431** |

413

He explains just a few of the arcane secrets of his sect. Roll one die, and if the number rolled is higher than your MAGIC score then increase it by 1.

Ask him to teach you more	turn to **373**
Go into the shrine	turn to **352**
Thank him and leave	turn to **398**

414

You can leave possessions and money here at your town house. Record anything you leave in the box below. Each time you return, roll two dice to see what's happened in your absence:

Score 2-9	Your belongings are safe
Score 10	Theft; all the money you left here is gone
Score 11-12	Fire; the town house and its contents have been destroyed

If your town house has burned down, turn to **155** and erase the tick beside the town house option there. Otherwise read on.

The town house is a good place to relax after your travels. If injured, restore your Stamina to its normal score. When you are ready to leave, turn to **155**.

ITEMS AT TOWN HOUSE

415

You catch sight of a fabulous golden animal standing above you on a ridge. It has the body of a stag, a long feathery tail, wings like forks of lightning and a dragon-like face with a single horn set above large thoughtful eyes.

Check your codewords. If you have *Bullion*, *Clanger*, *Fracas*, *Iota*, *Judas*, or *Kink*, turn to **314**. If not, turn to **492**.

416

You are crossing the northern reaches of Oni Province, a place of baleful repute.

Strike out east towards Narai	turn to **493**
Go south	turn to **356**
Cross the Gai River to the south-west	turn to **97**

417

You arrive at a wayside inn. A woman with a tiny baby slung on her back hurries out into the road to offer you a welcoming cup of green tea as thick as soup.

Stop at the inn	turn to **437**
Follow the road north	turn to **73**
Follow the road south	turn to **495**
Strike out due west	turn to **515**

418

If you have the codeword *Fire*, turn to **516**. If not, turn to **99**.

419

The boat takes you upriver as far as a little village, where you are made welcome by the locals who are curious for any news. You stay with them for a few days, regaling them with the tales of your travels. Recover 1 Stamina point if injured.

Soon it is time for the barge to make its return journey. 'Will you come back with us?' asks the barge master. 'Or do you intend to go looking for that shrine?'

Go back to Chambara	turn to **79**
Go further upriver	turn to **517**
Travel east	turn to **672**
Travel west	turn to **337**

420

Streams trickle over hard-packed earth carpeted with dead brown pine needles. Mushrooms squat like old toads in the hollows, thriving on the dank gloom. You are on the outskirts of Kwaidan Forest, but as you emerge into open country you find you have quite lost your

bearings.
Roll two dice.

Score 2-4	turn to **2**
Score 5-6	turn to **337**
Score 7	turn to **97**
Score 8-9	turn to **493**
Score 10-11	turn to **672**
Score 12	turn to **515**

421

You can buy a **lotus talisman (SANCTITY +1)** for 200 Shards, or a **paradise talisman (SANCTITY +2)** for 400 Shards.

'You probably won't be able to sell them outside Akatsurai,' warns a beggar sitting at the temple gates.

'Sell them?' snorts a priest. 'Why would anyone want to do that?'

Decide if you are buying either talisman and cross off the money. Then turn to **79**.

422

Recover 2-12 Stamina points (the roll of two dice) if injured. After several days you collect your belongings and prepare to set out again into the world. The monks gather to see you off.

'You are always welcome here,' says the abbot. Turn to **675**.

423

Takakura heaps every honour on you, to the envy of all the other courtiers. He presents you with a **golden katana**, a **lute (CHARISMA +3)** and personal apartments here in the palace. Note these gifts on your Adventure Sheet and then turn to **576**.

424

It is a long steep climb. The sun is sinking towards the horizon as you emerge from the trees and look along the clifftop. The late afternoon light is the colour of blood.

Lord Kiyomori and his guards stand in a circle around a man who is kneeling with his hands tied behind him. The breeze whips his long loose hair around his face as he looks up at them with a scowl of almost demonic ferocity.

'So, Akugenda,' says Kiyomori, 'you are unrepentant even now.'

The man called Akugenda spits on the ground. 'Repentance, you pious hypocrite? I call upon the Thunder Spirit to hear this vow: I'll be revenged on the pack of you!'

Kiyomori looks away in distaste. 'Enough of this. Jiro, kill him.'

Stop the execution	turn to **474**
Stand and watch	turn to **697**
Leave before they spot you	turn to **362**

425

He floats higher in the air, trying to stay out of your reach, and starts to veer off back towards the woods. To bring him down you must make a MAGIC roll at a Difficulty of 15.

Successful MAGIC roll	turn to **503**
Failed MAGIC roll	turn to **475**

426

One afternoon the sky darkens and the wind turns cold. Soon you are caught in a downpour. Seeing a light, you make for it and come to a ramshackle cottage where two men and a woman invite you inside until the rain stops. Your hosts cannot be peasants; their manners are too refined. Are they courtiers, exiled from the capital for some reason?

Ask them who they are	turn to **85**
Make casual conversation	turn to **504**
Tell them you must be going	turn to **476**

427

He is still alive, although highwaymen have stolen all his money. You help him to a roadside inn where you learn that he is a member of the prestigious Wistaria Clan.

'These are troubled times and evil men abound in the land,' he says. 'It is heartening to meet a good person like yourself. You are always assured of a warm welcome in Chompo.'

Get the codeword *Fuchsia* if you didn't already have it, then turn to **671**.

428

Your aerial journey gives you a marvellous opportunity to study the lay of the land, but it is hard to drink in all the details. Roll two dice, and if you get higher than your SCOUTING score you can increase it by 1.

'An extraordinary craft,' you say to the wizard. 'How do you steer it?'

'You have put your finger on the one aspect of the design that I have yet to perfect. For the nonce we must rely on fate, prayer, chance and wishful thinking.'

Eventually the balloon comes to rest in the upper branches of a tree and you hastily disembark. Roll two dice to see where you are.

Score 2-4	turn to **632**
Score 5-6	turn to **298**
Score 7	turn to **609**
Score 8-9	turn to **296**
Score 10-12	turn to **44**

429

Your men are surprised to see you return alive. 'Let's get going without delay, captain,' urges the first mate.

Set to sea	turn to **250**
Go ashore	turn to **568**

430

A hard-won victory like that must have taught you a thing or two. Advance one Rank. You can increase your unwounded Stamina score by 1-6 points permanently. Remember that going up in Rank also increases your Defence by 1.

Now turn to **479**.

431

You enter a glade where an old tree has toppled. Beetles scurry across it, burrowing into the dead wood, and a profusion of brightly stained flowers have taken root in the bark. On all sides
of the clearing there are saplings stretching hopefully up towards the bare patch of sky, engaged in a slow, silent and deadly

competition to be the fallen tree's replacement.

Press on across the clearing	turn to **583**
Turn back and find another route	turn to **351**

432

At the slightest touch of your foot on the porch step, the figure swings around, as weightless as an empty wasps' nest. You find yourself staring into the rigid parchment face of a cadaver. It dangles puppet-like, held up by a mass of fine silken strands. Then you see a long bristly leg extend out across the porch, and terror turns the warmth of daybreak to ice. Turn to **481**.

433

Here you can buy a ship or set sail if you already have one. Alternatively, you could pay for passage on a vessel bound for these destinations:

Chambara, cost 20 Shards	turn to **27**
Hagashin, cost 30 Shards	turn to **302**
Kaiju, cost 30 Shards	turn to **128**

If you can afford to buy a ship of your own then you can sail wherever you want. Three ship types are available.

Ship type	*Cost*	*Capacity*
Barque	240 Shards	1 Cargo Unit
Brigantine	480 Shards	2 Cargo Units
Galleon	990 Shards	3 Cargo Units

If you already own a ship you can sell it for half these prices. If you do buy a ship, record its details on the Ship's Manifest. The crew quality is average, but you can upgrade it to good for 75 Shards and to excellent for a further 150 Shards. Once you own a ship you can stock it with local goods or sell cargo that you have transported here from other ports.

Buy and sell cargo	turn to **482**
Set sail (if ship docked here)	turn to **224**
Return to the town centre	turn to **155**

434

'The merchant houses keep their doors closed to outsiders,' a Sokaran spice trader tells you. 'You need a letter of introduction to show that you're trustworthy.'

'Where can I get one?'

He shakes his head. 'Not here. Try asking in Chambara.'

Turn to **8**.

435

The wizard emerges from his home to demand that you pay a toll. He wants you to give him 200 Shards for crossing his lawn.

If you are willing to pay, cross off the money and go on your way by turning to **44**. If you can't or won't pay, turn to **441**.

436

A distraught fisherman tells you how he left his boat pulled up on the shore while he went to call on a friend.

'I got talking and forgot about the time,' he says. 'The tide came in and my boat drifted off – along with my little son and daughter who were on board!'

Swim out to the boat	turn to **265**
Decline to help	turn to **514**

437

The inn is run by a young widow who has several small children. She charges only 1 Shard a day, though you might like to give her a little more if you're feeling charitable. Each day you spend at the inn allows you to recover 1 lost Stamina point, up to the maximum set by your normal Stamina score when unwounded.

When you are ready to move on, turn to **494**.

438

The Urushi Mountains are a great blue bruise against the limpid sky at dusk. North is the city of Mukogawa, centre of Moonrise Clan power. Across the Ugetsu Straits lies the island of Toho, the untamed outpost of the Akatsurese empire.

Go south	turn to **535**

Go west	turn to **220**
Go up into the mountains	turn to **359**
Go north to Mukogawa	turn to **178**

439

Glistening darkly in the sunlight with its eyes closed, the river serpent really does look like a large flat rock.

Either you'll have to go the long way round, up to the point where the stream gushes out of the rocks, or maybe you can cross so quickly that the serpent doesn't react?

Use the serpent's head as a stepping stone	turn to **197**
Go the long way round	turn to **101**

440

If you have any of these codewords, delete them now: *Almanac*, *Bastion*, *Catalyst* or *Eldritch*.

You can invest money in multiples of 100 Shards. Hofuna will use this money to buy and sell commodities on your behalf while you are away from the city.

Write the sum you are investing in the box below or withdraw a sum you invested previously. When you have completed the transaction, turn to **8**.

```
MONEY INVESTED



```

441

The wizard starts chanting a spell. A dark cloud blots out the sun. As it gets closer you can hear the buzzing of a million angry wasps.

If you have the codeword *Flood*, turn to **484**. Otherwise the wasps sting you repeatedly, causing the *permanent* loss of 1-6 points from your Stamina score. If still alive you are forced to flee: turn to **44**.

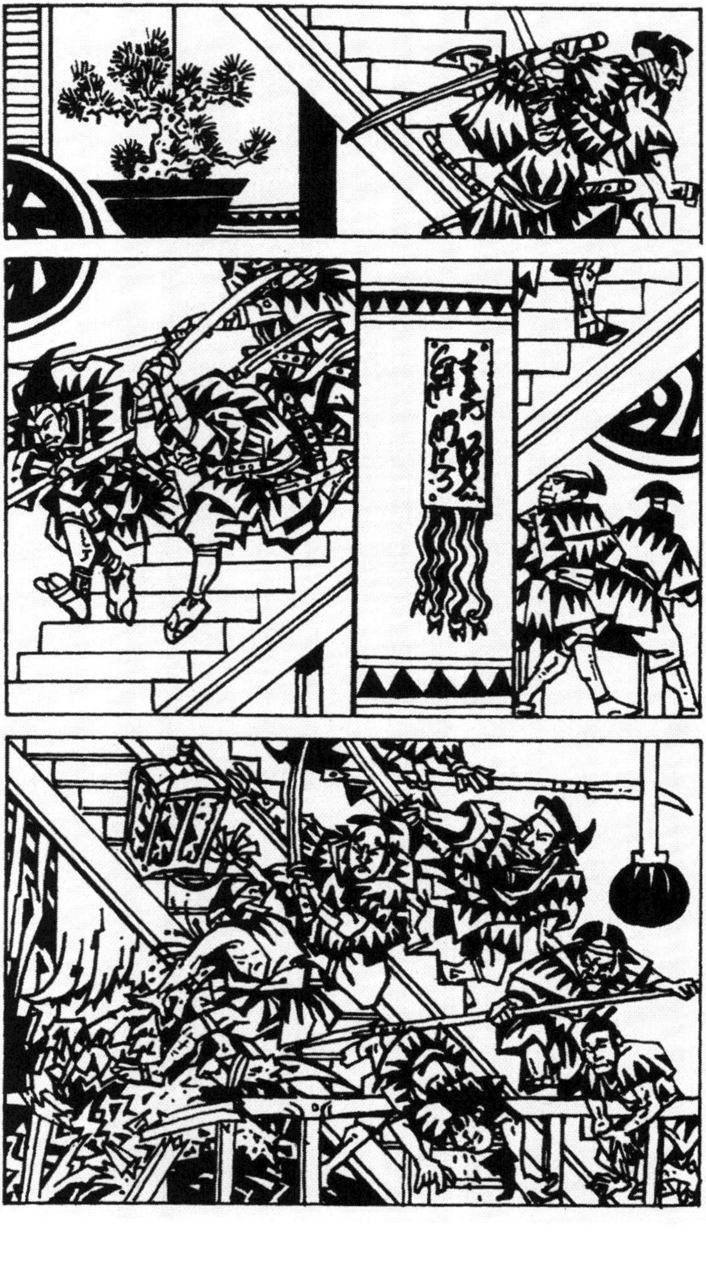

442

'The dragon has entered the palace!' screams a footman. The courtiers fly to and fro in panic while you marshal the best of the paladins and lead them down the long staircase. The dragon squats in the vast hall below chewing the palace's valiant defenders in its jaws. Its head alone is longer than your ship!

You give the order to attack, leading the paladins down the staircase in a reckless charge. The dragon bares its fangs and spits venom. Make COMBAT and CHARISMA rolls, both at a Difficulty of 15.

Both rolls successful	turn to **709**
Either or both rolls failed	turn to **692**

443

If you are in an adventurous mood, you are spoiled for choice. Should you strike out across Gashmuru Gulf towards the forbidden city of Dangor? Or venture over the Sea of Hydras to the Feathered Lands? Or put in at an Akatsurese port?

Go east	turn to **450**
Go south-east	turn to **550**
Go west	*Over the Blood-Dark Sea* **98**
Go north	turn to **80**
Go south	*The City in the Clouds* **77**

444

To the west are fertile rice paddies, but here the long grass lies withered across lanes of dry earth.

Roll two dice.

Score 2-8	A quiet journey	turn to **31**
Score 9-12	An unearthly gleam	turn to **121**

445

The innkeeper charges 1 Shard a day. For each day you spend here you can recover 1 Stamina point, up to the limit set by your normal (unwounded) Stamina score.

When you have either fully recuperated or run out of money, it is time to move on: turn to **591**.

446

A narrow, desolate strip of land separates the jagged smoke–blue shadow of the Kenen Mountains from the gunmetal grey of the Unbounded Ocean.

Roll two dice.

Score 2-8	No one and nothing	turn to **33**
Score 9-12	Hungry ghosts	turn to **734**

447

A storm sweeps with relentless speed across the sky, blotting out the sun. If you have a blessing of Safety from Storms, cross it off and turn to **87**. Otherwise turn to **222**.

448

The **cursed sword** is securely stuck to your hand. You must fight with it in every battle until you manage to remove the curse. The curse will vanish automatically the next time you enter a temple. (Shrines and monasteries don't count; it must be a building specifically described as a temple.)

There is one bit of good news. When the curse is lifted, the weapon will become a **sword (COMBAT +2)**.

Now turn to **58**.

449

From your hiding-place you watch the man with the lamp glide past. He is tall and thin as a candle, with deep-set eyes and a face of ascetic concentration. From his bizarrely patterned robes you guess he might be a sorcerer – that, and the way the lantern floats obediently in the air just above his head. A good thing you stayed out of sight.

You slip out into the street. Turn to **79**.

450

Not far off the starboard bow, hidden rocks break the waves into surging white froth. On the port side lies open ocean. Roll two dice.

| Score 2-9 | A safe voyage | turn to **543** |
| Score 10-12 | Attacked at sea | turn to **145** |

451

A group of patrolling sentries accost you on your way up the path to Kiyomori's villa.

'You were a fool to come here,' says the captain. 'Your description has been circulated throughout the west.'

They mean to arrest you. To fight your way free and escape back into the town you must make a COMBAT roll at a Difficulty of 17.

| Successful COMBAT roll | turn to **362** |
| Failed COMBAT roll | turn to **452** |

452

You are shackled and flung into the hold of a slave ship bound for the distant land of Uttaku.

The man chained to the bench next to you gives a deep groan that turns into a bitter chuckle. 'I almost got the death penalty,' he says, adding after a doomful pause, 'but my crime was too serious, so I was sentenced to slavery in Uttaku instead.'

To see what fate has in store for you now, turn to **321** in *The Court of Hidden Faces*.

453

Lose the codeword *Fruit* and get *Fossil* instead.

Your town house is attacked by a gang of the tonsured youths employed by the chancellor as his enforcers. Yelling madly, they pour in through the windows and start to smash everything in sight. By the time you succeed in driving them off you can smell smoke. They have set fire to the building!

Turn to **284** to rescue any possessions stored in the town house. You can only rescue items if there is room on your Adventure Sheet to carry them. Delete any you cannot carry as well as any money you may have left at the town house (there's no time to gather it up). After doing that, you can only stand in the street and watch your town house burn to the ground, then turn to **79**.

454

It is not unlike slamming your fist against a tombstone. Still smiling, Mister Dragon takes hold of your wrist and puts you on the ground with a single deft movement.

Turn to **63**.

455

You meet an actor who wishes to return to the town where he was born, to see his aged mother. 'But I have not had much success in my chosen profession,' he explains. 'If my mother sees me in these poor rags she will die a disappointed woman. I don't want her last thoughts to be full of worry for my future.'

He offers to sell you his only possession, a finely made **dragon mask**. He will not sell for less than 100 Shards, and obviously would not normally even go as low as that.

Pay him whatever you are willing to give (if anything) and turn to **43**.

456

The guards were expecting you to back off and make a run for it, so when you run further into the villa it takes them unawares. They chase you through to the courtyard at the back. 'We've got you cornered now!' shouts one. 'There's no way out!'

At the back of the courtyard stands a plain building of unpainted wood with a moss-lined roof. Only the large bronze bell gives any clue to its function. Rushing inside, you come across a statue that gazes down at you with a look of great serenity.

A man in priest's robes looks up from his prayers. 'Who dares invade the temple of the Sage of Peace?' he says sternly.

The guards are right behind you. Unless you can think of an escape route, this is where you must make your stand.

Get the codeword *Fracas* and turn to **385**.

457

You go for a walk in the entrancing countryside of Shaku Isle.

Roll two dice.

Score 2-5	A plaintive cry	turn to **263**
Score 6-8	Nothing disturbs your reverie	turn to **44**
Score 9-12	A wizard's mansion	turn to **279**

458

Since defeating the giant was possibly the toughest challenge of your life, you also deserve to advance one Rank. This means you can increase your unwounded Stamina score by 1-6 points permanently (the roll of one die). Remember that going up a Rank also means your Defence will increase by 1.

Now turn to **566**.

459

The vampires take the precaution of removing any weapons you may be carrying and throwing them into the undergrowth. (Cross these off your Adventure Sheet.) Then they each take hold of one of your limbs and carry you jerkily for miles into the wild depths of the forest, depositing you at last in front of a grim stone doorway. As the tallowy gleam of dawn shows beyond the treetops, the vampires retire rapidly back into the darkness. You are left alone.

Turn to **391**.

460

Dawatsu stands blinking in the entrance of the tomb. He is inconvenienced by the light, but after a moment's hesitation he follows you outside.

'Pathetic,' he jeers. 'I am no mere sheeted ghoul, to be sent cowering back to my coffin by the light of day. I am Morituri of the Dawatsu; I am next to the gods themselves!'

Dawatsu Morituri, COMBAT 10, Defence 20, Stamina 38 (Remember to reduce his Stamina score if you have managed to wound him already.)

There is no retreating now. If you prevail, turn to **489**.

461

You remember to prise the magic **tatsu pearl** out of the roof of the dragon's mouth. Add it to your list of possessions.

Swallow the pearl	turn to **68**
Explore the dragon's lair	turn to **488**

462

The local sea captains no longer ply their trade with the western ports because of the threat posed by the fleet owned by the Starburst Clan.

'To make a living these days, we have to make the long haul all the way to Yarimura,' complains one.

You can get passage to these destinations:

To Kaiju, cost 15 Shards	turn to **128**
To Yarimura, cost 30 Shards	turn to **749**
To Dangor, cost 35 Shards	*The City in the Clouds* **197**

Don't forget to pay the fare before you travel. If you decide to stay in Mukogawa for the time being, turn to **281**.

463

He tells you his sob story whether you want to hear it or not.

'I am an expert thief, if an indifferent fighter, but the old established burglars' clans will not allow me to ply my trade in the towns. Thus I've had to try my luck as a highwayman, and I'm just not cut out for it!'

'That's for sure.'

'Well, thanks anyway for sparing my life,' he says. 'In return let me give you this advice. The bridge over the Chu River is a favourite place for the Black Swan sisters to waylay travellers. Don't trust them an inch!'

If you have a **dragon mask**, turn to **50**. If not, turn to **316**.

464

If you previously left a **sealed letter** here, turn to **28** at once. Otherwise read on.

Like any knight of Akatsurai you are expected to live simply. Your room contains only a pallet, a low table, and two floor cushions. A maid has left a single flower in a celadon vase.

You can rest from your adventures here, restoring your Stamina to normal if wounded.

Possessions and money can be left without fear of robbery; just record them in the box below.

When you are ready to leave, turn to **553**.

PRIVATE APARTMENTS

465

You turn aside from the Unbounded Ocean. The prospect of adventure may be tempting, but no ship has ever returned from crossing those leaden waters.

Go south-east	turn to **72**
Go west	*Over the Blood-Dark Sea* **55**
Go south to Dragon Isle	turn to **90**
Go north to Druids' Isle	*The War-Torn Kingdom* **136**

466

The cool breeze on your face is at odds with this scene of fiery desolation. You pass your fingers across your eyes, muttering a charm to dispel illusions.

Get the codeword *Fire* and turn to **516**.

467

If you have the title Hatamoto, turn to **553**. If not, you can stay as a guest at the mansion (if injured, restore your Stamina to its unwounded score) and, when you're ready to leave, turn to **178**.

468

The crew refuses to remain in this hellish place. Many of the men are so terrified that they swear they will never put to sea again once this voyage is over. To convince them otherwise requires a CHARISMA roll of Difficulty 14. If you fail this roll, you must reduce your crew quality by one step – i.e. from excellent to good, from good to average, or from average to poor.

Turn to **122**.

469

Chomei of the Green Lodge family is widely acknowledged as the greatest swordsmith in Akatsurai. You also discover that he is a little eccentric. He makes you wait on the veranda of his house for three hours because he refuses to talk to anyone before taking his midday meal.

If you have the codeword *Frame*, turn to **498**. If not, turn to **519**.

470

Shingen is set in a small bay at the mouth of the Chiku River. Note that your ship is now docked here and then turn to **362**.

471

You are sailing past steep cliffs like the flanks of a titan's fortress. Swirls of darkness seem to emanate from a point somewhere along the coast. Your charts show you are not far from the Black Pagoda.

Put in at the mouth of the Gai River	turn to **410**
Follow the coastline east	turn to **300**
Steer north	turn to **100**
Make for the open sea	turn to **202**

472

The Black Pagoda is a seven-storeyed tower set above sheer cliffs where the sea crashes furiously against the rocks, sending up high spouts of white foam. The stone from which the pagoda is built was reputedly quarried from the doorway of hell itself. Its colour is so deep a black that the pagoda looks like a hole in space.

Knock at the door	turn to **507**
Sneak inside	turn to **567**
Turn away	turn to **501**

473

You jump up on to the roof and run along boldly to strike the creature. You can see it a little more clearly now, glaring from the black cloud like an old pike hidden in the depths of a muddy pond.

In this fight, attack as normal but do not use your normal Defence score. Instead, use your SANCTITY score in place of your Defence.

Chimerical Beast, COMBAT 8, Defence 9, Stamina 20

If you manage to kill it, turn to **423**.

474

Kiyomori and his retinue could not be more astonished if a faery creature from the overworld had just fallen into their midst.

Jiro, the chancellor's executioner, rests the tip of his two-handed sword on the turf and shakes his head. 'Now what do you think you're up to?' he says.

'Who is this fool?' demands Kiyomori. 'Jiro, execute them both.'

Jiro hefts his sword and steps closer. Two other guards are moving to get behind you. What now?

Fight all three	turn to **618**
Cut Akugenda's bonds	turn to **598**
Run for it	turn to **577**

475

As he fades off into the darkness he hurls a curse back at you. Lose any blessings you have noted on your Adventure Sheet, then turn to **610**.

476

The rain does not let up and by nightfall you are drenched. You slog over muddy fields in search of shelter, but all you can find is a solitary tree. You lay your head on a mossy root and the patter of rain lulls you off to sleep.

If you have the codeword *Future*, turn to **526**. If not, turn to **296**.

477

He is quite dead, but in their haste to rob him the highwaymen missed a **rabbit's foot charm**, a **four-leaf clover** and a **silver horseshoe**. Take these if you think they are worth having and then turn to **671**.

478

If you have **salt and iron filings**, turn to **705**. If not, read on.

The ghoul arrives at midnight but is undeterred by the benediction you spoke over the girl's body. It climbs in through an open window and lopes on long thin legs over to the trestle where the body lies. You are watching from behind a door, and when you see the ghoul begin its grisly meal you know it is time to decide: will you step out and confront it, or slip away into the night?

Fight the ghoul	turn to **527**
Leave while it's eating	turn to **53**

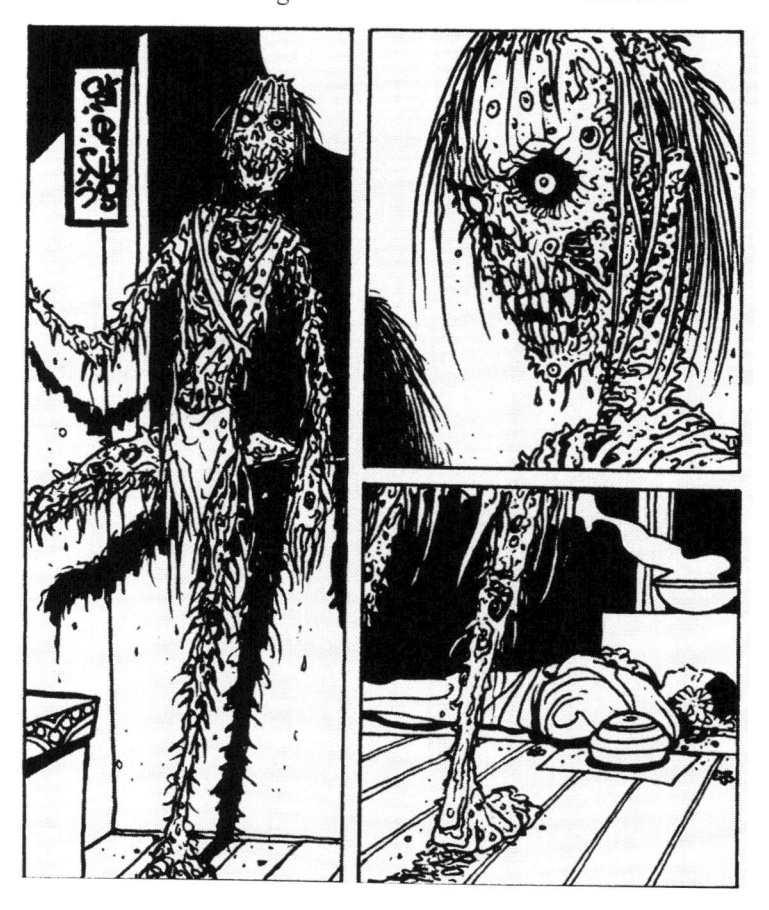

479

All your injuries are mysteriously healed. You are standing over the body of your own twin. Then you take a closer look, blink, and the scene melts away. Now you are sitting cross-legged in front of the altar in the great hall. The abbot puts a hand on your shoulder. 'You have been meditating for forty-nine days,' he says, 'and now you have truly attained enlightenment.'

You describe your experiences. 'The labyrinth represented the false paths you might have taken in your life,' explains the abbot. 'The book was the true teaching of the Sage of Peace, which you gained by confounding the Five Great Sins. Lastly, you faced the embodiment of your own passions. Victory or defeat means nothing in that encounter; you cannot overcome your inner self, you can only learn to live with it.'

Increase your SANCTITY score to 12 and get the title Enlightened One. Then turn to **383**.

480

The snake slides off into the undergrowth having sunk its fangs in your ankle. Pain floods into your veins, icy cold and lava-like at the same time. To survive you must either use up a blessing of Immunity to Disease/Poison (if you have one) or suck out the poison by succeeding in a SCOUTING roll at Difficulty 14.

Survive	turn to **412**
Succumb	turn to **140**

481

It stalks out of the darkness, its body hanging between long ebony legs like a fat oilskin full of poison. It would take a brave man to face such a thing without flinching.

Spider Creature, COMBAT 10, Defence 20, Stamina 33

Run for your life	turn to **585**
Fight and win	turn to **605**

482

In order to trade you must have the codeword *Frame*. If you don't, the local merchants refuse to have anything to do with you and you should turn to **155**. If you have the codeword *Frame*, read on.

You must have a ship docked in Narai harbour to transport goods. The prices given here are for single Cargo Units, which are much more than one person could hope to carry. Any cargo you buy will be delivered to your ship in the harbour, so note it on the Ship's Manifest.

Cargo	To buy	To sell
Furs	220 Shards	150 Shards
Grain	100 Shards	75 Shards
Metals	700 Shards	550 Shards
Minerals	550 Shards	500 Shards
Spices	700 Shards	600 Shards
Textiles	180 Shards	150 Shards
Timber	180 Shards	140 Shards

When you have completed your business arrangements, turn to **155**.

483

To find out how well your investments have done, roll two dice. Add 1 to the score if you are an initiate of the Three Fortunes. Also add 1 for each of the following codewords that you have acquired on your travels: *Almanac*, *Bastion*, *Catalyst* and *Eldritch*.

Score 2-3	Lose entire sum invested
Score 4-5	Loss of 50%
Score 6-7	Loss of 100%
Score 8-10	Investment remains unchanged
Score 11-12	Profit of 10%
Score 13-14	Profit of 25%
Score 15-16	Profit of 50%
Score 17	Profit of 100%

Now turn to **440**, where you can withdraw the sum recorded in the box there after adjusting it according to the result you've just rolled.

484

Instead of attacking you, the wasps turn on the evil wizard. There are so many that the noise is deafening. The wizard has no defence and is soon lying dead on the veranda of his mansion. The wasps rise into the air and go swarming off to the north-east.

Inside the mansion you find a **celestium wand (MAGIC +5)**, a **fretwork key**, a **green gem**, a **scarab amulet** and a bottle of **faery mead**. Take anything you want and get the codeword *Faded*, then turn to **44**.

485

She recognizes the pendant and allows you to pass.

Go west towards Oni Province	turn to **568**
Go east to Sakkaku	turn to **522**

486

You duck out of sight just seconds before the person with the lamp arrives at the far end of the corridor.

Make a THIEVERY roll at a Difficulty of 14.

Successful THIEVERY roll	turn to **449**
Failed THIEVERY roll	turn to **722**

487

Knocking at a narrow green door, you are admitted to a muddy courtyard where a beautiful lady sits with a flute in her lap. She calls you up on to the veranda beside her and listens without surprise as you tell your tale.

'I knew my lord would find me!' she says. 'But you must explain to him that I cannot return to court. I say this for his own good. The Lord Chancellor bears a grudge against me, and it is dangerous to antagonize him.'

You listen with a frown, suspecting that it would not go well for you if you returned to the palace empty-handed. You must try your best to convince her to come with you.

Make a CHARISMA roll at Difficulty 14.

Successful CHARISMA roll	turn to **12**
Failed CHARISMA roll	turn to **38**

488

You enter a long hall whose walls sparkle and gleam. The dragon's throne is a long stone bench against the far end of the chamber.

Treasure lies in great heaps on the polished white tiles. You fill your haversack with between 1000 and 6000 Shards (roll one die).

If you have the codeword *Fresco*, turn to **166**. If not, turn to **646**.

489

You can help yourself to the pick of Lord Morituri's funerary treasures – not only the spear that you already have, but a **hyperium wand (MAGIC +6)** and 2500 Shards in bizarrely shaped antique coinage. Note it all on your Adventure Sheet and then turn to **583**.

490

Giving a war-cry that sounds like a chicken breaking wind, the little fellow runs forward and pokes his knife towards you with an extravagant flourish. 'Have at you!' he cries.

Ridiculous Rogue, COMBAT 4, Defence 16, Stamina 30

You can try to take him alive if you want. To do that, you must fight without a weapon and taking a COMBAT penalty of 1. You can then treat any wounds you deal him as subdual damage only, and he will still be alive when his Stamina reaches zero.

Whether you kill him or not, you can take his **ring mail (Defence +2)**, his **knife** and his money pouch containing 15 Shards. Then, if you were fighting to subdue him, turn to **463**. If you decide to kill him, turn to **316**.

491

You cross the bridge leading to Lord Yoritomo's audience hall. Here he sits among his generals, absorbed day and night in planning the battle for dominance of these islands.

If you have a **sealed letter**, turn to **51**. If not, turn to **71**.

492

The animal swoops off into the woods. It was the kirin, the celestial stag that roams the world meting out justice. If you are a Troubadour you might be able to make up an impressive song about this encounter: roll two dice and if you get higher than your CHARISMA score you can increase it by 1.

Turn to **379**.

493

Journeying on, as the days pass, you see the full moon rise above forests of pine and sunlight mingle with the gushing spring waters from the hills.

Roll two dice.
Score 2-9	A quiet journey	turn to **514**
Score 10-12	Lost children	turn to **436**

494

The road runs from Chompo to Mukogawa, both the centres of power of great aristocratic clans.

Take the road south	turn to **495**
Take the road north	turn to **73**
Travel west	turn to **515**

495

This close to Mukogawa, you cannot go half a league without seeing parties of soldiers on horseback. All bear the white banner of the Moonrise Clan, and all have the hard-bitten look common to the warriors of the eastern provinces.

Which way are you headed?
North	turn to **417**
South	turn to **178**
West	turn to **515**

496

The priests will accept a donation of 10% of your cash and any one possession listed on your Adventure Sheet. If you refuse to hand these over, turn to **291**. If you agree, decide which item you are handing over, cross it off along with the money, and turn to **149**.

497

The Akatsurese are not great seafarers, and these are the best prices you can get for a second hand vessel:

Ship type	Sale price
Barque	180 Shards
Brigantine	450 Shards
Galleon	700 Shards

If you go ahead with the sale, remember to cross the ship off the Ship's Manifest. Turn to **612**.

498

Chomei flatly refuses to forge a sword for a you.

'I do not deal with merchants!' he says. 'My swords are of the highest quality. They are works of art, and not to be handled by those whose fingers are grubby with coinage.'

His servant shows you out. Turn to **79**.

499

You get three **moon spades (COMBAT +1)**. The bosun advises against looting the shrine itself. If you ignore him you can strip the altar of gold plate worth 1000 Shards but you must also lose all blessings and reduce your crew's quality to poor.

The crew is anxious to set sail. Turn to **745**.

500

You are on the road that runs from Sakkaku to Chambara. In places it is covered with gravel or even paved, but more often it is no more than a bare track running through tall grass. The pine trees to the north look as blurred and colourless as if they had been drawn in watered ink.

Go west to Sakkaku	turn to **522**
Go north off the road	turn to **378**
Head for Chambara	turn to **221**

501

The pagoda stands malevolently on the cliff top: a lighthouse built by demons to lure sailors to their doom. You cannot look at it without shuddering.

Travel north	turn to **395**
Make for Sakkaku to the east	turn to **568**
Follow the Gai River to the sea	turn to **20**

502

You strike up a conversation with a hermit who you meet on his way home. His name is Jobutsu. You cannot help noticing that he has very courtly manners, which he explains by telling you how he was once a nobleman at the imperial palace in Chambara.

'But I was undone by pride,' he says sorrowfully. 'I came to the Sovereign's notice because of my musical skill, you see. One day I was asked to play a very ancient flute that had been handed down through the generations. Alas, I did not think to examine it before I started to play. It was full of dust because it had not been played for so long, and so I was reduced to a coughing fit. Unable to bear the shame, I retired from court and came to live out here in the countryside.'

A sad story indeed, and perhaps cautionary. Get the codeword *Flux* and then turn to **652**.

503

Lose the codeword *Fusty*.

Something falls out of the sky with a plop. It didn't look big enough to be the monk, but you cannot see any sign of him now. When you go to investigate, you find an old badger lying dead among the pine needles.

Cook and eat the badger	turn to **344**
Go to bed	turn to **610**

504

Get the codeword *Future*.

The woman gives you a cup of hot green tea. It drives away the chill, but the longer you sit in the cottage the more uncomfortable you become. You start to notice the insects crawling over the bare earthen floor, the rustling of rodents in the thatching and the way the wind blows in through cracks in the walls.

Make your excuses and leave	turn to **476**
Spend the night here	turn to **683**

505

You run into a group of soldiers from the capital, immediately recognizable as the Lord Chancellor's troops by the many-pointed red star embossed on their breastplates.

If you have the codeword *Fracas* but not the codeword *Face*, turn to **18**. Otherwise the soldiers pass by without a word and you can turn to **196**.

506

It is only when you have gone a mile down the road that you realize you have left your money behind. Cross it off your Adventure Sheet and turn to **53**.

507

Your knocking is answered by heavy footfalls as something drags itself over to the door. There is a rusty screech as the bolts are drawn back.

Run away	turn to **501**
Stand your ground	turn to **528**

508

The abbot is amused by your little joke.

'You mean, of course, that one's training never ends,' he says, laughing. 'Well, I am glad you found the time to visit us again but I am sure you have better things to do elsewhere.'

Turn to **211**.

509

The tree stands at the brink of a precipice of weathered rock that has sloughed off into a small gully. Stalks of grass protrude from between the chunks of stone. Then you notice something else: a doorway of pitted granite, half buried in the debris.

Climb down to the door	turn to **391**
Go back	turn to **583**

510

Warily, you edge closer to the unmoving figure.
   Make a THIEVERY roll at a Difficulty of 15.

Successful THIEVERY roll	turn to **531**
Failed THIEVERY roll	turn to **432**

Browsing around the many tiny shops and market stalls, you soon discover that you have to haggle if you want a bargain.

Armour	To buy	To sell
Leather (Defence +1)	50 Shards	45 Shards
Ring mail (Defence +2)	100 Shards	90 Shards
Chain mail (Defence +3)	200 Shards	180 Shards
Splint armour (Defence +4)	350 Shards	300 Shards

Weapons (sword, axe, etc.)	To buy	To sell
No COMBAT bonus	50 Shards	35 Shards
COMBAT bonus +1	250 Shards	180 Shards
COMBAT bonus +2	550 Shards	380 Shards

Other items	To buy	To sell
Compass (SCOUTING +1)	400 Shards	350 Shards
Lockpicks (THIEVERY +1)	–	300 Shards
Candle	2 Shards	1 Shard
Parchment	8 Shards	5 Shards
Tatsu pearl	1000 Shards	900 Shards
Platinum earring	–	790 Shards

Items with no purchase price are not available to buy, although if you have one you can sell it. When you have done all your shopping, turn to **155**.

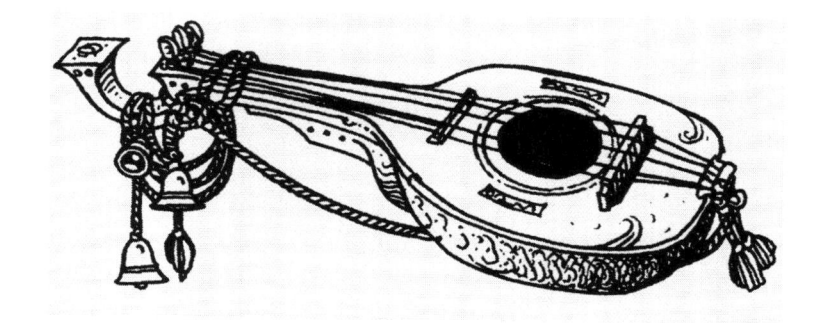

512

Ladies-in-waiting come to your room with little trays of spiced nut cakes, rice, pickled squid, roast pheasant, carrot and garlic salad, and various fruits mixed with liana syrup and shaved ice. After a hot bath, a good meal and a massage you soon begin to feel in the pink. Restore your Stamina to its normal unwounded score.

Your room contains a lacquer cabinet where you can store up to 5000 Shards and six possessions. To leave something here, just cross it off your Adventure Sheet and note it in the Cabinet box below. It will be here when you return.

When you are ready to leave, turn to **565**.

```
CABINET



```

513

The raven slips out of its cage and, taking the rope in its beak, flies swiftly in circles around the giant. Just as it is tying the knots, the giant opens a bleary eye. 'What's going on?' he says in a voice like a hippopotamus gargling with mud.

'Quick' says the raven. 'Kill him before he breaks the rope.'

Make a COMBAT roll of Difficulty 14 to do the deed in time.

Successful COMBAT roll	turn to **549**
Failed COMBAT roll	turn to **712**

514

You are travelling in north-west Akatsurai, in a district that the locals tell you is called Satsu Province. 'West lies Oni Province,' a young woodcutter tells you. 'It is the home of bone-eating demons!'

Go east to Narai	turn to **155**
Go west to Oni Province	turn to **395**
Go south	turn to **609**

515

Above muddy rice fields where the water lies in pools as still as mirrors, dragonflies dance metallically in the sunbeams.

Roll two dice.

Score 2-8	A quiet few days	turn to **3**
Score 9-12	Uncanny happenings	turn to **168**

516

The place that mortals know as the Dragon Isle is in reality Horai. It is the home of the sea elves, who keep it veiled under a frightening illusion to deter visitors. You are able to see it as it really is: pretty green gardens dotted with crystal lakes and phantasmagoric woodland. The air is filled with perfume and sweet music and the animals are so tame that they will eat from your hand.

The sea elves come down to the shore to greet you – a carefree company in pastel silks with pale eyes and long hair that floats like golden mist on the breeze. They give you magic fruit that restores your Stamina to normal if you were injured. Also increase your crew's quality by one step (poor to average, average to good, or good to excellent). When you are ready to sail away, turn to **122**.

517 ☐

You traverse a flower-filled valley towards a ridge of sombre pine trees. Arriving at a stream, you are about to cross when you notice that a large lump in mid-stream that you had mistaken for a boulder is actually the head of an enormous river serpent. You were just about to use it as a stepping stone.

If the box above is empty, put a tick in it and turn to **439**. If it was already ticked, turn to **101**.

518

'Why not buy this excellent vessel?' says a man whom the harbourmaster introduces you to. He gestures to a sturdy craft whose triangular sails remind you of a folded paper fan.

'What do those characters mean that are written along the side?' you ask him.

'They spell out the name of the ship: *Hell Spawn*.'

You examine this and many other ships. Choose from the types listed below.

Ship type	Cost	Capacity
Barque	200 Shards	1 Cargo Unit
Brigantine	450 Shards	2 Cargo Units
Galleon	900 Shards	3 Cargo Units

Record the details of your ship on the Ship's Manifest; you can name her if you wish. Remember to cross off the cost from the money recorded on your Adventure Sheet. The crew quality is average. Each time you arrive at a new destination, remember to change the entry in the Docked column. Currently, of course, the ship is docked at Chambara.

Go aboard	turn to **571**
Return to the city centre	turn to **79**
Hire better crew	turn to **536**

519

Chomei will forge a sword for you for the following prices:

COMBAT bonus +1	250 Shards
COMBAT bonus +2	450 Shards
COMBAT bonus +3	900 Shards
COMBAT bonus +4	1200 Shards
COMBAT bonus +5	1600 Shards

He is not interested in buying anything from you. If you buy a sword, remember to cross off the money before turning to **79**.

520

The road leads in only one direction: east, to the capital. Few travellers care to venture over the Chu River into the goblin-infested countryside of Oni Province.

Take the road to the capital	turn to **500**
Go north cross-country	turn to **378**
Go west across the Chu	turn to **594**

521

The morning dawns clear and bright. There is no sign of what became of the funeral procession. You cannot even see where they could have been taking the coffin.

You breakfast on a stew of herbs and mushrooms, watched from a distance by a solitary fox crouched on a log. Now it is time to set off again.

Turn to **611**.

522

Sakkaku is a town built from the near-black timber of Kwaidan Forest. It would present a very baleful sight if not for the locals' custom of planting flowers in the mossy thatching of their roofs, which in spring and summer transforms the town into a phantasmagoric idyll.

Take a room at an inn	turn to **278**
Visit the local shrine	turn to **293**
Leave the town	turn to **520**

523

If you have the codeword *Fracas*, turn to **451**. If not, turn to **569**.

524

You are skirting the west coast of Yodoshi, the main island of the Akatsurese group. The navigator's chart, based on a map painting he once saw on a paper fan in Yarimura, indicates your position to be roughly on a latitude with Noboro Monastery.

Steer for open ocean	turn to **102**
Follow the coast south	turn to **450**
Follow the coast north	turn to **200**

525

'I can show you the way to the Pure Land,' he says, 'but you will only be able to remain there until daybreak.' He scatters some dust from his hand and a shining path appears leading up into the western night sky. 'This path will take you there. Be sure that you do not stray off it! When you hear me ring the gong in my temple you must drop whatever you are doing and return at once, because at sunrise the path will vanish.'

Set out along the path	turn to **542**
Stay here after all	turn to **610**

526

You have a horrid dream that three disembodied heads come flying over the moor while you are asleep and start to devour you from the feet up. You half wake, feeling warm and numb as though you have been drugged. The heads look up with gory grins, then resume their meal. What is left of you goes back to sleep.

Lose the codeword *Future* and turn to **140**.

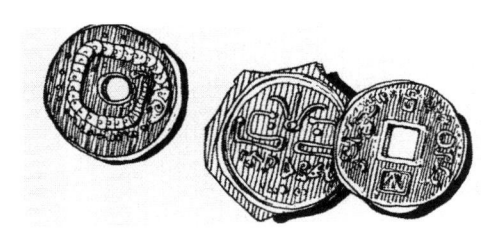

527

The ghoul gives vent to a loud screech and lashes out with its dirt-caked claws.

Ghoul, COMBAT 7, Defence 12, Stamina 15

If you flee it will get a free parting blow as you run off.

Turn and run	turn to **506**
Fight and win	turn to **544**

528

If you have the codeword *Fright*, turn to **545**. Otherwise turn to **561**.

529

You are surrounded by dense forest. Splashes of gold sunlight penetrate the green gloom by day, but after nightfall the darkness becomes absolute.

Press deeper into the woods	turn to **562**
Look for a path out	turn to **420**

530

To enter the tomb you must have something to light your way: a **lantern** or **candle** for instance. Otherwise your only option is to come back and explore it another time – assuming you can ever find your way to this spot again.

Enter the tomb	turn to **546**
Leave	turn to **583**

531

As you tiptoe past you discover why he didn't notice you. He is long past caring about the affairs of this world. His dead dry limbs are held up by a giant cobweb, making him look like a grotesque puppet left hanging in front of the shrine.

The web tells you what to look for – and sure enough, crouching just inside the entrance, you make out a tense clump of bristly legs and tiny jewel-like eyes.

Attack the creature	turn to **547**
Run away	turn to **398**

532

The Akatsurese draw a distinction between temples, which are dedicated to the mortal prophet they call the Sage of Peace, and shrines, where you can make offerings to their many deities. In Narai the only significant religious building is of the former type.

The monks can provide you with medicinal herbs if you are unwell, at a cost of 5 Shards. The treatment allows you to regain 2-12 lost Stamina points, up to the limit of your unwounded Stamina score.

Discuss initiation	turn to **725**
Get a blessing (if an initiate)	turn to **45**
Leave the temple	turn to **155**

533

The swordsmith is an ancient fellow as thin as a mantis. To convince him that you are worthy to buy one of his swords, you need to offer a goodwill payment of 40 Shards and then make a CHARISMA roll at a Difficulty of 20 if you're a Warrior, or Difficulty 22 if you belong to another profession. If you have the title of Junior Court Rank or Senior Court Rank you can add 2 to the dice roll. If you have the codeword *Fuchsia* you can add 3.

Assuming the swordsmith thinks you measure up, he will charge the following for a **sword** depending on the quality you require:

COMBAT bonus +2	350 Shards
COMBAT bonus +3	750 Shards
COMBAT bonus +4	900 Shards
COMBAT bonus +5	1400 Shards
COMBAT bonus +6	2800 Shards

If you purchase a sword, remember to cross off the money before turning to **572**.

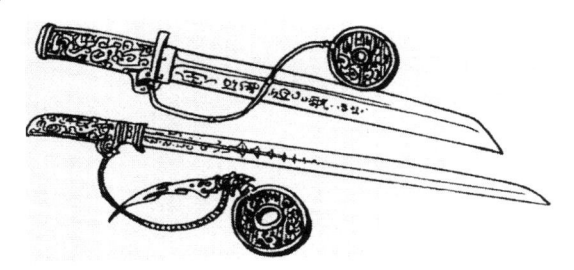

534

The giant wakes instantly. 'Eh?' he says, lurching to his feet. 'I'll crack open your bones and use them for soup!'

Turn to **712**.

535

A narrow alluvial plain separates the high-thrust Urushi Mountains from the eastern shore. Here the peasants grow rice and cotton, and weave silk for the clothes of great lords.

Go up into the mountains	turn to **359**
Go north	turn to **438**
Go south	turn to **74**

536

In the quayside taverns there are sailors from every part of the Fabled Lands, all eager to sign on and resume their life at sea. It will cost you 15 Shards to upgrade a poor crew to average, 50 Shards to upgrade average to good, and 100 Shards to upgrade good to excellent. These prices are cumulative, so upgrading a poor crew to excellent requires 165 Shards.

Once you've recorded any changes on the Ship's Manifest, turn to **612**.

537

There are sentries at the gate leading to the inner keep. They draw their swords as you approach and regard you with scowls of derision. 'Dog of a merchant, your presence would defile the House of Wistaria.'

You must remain in the outer town. Turn to **8**.

538

A long tunnel stretches off into the glistening subterranean darkness.

Follow the tunnel	*Over the Blood-Dark Sea* **445**
Climb back up	turn to **79**

539 ☐

If the box above is empty, put a tick in it and turn to **751**. If it was already ticked, turn to **576**.

540

You dive through a side door leading to a terrace and run off across the garden. But the grass is slippery because of the rain and you lose your footing and go sprawling. As you jump to your feet the old scholar comes gliding rapidly across the lawn towards you, his robes belling out around him. He casts a spell that manifests a swarm of venomous sprites who start buzzing around your head.

Make a MAGIC roll at a Difficulty of 16.

Successful MAGIC roll	turn to **637**
Failed MAGIC roll	turn to **658**

541

In the topmost chamber you see a tiny hunchbacked man dozing in a chair. There is nothing here any more to interest you.

Turn to **501**.

542

You have to leave your weapons, armour and money behind because these things are not permitted in the Pure Land. The path takes you up beyond the stars to a place of invigoratingly cold air. Here you meet a venerable sage who explains many mystic truths.

Suddenly you hear the gong. At the same time, the venerable sage breaks off from his sermon to shout, 'Cock-a-doodle-do!' You jump up to look for the path, but the clouds underfoot have become dingy and dry, rustling like straw. They give way and you plunge downwards with a scream, expecting to fall miles back to earth, but in fact you land with a solid thwack in the middle of the kitchen table. The proprietor of the lodge pauses in the act of striking the breakfast gong to stare at you in amazement. You gaze up through the hole in the roof to see a beady-eyed rooster watching you with haughty disdain.

Racing back to your room, you discover that your weapons, armour and money have gone. Cross them off your Adventure Sheet and lose the codeword *Fusty*, then turn to **654**.

543

You are sailing the coastal waters west of the straits that separate Shaku, the small southern island, from the main part of Akatsurai. The helmsman looks to you to set the course.

East	turn to **649**
North	turn to **350**
West	turn to **102**

South	turn to **550**
Put in at Hagashin	turn to **340**
Put in at Hidari	turn to **361**

544

'Now we can take our daughter's body to the cremation ground,' say the old couple. They have no money to repay you for your help, only the assurance that you will always be a welcome guest at their cottage.

Turn to **53**.

545

You look down to see a tiny hunchbacked man with a thin dark face and long nose. 'So you're back again,' he says grumpily before turning and strutting off. The size of the stairwell magnifies the echo of his footsteps, which is what made it sound as if a giant was corning to answer the door.

There is nothing here any more to interest you. Turn to **501**.

546

You are immediately presented with two routes: low brick lined tunnels extending straight back into the ground.

Take the left-hand tunnel	turn to **604**
Take the right-hand tunnel	turn to **162**

547

If you have a **crimson arrow**, turn to **564**. Otherwise, turn to **481**.

548

The armoury is run by the Thunderhead Clan, whose members maintain a proud tradition stretching back five hundred years. They will not make a suit of armour for just anybody. You have to convince them you are worthy by paying 50 Shards and making a CHARISMA roll at a Difficulty of 21. You can add 2 to the dice roll for having each of these codewords: *Fuchsia*, *Fleet* and *Frog*.

If you're accepted you can buy one suit of armour only at the following prices.

Leather (Defence +1)	25 Shards
Ring mail (Defence +2)	75 Shards
Chain mail (Defence +3)	150 Shards
Splint armour (Defence +4)	280 Shards
Plate armour (Defence +5)	600 Shards

When you have finished your business here, turn to **572**.

549

The giant's body slumps to the floor with a noise like a collapsing sack of potatoes. 'Phew!' snaps the raven. 'You cut it a bit fine, didn't you? Call yourself a hero?'

Turn to **566**.

550

You are sailing in the placid coastal waters south-west of Shaku Island.

Head south into Gashmuru Gulf	*The City in the Clouds* **77**
Follow the coast eastwards	turn to **601**
Go north	turn to **450**
Make for the open sea	turn to **102**

551

A farmer puts you up for a couple of days; recover 1 Stamina if injured. As you make ready to set out, the farmer tells you that Gaman Monastery lies to the north.

Go north	turn to **609**
Go east over the Chu River	turn to **735**

Go south	turn to **568**
Go west to Oni Province	turn to **356**

552

The Great Saddle Road is a metalled highway linking the country's two great centres of power: Chambara, the imperial capital, and Mukogawa, where the rule of the Moonrise Clan lords is unchallenged. Where are you headed?

Westwards	turn to **590**
Eastwards	turn to **178**
North over open country	turn to **515**
South towards the Clearwater Shrine	turn to **444**

553

You are one of the Shogun's trusted lieutenants and can roam the inner precincts unchallenged. Ranks of guards bow deeply as you pass between them along the quiet corridors. A servant waits in front of the door to your private apartments.

Enter your apartments	turn to **464**
Request an audience with the Shogun	turn to **491**
Go to see his spymaster	turn to **32**
Leave the manor	turn to **178**

554

The rural estates of the lords of Toho are very different from the dwellings of their cousins on the western island. Here you see great log-built manor houses with thatched roofs as big as a temple's. The peasant huts are clustered close to the home of their lord, in fear of attacks from the upland barbarians.

Go north	turn to **633**
Go into the mountains	turn to **319**
Travel to Kaiju	turn to **270**
Cross the river	turn to **592**

555

Several merchant ships from distant lands are riding at anchor in the harbour. Passage to Dweomer on the Sorcerers' Isle will cost 35

Shards, to Metriciens will cost 35 Shards, to Aku will cost 40 Shards, and to Yarimura will cost 25 Shards.

Travel to Dweomer	*Over the Blood-Dark Sea* **242**
Travel to Metriciens	*Over the Blood-Dark Sea* **260**
Travel to Aku	*The Court of Hidden Faces* **502**
Travel to Yarimura	turn to **749**
Stay in Chambara	turn to **612**

556

Note on the Ship's Manifest that the ship is now docked near to the Inn of Perfect Contentment, on the west coast of Yodoshi Island. Then turn to **733**.

557

Get the codeword *Flimsy*.

The play concerns a knight who is given hospitality at a lonely house where the inhabitants are flying-head goblins. During the night he overhears the flying heads plotting to kill him but foils the plan by destroying their bodies, which kills them. The whole thing is artfully portrayed using masks, with the effect of the flying heads being achieved by having black-garbed actors standing against a black backdrop so that only their terrifying white masks are visible.

When the play is over, one of the actors offers to sell you his **paper sword** as a souvenir for 5 Shards. Buy it if you wish and then turn to **289**.

558

With the corning of night a paper lantern is lit. It gives no warmth, but you are better off here than outside. The rain is falling heavily by now. You can hear it rustling the thatch and pouring in rivulets on to the porch.

You doze off, waking in the middle of the night to see a horrific sight. Three headless corpses are lying against the far wall – the bodies of your hosts!

Leap up and look around	turn to **600**
Wait and watch	turn to **579**

559

'It's your funeral,' says the priest.

You stomp off back to your bed of straw, determined to get a good night's rest even if it really should turn out to be your last. You hear no more noise from the funeral procession, and in the morning you feel very far from dead. In fact you feel famished. Seeing a fox hanging around outside, you startle it with a loud cry. It bolts off into the trees, which seems to prove you are no ghost.

You laugh at the fox's fright, but also out of relief. What a strange experience. Or was it but a dream?

You continue on your way. Turn to **611**.

560

An object resembling a giant paper lantern comes drifting over the fields. Intermittently it gives off a gleam of fiery yellow light. As it descends you can make out a man in wizard's robes standing in a basket slung underneath the lantern, conjuring gouts of flame that he sends shooting up inside it.

The strange craft bumps to a landing on a nearby hillock.

'Hallo,' calls the occupant of the basket. 'Want a lift anywhere?'

Get into the basket	turn to **581**
Thank him but say no	turn to **266**

561

The door swings open, releasing a gust of thick foul air. You are confronted by a face that almost fills the doorway. A lumpish skull covered with warty hide sits between shoulders as wide as a log. Muscles like huge sacks of flour strain in a torso weighed down with fat and hair. Then the giant opens his mouth to speak, and all of sudden you know where that smell is coming from.

If you have the **seal of the Black Pagoda**, turn to **582**. If not but you have a **lady's court robe**, turn to **602**. If you have neither, turn to **623**.

562

The rise of the land is your only clue as to which way to go.

Make a SCOUTING roll at a Difficulty of 13.

Successful SCOUTING roll	turn to **583**
Failed SCOUTING roll	turn to **398**

563

It is not easy to fight a foe you cannot see. Roll only one die for your COMBAT rolls in this fight, not two as you normally would.

Haniwa Warrior, COMBAT 8, Defence 20, Stamina 21

If you win, turn to **752**. If you lose, turn to **140**.

564

Without a second thought you hurl the arrow straight at the monster, catching it straight in the middle of its cluster of eyes. It gives a series of spasms and drops from its web, horribly injured.

Turn to **481** to fight it but note that you have already reduced its Stamina by 3-18 points (the roll of the three dice).

565

To get in to see the patriarch you must have the codeword *Fuchsia*. If you don't, turn back to **572** and choose again. If you do have *Fuchsia*, read on.

Hidehira is always happy to welcome an ally of his clan. 'My house is your house,' he says. 'Stay as long as you like.'

Rest and recuperate	turn to **512**
Pray in the family shrine	turn to **648**
Leave	turn to **572**

566

Get the codeword *Fright*.

After a thorough search of the pagoda you find 2500 Shards, a canister of **rat poison**, a **pirate captain's head**, three suits of **chain mail (Defence +3)**, a **battle axe (COMBAT +3)**, a **dragon's head** and a **pink rice grain**.

Take whatever you want and turn to **501** when you're ready to resume your travels.

567

You climb up to the first balcony and slip in through a narrow window. The interior of the tower is an architect's nightmare of long shadows, twisting stairs and crazy angles.

If you have the codeword *Fright*, turn to **541**. Otherwise, turn to **753**.

568

Shrines to the rice god are a common sight at the end of every country lane, here in the rich farmlands of western Akatsurai.

A shrine warden gives you directions. 'East lies the town of Sakkaku,' he says. 'West over the Gai River is Oni Province, where it is easier to tell the devils from the men.'

Head towards Sakkaku	turn to **7**
Cross the Gai River to the west	turn to **356**
Travel north	turn to **97**
Go to the Gai estuary	turn to **20**

569 ☐

If the box above is empty, put a tick in it and turn to **597**. If it was ticked previously, turn to **617**.

570

Down in a gully you see an overturned sedan chair. Half a dozen knights wearing white pennants are struggling against a larger force of hairy fur-clad barbarians.

Help the knights	turn to **240**
Help the barbarians	turn to **264**
Continue on your way	turn to **280**

571

The mate calls the men to attention. 'We're ready to sail, skipper,' he informs you.

Put to sea	turn to **150**
Go ashore	turn to **612**

572

No merchants are allowed into the inner stockade, where the mansions of the Wistaria Clan stand proudly on the hillside. Over all looms the massive curved roof of the palace of Lord Hidehira, the patriarch of the clan.

Find a swordsmith	turn to **533**
Find an armourer	turn to **548**
Visit the patriarch	turn to **565**
Pray at a shrine	turn to **587**
Leave the inner keep	turn to **8**

573

Your stay at the inn has been so restful that you are reluctant to leave. Nonetheless, it is time to resume your travels.

Take the road to Narai	turn to **2**
Take the road to Chompo	turn to **30**
Go south cross-country	turn to **336**

574

Masayori, Secretary of the Council of the Left, comes out to greet you as you cross the lawn.

'Ah, you are here at last,' he says.

'Was I expected?' you retort in surprise.

Masayori puts a flute into your hands. 'This is the famous flute Twilight Mourner. It is a priceless heirloom handed down by the Sovereign's ancestors. The Sovereign is waiting at this very moment for you to play to him.'

You are hurried through to the inner apartments, where Takakura sits impatiently on a raised dais surrounded by courtiers.

'Ah!' he says brightly as he sees you enter. 'Masayori has spoken of your great talent which, if not for him, would have remained forever hidden by modesty. Come, give us a tune.'

Everyone is waiting. What will you do?

Play as the Sovereign requests	turn to **156**
Tell him that you cannot	turn to **179**

575

The old scholar raises his hands, displaying nails as long as a hawk's talons. He flings a glittering trail of dust in your direction, which settles on the painted screen. Suddenly a great wind sucks you backwards and you plunge into the painting. Now you are surrounded by demonic horsemen with nothing but clouds in all directions.

Make a MAGIC roll at a Difficulty of 18.

Successful MAGIC roll	turn to **616**
Failed MAGIC roll	turn to **596**

576

You go to your personal apartments, located in the east wing of the palace.

Outside your room is a terrace that overlooks a serene courtyard of raked white sand on which rocks have been laid out in a mystical pattern. The pattern is supposed to represent the forces of nature and you find it relaxing to gaze on while meditating.

You can rest in your apartment to recuperate any lost Stamina points. Also you can leave money and possessions here to save having to carry them around with you. Each time you return, roll two dice.

Score 2	You receive a gift of 50 Shards
Score 3	Bad tidings; turn immediately to **739**
Score 4-9	Everything is fine
Score 10-12	There has been a fire; cross off any money and possessions left here

When you are ready to leave, turn to **79**.

APARTMENTS

577

You turn and scramble back down the cliff path. Kiyomori's guards don't bother to give chase. Fortunately, because you had the setting sun at your back, you doubt if any of them got a good look at your face. Even so, the wisest course seems to be to leave town at once. You decide not to travel by road in case Kiyomori sends out patrols.

Go north-east	turn to **704**
Go south-east	turn to **653**
Go upriver	turn to **359**

578

You are strolling around the great metropolis of Chambara, whose canals and wide, gravelled thoroughfares are lined with cherry trees.

Roll two dice.

| Score 2-5 | A queer duck | turn to **682** |
| Score 6-12 | Skinheads | turn to **599** |

579

After half an hour the disembodied heads of the three come drifting in out of the night. They all have purple juice dribbling down their chins and insects' legs stuck between their teeth.

'Beetles again, yuk!' says the woman's head, glaring in your direction. 'Why can't we have a succulent bite of human flesh for a change?'

'Ssh!' says the chief head. 'You'll wake our guest. You know we daren't harm someone with such powerful friends. They would send priests and wizards to exact revenge.'

The heads attach themselves to their bodies and appear to sleep. The rest of the night passes uneventfully. You set out on your way before dawn, anxious to get far away from here. Turn to **296**.

580

There is a grey mist covering the sea as you rise early in the morning to set the new course.

Follow the coast north	turn to **641**
Sail west towards the Sea of Hydras	turn to **450**
Go south towards Gashmuru Gulf	turn to **601**

581

He mutters a spell and another jet of flame takes the balloon aloft. You watch the ground drop away until the fields and treetops look like tiny details in a painted mural. If you have the codeword *Cheese* but not the codeword *Fortress*, turn now to **19**. Otherwise read on.

The wizard tells you his invention uses hot air to stay airborne. 'Let's face it, that's a commodity that will never be in short supply,' he says with a laugh.

Roll two dice.

Score 2	turn to **622**
Score 3-12	turn to **428**

582

The giant takes the seal and puts it close to his eyes. In his shovel-like hands it looks no bigger than a pinhead.

After a moment he gives a grunt, half satisfied and half disappointed, and beckons you inside. The door booms shut. You stand waiting until the giant points towards a staircase at the back of the hall. 'Come this way ' he growls.

Turn to **643**.

583

Gnarled branches dripping with rampant foliage twine high overhead, choking out the daylight and leaving the ground in a perpetual pall of green dusk.

Penetrate deeper into the forest	turn to **644**
Search for a way out	turn to **603**

584

In your pell-mell flight you drop the light. There is no going back for it now; cross it off your Adventure Sheet. Seeing a gleam of daylight ahead you give a gasp of relief, only to notice that the doorway is sliding inexorably shut.

To squeeze through before it has closed entirely requires a THIEVERY roll at a Difficulty of 12. Failing that, you will be sealed inside the tomb until your air runs out.

Successful THIEVERY roll	turn to **583**
Failed THIEVERY roll	turn to **140**

585

You have not gone half a dozen steps when a web shoots out to engulf you. A heavy weight bears you to the ground and sharp horny fangs dig repeatedly into your flesh. Your struggles grow weaker and weaker. Soon, utterly paralysed, you can only watch numbly like one already dead as the spider creature hauls you into the shrine and hangs you in its larder.

Turn to **140**.

586

In every port there are always unemployed sailors in search of work. You can upgrade a poor crew to average for 25 Shards, an average crew to good for 50 Shards, and a good crew to excellent for 90 Shards.

Once you've recorded any changes on the Ship's Manifest, turn to **302**.

587

The shrine is lit by hundreds of candles, each illuminating a tiny niche in which there is a statue of a different god. You can make an offering of 25 Shards if you wish, in which case roll one die to see what response you get. If you roll a blessing that you already have then the offering is wasted, because you can only have one blessing at a time of each type.

Score 1	The gods ignore you; no blessing
Score 2	A blessing of Safety from Storms
Score 3	A blessing of Immunity to Disease/Poison
Score 4	A COMBAT blessing
Score 5	A MAGIC blessing
Score 6	A THIEVERY blessing

Ability blessings can be used once to reroll the dice when using that ability.

You can also buy wands from the sorcerer's booth at the side of the shrine. His stock is small but inexpensive.

	To buy	*To sell*
Amber wand (MAGIC +1)	400 Shards	250 Shards
Ebony wand (MAGIC +2)	800 Shards	450 Shards
Cobalt wand (MAGIC +3)	1500 Shards	900 Shards

When you are through here, turn to **572**.

588

The ship's hull smashes into the sharp ridge of a reef. 'She's going down!' cries the first mate. 'It's every man for himself!'

Turn to **126**.

589

The sky becomes overcast, casting a dreary shadow over the land. You sense the displeasure of the gods. Roll one die.

Score 1-2	Ill-fated; lose all blessings
Score 3-4	Doomed; lose resurrection deal
Score 5	Forsaken; lose initiate status (if any)
Score 6	Cursed; lose 1 Stamina permanently

The gods treat mortals in the same way that small boys treat insects – toying with us for their amusement. Turn to **630**.

590

You come to a large hunting lodge beside a grove of pine trees. Here you could rest for a few days.

Take a room at the lodge	turn to **610**
Continue on your way	turn to **654**

591

You are outside the quaintly named Inn of Perfect Contentment on the road between Shingen and Hidari. If you have a ship moored here you can set sail; otherwise you must continue your journey on foot.

Put to sea (if ship here)	turn to **350**
Take the Shingen road	turn to **125**
Take the Hidari road	turn to **673**
Head due east	turn to **653**

592

The eastern island, Toho, is a very different place from Yodoshi. In remote rural areas you see constant reminders of the threat of barbarian raids – in the pinched faces of the field workers, the stout palings defending each village, and in the occasional burnt-out husk of a harvest shrine.

Roll two dice.

Score 2-6	A funeral	turn to **269**
Score 7-9	All is quiet	turn to **611**
Score 10-12	A storyteller	turn to **201**

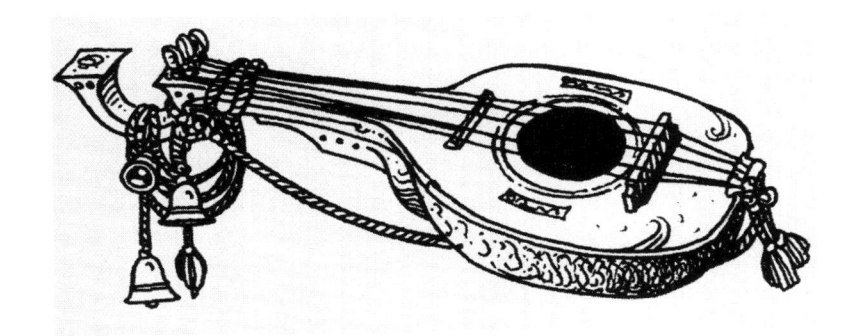

593

Passage on a barge will cost you 10 Shards. 'What is to be found at the source of the Moku River?' you ask the barge master.

'There is a shrine where the river emerges from Kwaidan Forest,' he replies. 'No one goes there any more. We simply carry goods from the villages along the riverbank.'

Pay 10 Shards to go upriver	turn to **419**
Stay in Chambara for now	turn to **79**

594

A long wooden bridge supported by heavy wooden pilings stretches across the Chu River. A woman in warrior's garb awaits you at the halfway point, announcing herself as the daughter of Lord Chudaifu of the Black Swan Clan. Apparently she wishes to test her martial prowess against you – she has drawn her sword and stepped out to block your path.

Accept her challenge	turn to **614**
Go back the way you came	turn to **522**
Show her an **agate swan** if you have one	turn to **485**

595

You go through to the outer royal apartments, where you spend a pleasant morning chatting with other courtiers. Servants bustle in with lunch, which consists of baked fish fresh from the Moku River, pickles, rice patties and iced sherbets. In the afternoon you take a nap while a lady-in-waiting strums idly at a lute.

Later you take a bottle of rice wine and sit on the terrace exchanging poems until the moon sets. Regain 1 Stamina for your peaceful sojourn at the palace, then turn to **79**.

596

The horsemen chase you for miles across the nebulous landscape. To escape their stinging spears you are forced to abandon every possession and all the money you are carrying. At last you lose your tormentors in a bank of fog. Their excited cries and the fierce snorts of their steeds gradually recede into the distance. The aftermath of your ordeal leaves you miserable and trembling, glad to have got away with your life.

The fog lifts and you find you are wandering the city streets. A cock crows and people start to open up their shops. They are astonished to see an exhausted and haunted-eyed wanderer stumbling by.

Cross off all your possessions and money before turning to **79**.

597

The Lord Chancellor's servant tells you his master has gone up to the cliffs. He points to a path winding through pine trees above the villa. 'Come back another time,' he suggests.

Go up to the clifftop	turn to **424**
Return to the town	turn to **362**

598

For a prisoner who has been chained up without food or water, Akugenda reacts with outstanding vigour. Leaping to his feet, he touches your throat in a caress that suddenly becomes a steel grip.

'Sorry to be such an ingrate,' he says, 'but I could really use a boost of life energy right now.'

You can hardly believe it – he is using sorcery to drain your soul! Make a MAGIC roll at Difficulty 15 to resist.

Successful MAGIC roll	turn to **638**
Failed MAGIC roll	turn to **140**

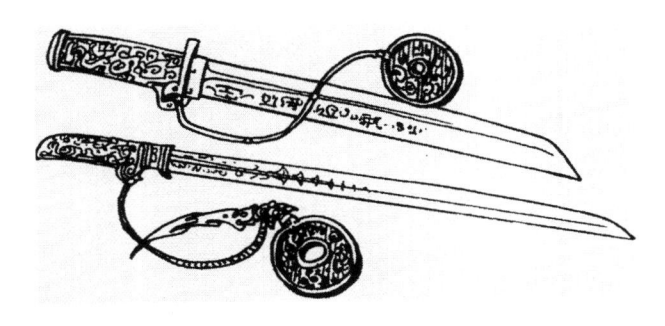

599

You see a group of youths persecuting an old man. The youths all have short hair and wear red robes, making them look like temple acolytes.

To your surprise, none of the people walking past is going to help the old man; they all look as if they'd rather not get involved.

Help the old man	turn to **660**
Ask what's going on	turn to **41**
Mind your own business	turn to **79**

600

If you have the codeword *Flimsy*, turn to **365**. If not, turn to **640**.

601

To the south lies the daunting expanse of Gashmuru Gulf. Only the most foolhardy mariners dare to strike out for the fabulous city of Dangor.

Tack around Shaku Island	turn to **550**
Head north for Yodoshi Island	turn to **649**
Strike out for Dangor	*The City in the Clouds* **77**

602

The giant peers at you, then sticks his huge paw out and pulls you inside. The door closes with a sound like a bell tolling.

'Don't get many visitors as delectable as you,' sniggers the giant obscenely, running his bloated sweaty fingers over your limbs.

'I'll bet,' you say, pulling away. 'Are you going to keep me standing in the hall?'

He gives you a look that is ingratiating and menacing at the same time. 'Come upstairs.'

Turn to **643**.

603

You feel as if you are wandering in an endless labyrinth of moss-clad rocks and ancient trees.

Roll two dice.

Score 2-7	A woodland path	turn to **529**
Score 8-9	A great black bear	turn to **624**
Score 10-12	An eerie grotto	turn to **189**

604 ☐

If the box above is empty, put a tick in it and turn to **666**. If it was already ticked, turn to **688**.

605

The spider's bite was poisonous. If it injured you even once then you are doomed unless you have a blessing of Immunity to Disease/Poison. If you have a blessing, remember to cross it off and then turn to **331**.

If the spider bit you and you don't have a blessing, turn to **140**.

606

If you have the codeword *Frame*, turn now to **627**. Otherwise read on.

You must have a ship docked in the harbour in order to transport goods. The prices given here are for single Cargo Units, which are much more than one person could hope to carry. Any cargo you buy will be delivered to your ship in the harbour, so note it on the Ship's Manifest.

Cargo	To buy	To sell
Furs	250 Shards	175 Shards
Grain	150 Shards	100 Shards
Metals	700 Shards	600 Shards
Minerals	550 Shards	500 Shards
Spices	580 Shards	540 Shards
Textiles	200 Shards	150 Shards
Timber	200 Shards	150 Shards

When you have made all your business arrangements, turn to **302**.

607

At the temple you can get medical treatment for only 8 Shards. The treatment allows you to regain 2-12 lost Stamina points, up to the limit of your unwounded Stamina score.

If you wish to become an initiate of the Sage of Peace, the monks will instruct you in the sacred doctrine. To comprehend this doctrine requires a SANCTITY roll at a Difficulty of 15. If successful you are accepted as an initiate. (The monks are open minded and don't mind if you were already an initiate of another god.) If you try the SANCTITY roll and fail, the doctrine turns out to be so confusing that you lose 1 from your SANCTITY score.

The advantage of being an initiate is that you can get a blessing. The Sage of Peace bestows these on his initiates for free. If you are an initiate, write Luck in the Blessings box on your Adventure Sheet. The blessing can be used once to allow you to reroll any dice result. After using the blessing, remember to cross it off your Adventure Sheet. You can have only one Luck blessing at a time.

When you are through at the temple, turn to **8**.

608

You are taken to a high-gabled wooden palace whose airy halls are patrolled by hundreds of magnificently armed guards. How can you have failed to notice it as you sailed in? The paladin takes you to the throne room where the hubbub of courtiers' chatter gradually subsides as everyone notices your arrival. The queen sweeps forward, her resplendent skirts of gold-laced black silk supported by a group of identical ladies-in-waiting.

She tells you that her realm has lately been menaced by a terrible dragon. She has heard of your heroic reputation and asks if you will slay the dragon for her.

| Do as she bids | turn to **442** |
| Ask what reward she will give | turn to **629** |

609

This is a picturesque region of sugarloaf hills, translucent clouds and ferns gently ruffled by the wind.

Roll two dice.

Score 2-4	Bad omens	turn to **589**
Score 5-9	Nothing of note	turn to **630**
Score 10-12	The monastery	turn to **402**

610

With its split-log walls and thatched roof, the hunting lodge looks like any rural inn. A night's lodging costs you 3 Shards. This includes a meal and a warm bed, allowing you to recover 1 Stamina point if injured. But, in addition to rest and relaxation, you can also enjoy some sport while you're here.

Go hunting	turn to **206**
Put your feet up	turn to **181**
Resume your journey	turn to **654**

611

'Up in the hills,' a peasant tells you, 'lurk the uncivilized *emishi* – the earth spiders who burn our crops and steal our womenfolk.'

'Earth spiders? Why do you call the barbarians that? Is it because they are hairy and unwashed?'

He shakes his head. 'No. It's because they're giant spiders.'

Where now?

North into the hills	turn to **319**
To Kaiju	turn to **270**
Across the Shi River	turn to **554**
South to Kumo Province	turn to **174**
Still further east	turn to **674**

612

Extensive quays enclosed by a broad sea wall comprise the dockland area of Chambara. Here you can set sail if you have a ship, or buy one if you do not. If you have neither a ship of your own nor the money to buy one, it is also possible to hire passage on a vessel bound for other ports.

If your ship is docked here	turn to **571**
Buy a ship	turn to **518**
Hire crew for your ship	turn to **536**
Sell a ship	turn to **497**
Hire passage to another port	turn to **555**
Go back into the city	turn to **79**

613

You walk briskly up the street leading to the stockade. If you have the codeword *Frame*, turn to **537**. If not, turn to **107**.

614

'If you wish, we can exchange weapons,' says the lady with a polite bow. 'I would not want you to think I had an unfair advantage simply because my father's wealth can buy the best swords in the land.'

Agree to exchange (if you have a weapon)	turn to **635**
Tell her to get on and fight	turn to **656**

615

Rain starts to fall just as you reach the gazebo, soaking the ivy and giving the evening air a delicious tang. But the occupant of the gazebo seems oblivious of the beauty of the moment. He is gazing sadly with many heartfelt sighs at a portrait in his hand.

Turn to **747**.

616

You counter the scholar's illusion with magic of your own, erupting out of the painted screen amid flooding tendrils of smoke. He reels back, covering his face with his sleeve, and retaliates by sending out a glowing web of energy to ensnare your wits.

Make a MAGIC roll at a Difficulty of 16.

| Successful MAGIC roll | turn to **637** |
| Failed MAGIC roll | turn to **658** |

617

If you have the codeword *Fleet*, turn to **82**. If not, turn to **13**.

618

This will be a hard fight. They all attack at the same time - meaning that you only get to strike one blow (against whichever opponent you choose) in the time that all three get to strike you.

Jiro, COMBAT 10, Defence 13, Stamina 10
Nunobiki, COMBAT 9, Defence 13, Stamina 14
Yoshio, COMBAT 9, Defence 13, Stamina 13

| Surrender | turn to **452** |
| Fight and win | turn to **738** |

619

If you did not have one already, you get a blessing of Safety from Storms. Note it on your Adventure Sheet. This will stand you in good stead when you are travelling at sea. It works exactly like a blessing from the western gods Alvir and Valmir, although this monk's blessing is spiritual rather than divine.

By now it is the early hours of the morning. Seeing you are tired, the monk bids you goodnight. Turn to **610**.

620

The ghoul arrives at midnight, poking its grey face in through the window of the room where the dead girl is lying. You watch from behind a door as it creeps inside, but as soon as it so much as licks the corpse it recoils with an agonized shriek and flees off into the night.

The next day you find it dead in front of its lair, poisoned by the holy aura you laid on the corpse. Inside the lair you find a jar of **faery mead** and 250 Shards. You can also take the **ghoul's head** as a trophy if you want.

Note anything you are taking on your Adventure Sheet and turn to **53**.

621

The storm whips up the sea into white-frothed grey breakers. If you have a blessing of Safety from Storms, cross it off and turn to **580**. Otherwise turn to **222**.

622

The wizard misjudges one of his spells and sets fire to the paper balloon. The balloon breaks up into charring fragments and the two of you plummet to the ground. Turn to **140**.

623

The giant slams the door shut on your leg, causing you the loss of 1-6 Stamina points and trapping you while he slams punishing punches into your gut. He knows how to maim, and any Stamina points you lose in this fight are permanently lost!

Giant, COMBAT 15, Defence 22, Stamina 51

Remember to keep track of each time he injures you and reduce your unwounded Stamina score by that amount if you survive the fight. If, somehow, you defeat him, turn to **458**.

624

You take shelter for the night in a cave that turns out to be occupied by an old bear. It lumbers forward with a growl, its shaggy coat blurring into a deep darkness at the back of the cave. You must fight it at a penalty of -2 to COMBAT unless you have a source of light such as a **lantern** or **candle**.

Bear, COMBAT 7, Defence 11, Stamina 17

If you win, you can continue on your way; turn to **529**.

625

You have gathered several handfuls of silver, worth a total of between 10 and 60 Shards (roll one die), when a sudden gust of icy wind extinguishes your light. You are plunged into utter blackness. Then you hear a soft sigh of laughter that can only bode evil, and you start groping your way hurriedly back towards the exit.

Turn to **584**.

626

Sharp peaks gleaming with snow pierce the sky. Far off you can make out a few thatched cottages huddled mournfully below a ridge of wind-blasted pines.

Descend out of the mountains	turn to **646**
Go higher	turn to **24**

627

You have a contact in the Autumn Moon clan who makes sure that you get a good deal. 'May I point out that Hagashin is famous for its textile industry?' he says.

Cargo	To buy	To sell
Furs	250 Shards	175 Shards
Grain	120 Shards	80 Shards
Metals	680 Shards	600 Shards
Minerals	550 Shards	500 Shards
Spices	550 Shards	500 Shards
Textiles	150 Shards	100 Shards
Timber	180 Shards	140 Shards

When you have made all your business arrangements, turn to **302**.

628

If you have the codeword *Cenotaph*, turn go **151** now. Otherwise read on.

The only place you can find to stay is a tiny rat-infested garret above a noisy tavern. At night the room fills with smoke from the taproom below, and the roof lets in the rain, the innkeeper wants 1 Shard a day for this hovel. Each day you spend here, roll a die. On a score of 1-5 you can regain 1 Stamina point if injured, but on a roll of 6 you get dysentery and lose 1 Stamina. When you are ready to leave, settle your bill and then turn to **8**.

629

The paladin presses his lance against your wrist. A shooting pain stabs up your arm. Turn to **692**.

630

It is not easy for a person to find Gaman Monastery if his mind is rooted in worldly matters. To locate the monastery you will need either a SCOUTING roll at Difficulty 15 or a SANCTITY roll at Difficulty 13.

Successful roll	turn to **402**
Failed roll (or not making the attempt)	turn to **675**

631

A seller of incense sticks tells you that this road is called the Great Saddle because of the lay of the land between Chambara and Mukogawa.

Roll two dice.

Score 2-8	A quiet journey	turn to **652**
Score 9-12	A hermit	turn to **502**

632

You are at the southern tip of Yodoshi, the main island of Akatsurai. The climate here is subtropical, and exotic scents tinge the breeze, but the mountains to the north wear caps of snow.

Travel up into the mountains	turn to **359**
Go west to Hidari	turn to **323**
Follow the coast up to Mukogawa	turn to **535**

633

This is wild cloud-swept moorland where the trees grow bent, like old man pushing wearily into a strong wind. Roll two dice.

Score 2-8	Nothing in sight	turn to **298**
Score 9-12	A woman in white	turn to **287**

634

Two roads leave Chompo – for Narai, far west along the coat, and Mukogawa to the south.

Take the road to Narai	turn to **194**
Set out for Mukogawa	turn to **73**
Go west over open country	turn to **282**
Explore the land to the east	turn to **242**

635

You must give her anyone weapon from among the possessions you are carrying. (You could give her a **paper sword** if you have one.) Do not cross the weapon off your list of possessions yet as you might get it back. She hands you her own sword in return. Turn to **677**.

636

Room after room is unlit, cold and deserted. From outside comes the growl of distant thunder and then the sound of light rain gusting against the shutters. You are about to leave when you notice a fine **golden katana** hanging on the wall. Add this to your list of possessions if you wish, then turn to **657**.

637

You utter a curse of undeflectable force and the aged scholar falls clutching his heart. You search his body and find a **spirit mirror (MAGIC +4)**. Add this to your list of possessions if you want it. Now it is time you made yourself scarce: turn to **79**.

638

Akugenda recoils with a grimace, like a man who had sipped at a wine-cup only to discover it contained vinegar.

'Never mind the foreigner,' says Kiyomori to his guards. 'Akugenda is the real threat. Concentrate your attacks on him.'

Akugenda only laughs, performing a series of complex magical gestures that cause a thick mist to spring up from the grass. You catch a glimpse of his silhouette rising into the air as the chancellor's guards mill about in confusion.

Grab Akugenda's ankle	turn to **681**
Wait to see what happens	turn to **659**

639

You strike the monk down. He does nothing to resist. Lose 1-6 points from your SANCTITY score permanently for attacking a blameless holy man. Your score, however, cannot go below 1.) The monk levitates away nursing his injuries. Are you at all ashamed as you slope off to your bed? Turn to **610**.

640

The door bangs open and the heads of the three hosts swoop in. They give vent to shrill cries of fury when they discover you are awake. With their faces contorted into devil masks of hatred and blood running down their chins, you wonder how you could have mistaken them for human beings.

Turn to **273**.

641

Night falls, the moon comes up, and the sky looks like ink against the polished slate of the sea.

Roll two dice.

Score 2-9	An untroubled journey	turn to **662**
Score 10-12	Attacked by pirates	turn to **145**

642

You race off down the stairs. The giant stands on the landing above, roaring and shaking his fist. Hauling the door open you dash outside, but then a massive chair comes hurtling down from the top of the pagoda and smashes to splinters on your head. Lose 2-12 Stamina points. (At least those are Stamina points you can get back by resting, unlike any you may have lost battling the giant in person.)

If you are still alive and kicking, turn to **501**.

643

The giant heaves his way up the stairs ahead of you. His wobbling bulk puts you in mind of two water buffaloes squeezed together in a sack full of dung – except that wouldn't small this bad.

At last you reach the top storey, where the giant invites you to sit at his dining table. What you thought at first was a dirty lace tablecloth turns out to be a thick layer of dust that is thrown up into the air the moment you sit down. While you are coughing, the giant fetches a couple of rusty goblets, tips out the family of spiders who were living inside them, and pours you some wine.

'Your health, sir giant,' you say for want of anything better.

'Call me Big Boy,' he says, slobbering wine all down his chin.

Drink the wine   turn to **664**

Pretend to drink	turn to **686**
Attack him	turn to **712**

644

The Akatsurese name for hell is *ne no kuni*, which means 'the Land of Roots'. You could easily believe that is where you are now.

Make a SCOUTING roll at Difficulty 14.

Successful SCOUTING roll	turn to **665**
Failed SCOUTING roll	turn to **603**

645

Add the **spear (COMBAT +4)** to your list of possessions.

The gaping hole in the man's chest slowly closes as the dead grey flesh knits itself together. His eyes open, gleaming like polished golden orbs with no sign of irises or pupils. You take a step back as he drifts into an upright position and unfolds his arms.

'I am Lord Morituri of the Dawatsu Clan,' he says in a voice made thick by centuries of silence.

You start to reply, 'And I am—'

Morituri holds up a long-taloned hand. 'That no longer matters. Your life is behind you now.'

If you have the title Chosen One of Nagil, turn to **711**. If not, turn to **742**.

646

You find a steep rocky trail that carries you down out of the mountains.

Head north	turn to **674**
Head south	turn to **174**
Head west	turn to **592**
Head east	turn to **706**

647

Hagashin is much more cosmopolitan than the other cities of Akatsurai. As you walk down the streets you might rub shoulders with wizards from Braelak, nomads from the Blue Grasslands of western Ankon-Konu, masked lords of Uttaku and even iron-dark priests from far Chrysoprais.

You soon strike up conversation with a foreign captain who is willing to take on a passenger. Choose from the following destinations:

Mithdrak, pay 70 Shards	*The Isle of a Thousand Spires* **8**
Dangor, pay 35 Shards	*The City in the Clouds* **197**
Dweomer, pay 35 Shards	*Over the Blood-Dark Sea* **242**
Metriciens, pay 35 Shards	*Over the Blood-Dark Sea* **260**
Aku, pay 55 Shards	*The Court of Hidden Faces* **502**
Smogmaw, pay 15 Shards	*Over the Blood-Dark Sea* **535**
Teleos, pay 80 Shards	*Legions of the Labyrinth* **18**
Chambara, pay 15 Shards	turn to **27**

Remember to pay the fare if you decide to travel. If you want to stay in Hagashin after all, turn to **302**.

648

Because the House of Wistaria is related to the royal family, they especially revere the goddess Nisoderu, spirit of the sun, who is believed to be the first ancestor of the Sovereign. Her shrine is in the east garden of the mansion. Two painted screens that show the veiled goddess arising from the cavern of night slides back to give entry to the inner chapel, a room whose bare wooden floor and walls have been polished until the gleam like red gold.

Speak to the goddess	turn to **668**
Leave the shrine	turn to **565**

649

The lookout says he can see Shaku Island to the south-west and Yodoshi Island to the north.

Roll two dice.

Score 2-10	An uneventful voyage	turn to **580**
Score 11-12	A storm brewing	turn to **621**

650 ☐

You lead your men ashore on one of the cliffs. Coarse tufts of grass sprout above weathered cliffs of chalk. A few ungainly flightless birds glare with disapproval at your insolent invasion.

If the box above is empty, put a tick in it before turning to **364**. If it was already ticked, read on.

You lay up in a cove for a couple of days while replenishing your stocks of fresh water. The men are glad to have something other than fish and ship's biscuit to eat for a change. Recover 1-6 Stamina points (the roll of one die) if injured, and when you are ready to set sail turn to **136**.

651

You get a couple of handfuls of jewels worth 200 Shards, but then the giant's pet raven peers out from its cage and gives a screech. The giant yawns like a volcano about to go off.

Run for it	turn to **501**
Do battle with the giant	turn to **712**

652

You are on the road not far from Chambara, the capital city. Decide where your travels will take you next.

To the capital	turn to **79**
East along the road	turn to **590**
Towards the Kwaidan Forest	turn to **672**
South over open country	turn to **704**

653

Pine trees line the flanks of the Urushi Mountains, where meltwater streams down in quicksilver torrents and the sunlight sparkles across fields of flowers.

Roll two dice.

Score 2-8	An uneventful journey	turn to **297**
Score 9-12	A challenge is issued	turn to **698**

654

The road leads in one direction to Chambara, in the other to Mukogawa. From your vantage point here in the hills you cansee the countryside tumble down to west and east in a profusion of fields, streams and scattered farmsteads.

Travel to Chambara	turn to **631**
Travel to Mukogawa	turn to **552**
Go north-east	turn to **515**
Go north-west	turn to **672**
Go south-east	turn to **444**
Go south-west	turn to **704**

655

The only ships available for sale are the ones rejected by the Moonrise

Clan as unsuitable for their fleet. After several days of persistent effort you find a small vessel with a worm-eaten figurehead that might just suit your purposes.

| *Ship type* | *Cost* | *Capacity* |
| Barque | 240 Shards | 1 Cargo Unit |

If you decide to buy it, cross off the money and record the ship's details on the Ship's Manifest. The crew quality at the moment is poor.

Each time you arrive at a new destination, remember to change the entry in the Docked column on the Ship's Manifest. So, if you don't intend to set sail right away, note that the ship is docked at Mukogawa.

When you have finished here, turn to **281**.

656

The woman takes a spinning leap towards you, whirling through the air so fast that her attacks comes thick and fast in a blur of furious motion. If you gave her a weapon, add its COMBAT bonus (if any) to her COMBAT and Defence scores.

Warrior Maid, COMBAT 8, Defence 16, Stamina 18

| Fight and win | turn to **746** |
| Surrender | turn to **36** |

657

You make your way back down the silent corridors towards the palace entrance. A glimmer of lamplight warns you that someone is coming this way. You look around. The only place to hide is behind a painted screen that shows hunters riding on horseback across a landscape of clouds.

| Hide behind the screen | turn to **486** |
| Stand your ground | turn to **678** |

658

'Regrettably I cannot afford the luxury of toying with you,' murmurs the old scholar. He throws out both hands, causing his long sleeves to make a snapping sound like a sail going taut in the wind. The occult force he propels at you is invisible but deadly. You drop as though poleaxed, clutching your sides as the spell turns your innards to mush.

Turn to **140**.

659

The mist blows away on the breeze. Akugenda by now is visible only as a small floating shape against the fiery sunset.

Kiyimori's eyes narrow in focused rage. 'Jiro,' he snaps, 'slay the interfering clod.'

Jiro and two other warriors spread out to encircle you. Get the codeword *Fern* and turn to **618**.

660

The youths back off, but they seem surprised rather than afraid of you. 'You should keep your nose out of things that don't concern you,' says the ringleader. He spits on the ground at your feet before leading his gang away.

The old man is Lord Yasutaka of the Wistaria Clan. He made his common mistake of opening criticising the Lord Chancellor. 'Those shaven-headed youths are Kiyomori's private army of thugs,' he says. 'It's deplorable what's happened to this country!'

Get the codewords *Fruit* and *Fuchsia* before turn to **79**.

661

One **dead head** sinks its teeth into your forearm and you cannot prise its jaw open even when it has stopped struggling. To dispose of it you have to make a MAGIC roll at a Difficulty of 11. Failing this, you must add it to your list of possessions and note that you can only dispose of it once you have visited a temple or shrine.

Now turn to **296**.

662

'There's no anchorage to be found here,' reckons the mate, pointing to the reef-bound shore. 'We'd be best off making for Mukogawa.'

Set a course north	turn to **745**
Steer due east	*The City in the Clouds* **77**
Follow the coast south	turn to **649**

663

Talanexor is a powerful mage and pyrotechnics is his speciality. To counter his fire jets you must make a MAGIC roll of Difficulty 16.

Successful MAGIC roll	turn to **718**
Failed MAGIC roll	turn to **140**

664

You knock back the wine before you have time to gag. It feels like your insides are being scoured out with a wire brush. An instant later the alcohol fumes hit your brain. The effect is similar to being half drowned and then held over a bonfire.

Lose 1 point permanently from all your ability scores except SANCTITY. One thing's for sure – you can't handle much of this stuff.

Offer him **faery mead** if you have it	turn to **740**
Attack him	turn to **712**
Make your excuses and leave	turn to **501**

665

Soaring pines lean overhead, virtually blotting out the sunlight. You are a solitary traveller adrift in the immensity of the Kwaidan Forest.

Search for a way out	turn to **687**
Go deeper into the woods	turn to **715**

666

The passage leads to a tomb chamber. On a catafalque of blue-veined white marble lies a man who might be either sleeping or dead. The spear driven right through his chest argues in favour of the latter. All around him on the floor of the chamber are scattered antique oblong coins.

Help yourself to some treasure	turn to **625**
Withdraw the spear	turn to **645**
Leave without rifling the tomb	turn to **583**

667

You take lodging at a quaint inn standing on stilts out over the main canal. Every morning you can buy fresh fruit for breakfast from punts that come right up to your window.

Each day you spend at the inn costs 2 Shards and allows you to recover 1 lost Stamina point, up to the limit of your unwounded Stamina score. When you are ready to move on, turn to **226**.

668 ☐

If the box above has a tick in it, the goddess does not deign to receive you: turn now to **565**. If the box is empty, do not put a tick in it just yet, but read on.

To obtain the favour of the goddess you must make a CHARISMA roll of Difficulty 16. If you fail this roll, put a tick in the box above and then turn to **565**. If you succeed, you have the ear of the goddess: turn to **691** *without* ticking the box.

669

You station yourself outside the Sovereign's apartments and wait.

About two hours after midnight, just as the moon has risen, a black cloud comes drifting from the woods west of the city and hovers over the roof of the palace. At the same time a baleful influence can be felt settling over everything like a chill wind from a graveyard. Peering into the depths of the cloud, you are sure you can make out a monstrous squirming shape.

Make a MAGIC roll at a Difficulty of 17.

Successful MAGIC roll	turn to **403**
Failed MAGIC roll	turn to **473**

670

You find your way into Kiyomori's private chambers. He is outside in the garden watching a play, so you have plenty of time to sort through his treasure chest. You can take 1000 Shards, a **tatsu pearl**, a **pole axe (COMBAT +2)** and **silver chopsticks**.

To sneak back out, turn to **79**.

671

You are on the road that follows the coastline between Narai and Chompo. Forested hills loom large as thunderclouds against the southern sky.

Go south	turn to **398**
Go east	turn to **703**
Go west	turn to **155**

672

Around the central mountains of Akatsurai, the terrain is rugged and wild. Swept by the wind, blue-tinted heather seethes like an ocean under a wide sky of racing clouds.

Roll two dice.

Score 2-8	An untroubled journey	turn to **296**
Score 9-12	Unexpected hospitality	turn to **426**

673

The Western Coastal Road runs all the way from Hidari to the Imperial capital, Chambara. It passes along cliff tops and down through fishing villages where you are offered cups of bitter green tea.

Follow the road north	turn to **733**
Go south to Hidari	turn to **323**
Strike out towards the mountains	turn to **653**

674

You are travelling through the central region of Toho Island, between the Kenen and Yasai mountain ranges. The only dwellings you see hereabouts are the log cabins of solitary hunters, nestled beside boulders or half-hidden in a copse of trees.

Go east	turn to **706**
Go west	turn to **592**
Go south	turn to **245**
Go north	turn to **319**

675

The hills rise steeply in the east, blue and tree-clad. This is the Kwaidan Forest, whose leafy paths are more often trod by sprites than mortal men.

Enter the forest	turn to **398**
Go north	turn to **493**
Go south	turn to **97**

676

Senior members of the Moonrise Clan supervise all trade at the warehouses to make sure that they have ample supplies for the coming war.

The prices quoted here are for entire Cargo Units – much more than a single person can carry. You will need a ship to transport goods in these quantities.

Cargo	To buy	To sell
Furs	200 Shards	150 Shards
Grain	300 Shards	250 Shards

Metals	950 Shards	800 Shards
Minerals	600 Shards	550 Shards
Spices	700 Shards	650 Shards
Textiles	250 Shards	180 Shards
Timber	300 Shards	250 Shards

When your business is complete, turn to **281**.

677

The sword she has given you is as heavy as an iron bucket. Worse, it seems to have magically welded itself to your hand. You have no choice but to fight with it, even though it is a **cursed sword (-2 to COMBAT)**! Note this on your list of possessions. Because it affects your COMBAT score, it also reduces your Defence.

If you gave her a **paper sword**, turn to **723**. Otherwise, turn to **656**.

678

If you took the **golden katana** from the other room, turn to **722**. Otherwise turn to **747**.

679

'How can you possibly find her?' laments Takakura, weeping bitterly into his long sleeves. 'Alas, poor Kokoro. I know only that she has been taken to a small house with a green door somewhere in the suburbs.'

If you are a Troubadour, turn to **721**. If not, turn to **736**.

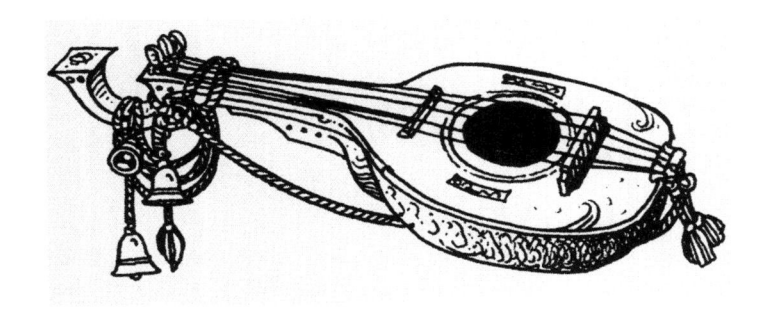

680

'You are brave enough, I'll give you that!' roars Tadachika, delighted at the opportunity of showing off his skill. Signalling the chancellor's guards to stay back, he draws his sword and advances on you.

Tadachika, COMBAT 11, Defence 17, Stamina 21

Turn and run off	turn to **696**
Fight and win	turn to **728**

681

Akugenda's spell carries both of you aloft. Kiyomori sends for his archers, but by the time they get up to the cliff top you are out of range. The breeze bears you steadily southwards.

'I expect you're wondering why the chancellor was going to have me executed,' says Akugenda.

'Actually I'm wondered how we're going to get down.'

'Oh, I'll drop you off right here,' he says laughing.

A kick sends you plummeting down into the sea. You swim ashore in time to see Akugenda drifting off into the sunset. You doubt if you've seen the last of him. Get the codeword *Fern* and turn to **733**.

682

You see a richly attired gentleman strutting down the street at a very smart pace for someone with such a dignified appearance. His eyes are fixed straight ahead of him and his stern expression as he brushes past is enough to deter you from saying anything. As you watch him go bobbing down the street, you notice a ticket sticking up out of his hat. Has he forgotten to remove the price tag? If so, and he is on his way to the palace, he could suffer serious embarrassment.

Run and catch him up	turn to **84**
Forget about it	turn to **79**

683

Lose the codeword *Future*.

You are soon fast asleep in spite of the hard clay floor, the constant trickle of rainwater and the draught coming under the door. In the small hours of the night you are confronted by three disembodied heads that come drifting through the air towards you. It seems like a nightmare until one of them tears a chunk out of your flesh with its teeth and you realize you are wide awake.

Lose 2-12 Stamina points (roll two dice). If you survive that, turn to **273**.

684

One of the Akatsurese sailors, a man named Narakami, fancies himself as something of a poet. Gazing out to sea he says: 'Under the wide sky, a scintillant refulgence: the lightning's flicker. I see it and am fearful, then it fades and I am sad.'

'Belay that talk of lightning,' shouts the mate superstitiously, 'or you'll see me with my lash, and that'll make you sad all right!'

Roll two dice.

| Score 2-5 | A flash of lightning | turn to **335** |
| Score 6-10 | A quiet voyage | turn to **713** |

685

Check your list of possessions. Do you have an edged weapon such as a **knife**, **sword** or other sharp implement with which to cut the balloon's ropes? (A **paper sword** will not do the trick.) If you do, turn to **699**. If not, Talanexor's spell hits you while you are still fumbling with the ropes – turn to **140**.

686

You pour away the wine when the giant isn't looking. There is a sizzling sound as it burns the varnish off the floorboards. 'Here, don't you like my wine?' says the giant, rearing upright with an angry look.

If you have a bottle of **faery mead**, turn to **740**. If not, turn to **712**.

687

The stench of loam and pine needles makes you feel slightly sick. The green half-light is gritty and filled with creeping shadows. This place is like a nightmare brought on by fever.

Roll two dice:

| Score 2-7 | You follow a stream | turn to **529** |
| Score 8-12 | Unseen tormentors | turn to **700** |

688

The tomb chamber is no longer occupied, but there are still plenty of those odd oblong coins strewn around.

Pick up some silver	turn to **625**
Get out of here	turn to **583**

689

You soon get into serious trouble. Dangling halfway up the cliff, you can see no way on and you aren't sure you can get back down. Make a SCOUTING roll at a Difficulty of 17. You can add 1 to the dice roll if you have **rope** and add 2 if you have **climbing gear**. A successful roll means you manage to get safely back to the base of the cliff. A failed roll means you slip and fall, losing 4-24 Stamina points (roll four dice).

If you survive, turn to **646**.

690

It is characteristic of the people of Hagashin that they do not bother with the usual distinction between temples to the Sage of Peace and shrines to the divine powers. 'All creation is divine,' says a priest, 'so heaven and earth are one.'

You can get a blessing for 35 Shards – or just 20 Shards if you're an initiate of the Sage of Peace. Blessings are available for CHARISMA, SCOUTING, COMBAT and MAGIC. Simply pay the money and note the appropriate ability in the Blessings box on your Adventure Sheet. The blessing works by allowing you to try again when you fail a roll for that ability. You can only use the blessing once; it is then used up and you should cross it off. Also, you can only have one blessing for each ability at any one time.

Now turn to **226**.

691

To become an initiate of Nisoderu you must now make a SANCTITY roll at a Difficulty of 15. If you succeed and were already an initiate of another god, lose that status and write Nisoderu in the God box on your Adventure Sheet. If you fail the SANCTITY roll, Nisoderu will not accept you.

If you are already a initiate of Nisoderu and want to renounce her worship, cross her name off the God box on your Adventure Sheet. Then make a CHARISMA roll of Difficulty 18 to see how she responds to your ingratitude.

If you want to obtain Nisoderu's guarantee of resurrection, make a CHARISMA roll at a Difficulty of 14 (or 20 if you're not an initiate). If successful, write *Lords of the Rising Sun* **710** in the Resurrection box on your Adventure Sheet. In the event that you should die, turn to **710** in this book. You can only have one resurrection arranged at a time.

Lastly, if you failed any of these CHARISMA or SANCTITY rolls, the goddess makes her displeasure known to the clan elders by a sign and they will ostracize you from now on; lose the codeword *Fuchsia*.

To leave the shrine, turn to **565**.

692

You wake up to find your feet in a pool of water. You must have dozed off on the beach and now the tide is coming in. The mate is bending over you. 'Were you having a dream, skipper?' he asks. 'We ought to be getting back on board.'

As you row back out to the ship, one of your crewmen mentions how he spent the afternoon watching a swarm of wasps fight a snake that was trying to get into their nest. For a fleeting moment it seems to evoke a familiar memory...

You give the order to weigh anchor. Turn to **136**.

693

A maid spots you skulking and raises the alarm. You are chased by Kiyomori's guards and soon apprehended. Get the codeword *Fracas* if you didn't have it already, then turn to **452**.

694

Shuriyoko turns the evidence in his fingers. His gaze is like acid. 'Why would you have this unless you are plotting against our master the Shogun? Now I'll see you get a traitor's reward.'

You are taken out into the courtyard and beheaded. Lose the codeword *Frog* and the title Hatamoto, then turn to **140**.

695

'I'm for setting sail without delay, captain,' advises the mate. 'If we stay here too long I reckon those Moonrise Clan officials will take our vessel for their navy.'

Give the order to sail	turn to **745**
Go ashore	turn to **281**

696

As you run away down the path to the town, Lord Kiyomori himself comes out on to the porch and calls for his bow. The arrow strikes you just as you reach the coastal path – a magnificent shot over a distance of a hundred and fifty paces.

Admiration gives way to pain as you tear the **crimson arrow** out of your thigh and hobble on. Lose 3-18 Stamina points (the roll of three dice), from which you can deduct your armour's Defence bonus.

If you survive that, acquire the codeword *Fracas* if you didn't have it already. Then turn to **362**.

697

Akugenda gives a defiant shout as Jiro lifts the two-handed sword and swings it towards his neck. *Slish*, the blade cleaves through; *thunk*, the head drops to the ground. Jiro lowers his blade and reaches for a pitcher of water to clean it.

Kiyomori and his retainers turn to depart, but then a sound makes itself heard. It begins as a low groan, building rapidly to a drawn-out scream of hatred that suddenly becomes an ugly laugh. The hairs on your neck stand on end.

All eyes turn to the body. Coalescing in the air above it is a shadowy image, tinged with the dark red of clotted blood, eyes burning like the heart of a storm. Akugenda's ghost.

Turn to **720**.

698

You are challenged to a bout of unarmed sparring by a short swarthy fellow called himself Mister Dragon.

'No weapons or armour permitted,' he says with a broad smile.

Accept the challenge	turn to **719**
Refuse	turn to **297**
Attack him fully armed	turn to **135**

699

You swiftly cut the balloon loose and grab hold of the dangling ropes. The basket drops away with Talanexor still firing bursts of wildfire at you. 'From hell's heart I stab at thee!' he screams, consumed by rage.

One of the fireballs hits you. Lose 3-18 Stamina points (the score of three dice). If you survive that, you watch Talanexor plunge to his doom and then wait while the balloon drifts gradually down out of the sky. You come to a rest in a dense forest.

Get the codeword *Fortress* and turn to **312**.

700

Loud shrieking laughter rings out from high above as a shower of pebbles, soil and pine cones is flung down on your head. Roll a die: the number you roll is how many Stamina points you lose, regardless of armour. If you get a six, roll the die again and take that many Stamina points as well – rolling yet again if you get another six, and so on.

If you survive, you hear a fluttering as your attackers flit off into the depths of the wood. Soon you find a stream which must surely lead down towards the forest's edge.

Turn to **529**.

701

You pull yourself up on the ledge. Sure enough there is an open doorway between pillars of translucent moonstone that have been polished smooth until they shine like ice. On the lintel is carved a cryptic motto: 'Heaven and earth are limitless.'

With a sound like the clanging of copper shields, a long blue dragon hauls itself out of the recesses of the cave. Your limbs are trembling after the exertion of the climb and the glow in the dragon's eyes is so dazzling that you feel sick, and yet somehow you must fight it.

If you have an **iron fan**, turn to **716**. If not, turn to **743**.

702

You find an inn that charges only 5 Shards a week. Each week you stay here, roll one die and that is the number of Stamina points you recover if injured. Your Stamina cannot go higher than its normal unwounded score. When you are ready to set out, turn to **270**.

703

You arrive at a roadside inn overlooking a reef-lined bay.

Stop at the inn	turn to **295**
Go east	turn to **30**
Go west	turn to **2**

704

One night, watching the moon pull free of a bamboo thicket, you hear flute music in the distance: it makes you think of the ancient Akatsurese poets.

Roll two dice.

Score 2-9	A peaceful few days	turn to **732**
Score 10-12	The urge to sing	turn to **216**

705

Iron filings act as a painful barrier to all uncanny creatures, and salt purifies the ground so that unclean spirits cannot cross it. You sprinkle them round the cottage. All night long you listen to the ghoul pacing around outside, whimpering and snarling, until finally it is driven back to its lair with the onset of dawn.

Cross the **salt and iron filings** off your list of possessions and turn to **544**.

706

The easternmost shore of Akatsurai. Beyond lies only the limitless cobalt expanse of the Unbounded Ocean, where each morning the sun is reborn from the underworld and begins a new day's dying.

Go north along the coast	turn to **446**
Go south to Kumo Province	turn to **174**
Go west towards Kaiju	turn to **674**
Go up into the mountains	turn to **245**

707

The Chu River is a fierce white torrent between rocky banks. You will need to be a strong swimmer to get across. Make a SCOUTING roll at Difficulty 13 if you try it, and if you fail the roll you must turn back after losing 1 Stamina point.

Turn back (or don't try to cross) turn to **378**
Get across turn to **97**

708

The play is about an extremely old frog with magical powers. It tricks a foolish scholar with the illusion of a beautiful girl. The frog uses this illusion to lure the scholar to his death in the marshes, but he is saved in the nick of time by his wise teacher. The teacher draws his sword and slices just to the left of the illusion, where he knows that the invisible frog must be standing, and it jumps into the water. As the ripples fade, so does the illusion that the scholar had fallen in love with.

Get the codeword *Flag* and then turn to **226**.

709

Dodging and hacking, you battle the dragon without a thought for your own life. The paladins join in too, swarming across its body and piercing its scaly flanks with their spears. It is a hard fight but at last the dragon lies dead.

'We shall not forget your valour this day,' says the queen. 'Henceforth you will be known as the mightiest of our champions.'

Get the codeword *Flood* and turn to **692**.

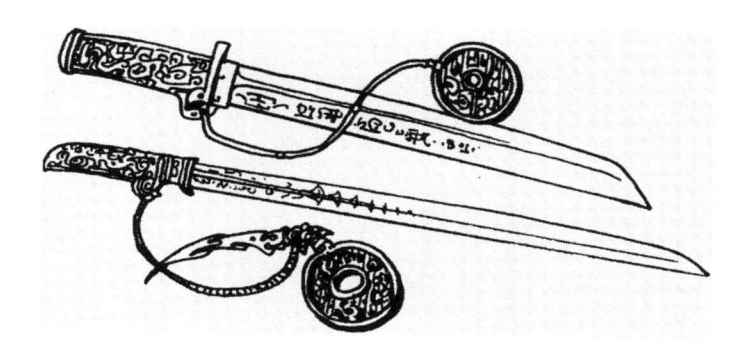

710

You are wandering in a murky place. Slowly you make you way up a steep path. The ground mist swirls away behind you and the world grows brighter.

You have lost all your possessions and money, but you are alive at least. A peasant passes you on the road and gives you an odd look. 'Don't you know that this road leads to the underworld?' he says. 'It is not safe to linger here at night.'

Dawn ensanguines the sky. 'Now it's day,' you reply.

Erase the entry in the Resurrection box on your Adventure Sheet and then turn to **146**.

711

He steps closer, scrutinizing you with his strange luminous gaze, then pauses in the act of raising a hand to your throat and gives a vexed sigh.

'Ah, your soul is forbidden fruit. Well, no matter – I sense there are others wandering in the woods nearby. I shall have them instead.'

You are not sure whether to broach the subject of a reward, but Morituri shows he is not ungrateful by offering you a **hyperium wand (MAGIC +6)**.

'This would be a great gift, lord,' you say.

He spreads his hands, displaying talons like kitchen knives. 'It is yours for just a few drops of blood, sufficient to sustain me until I can find another source to feed on.'

Let him drink some of your blood	turn to **23**
Refuse to co-operate	turn to **742**

712

The giant may look clumsy, but he strikes with unstoppable strength and he knows how to break bones. Any Stamina points you lose in this fight are permanently lost

Big Boy, COMBAT 15, Defence 22, Stamina 51

Remember to keep track of each time he injures you and reduce your unwounded Stamina score by that amount if you survive the fight. Fortunately the giant is not fast on his feet, so you can flee at any time.

Run off before he kills you	turn to **642**
Fight and (somehow) win	turn to **458**

713

Your vessel is skirting the north coast of Akatsurai's largest island. It is up to you to set the course.

Go east	turn to **161**
Go west	turn to **224**

714

You perform a rite of purification that restores the official's sacrosanct status. He is so impressed that he tells all his friends, who come to you requesting blessings and sacred talismans. You are showered with presents to the value of 100 Shards. Add this sum to the money on your Adventure Sheet, then turn to **79**.

715

The heart of the wood is as dark a spot as you are likely to find this side of the grave. The trees stand on all sides like the pillars of an immense cathedral.

There is a fluttering sound. Something drops lightly to the ground behind you. You turn to see a strange hunched creature with a long black beak, gnarled leathery talons and a mantle of glossy black feathers. It winks at you mischievously and points to the upper branches, where you can now make out many other such creatures like smudges of ink in the bosky gloom.

The nearest creature plucks at your sleeve. 'We don't get many of your kind in these parts,' it says in a harsh croaking voice.

To impress the tengu you must make a CHARISMA roll at a Difficulty of 15. Add 2 to the dice if you are a Rogue (they can relate to that) but subtract 2 if you are carrying more than 750 Shards, because tengu are extremely avaricious.

Successful CHARISMA roll	turn to **164**
Failed CHARISMA roll	turn to **139**

716

Holding the fan in front of your eyes at least gives some protection from the dragon's baleful stare. It rears up, clawing at you and spitting gouts of blistering plasma.

Dragon, COMBAT 9, Defence 19, Stamina 27

If you manage to defeat it, turn to **461** if you have the codeword *Farm* or to **488** otherwise.

717

Lord Yoritomo of the Moonrise Clan has sent out the call to arms to all his loyal vassals in the east. Troops are arriving every day and there is hardly room in the city to billet them. Perhaps that is why the innkeeper feels justified in charging 4 Shards a day. Still, that price includes a comfortable bed and good food, allowing you to recuperate 1 Stamina point each day until fully healed.

When you are ready to move on, pay your bill and turn to **178**.

718

Swaying precariously in a flimsy basket a thousand yards above the ground, you join in battle with one of the foremost sorcerers of the age. He lunges at you, hands surrounded by hot white plasma, spitting molten sparks.

For this battle only, your Defence score is the sum of your MAGIC score plus your Rank. Armour does not count.

Talanexor, COMBAT 11, Defence 17, Stamina 17

If you win, get the codeword *Fortress*. You can take Talanexor's **cobalt wand (MAGIC +3)** while waiting for the balloon to drift back to the ground, where it lodges in a tree.

Turn to **312**.

719

Mister Dragon stands in front of you, apparently as unassailable as a slab of rock. He invites you to make the first attack. What will you try?

A hammer blow to the crown of his head	turn to **112**
A finger strike to the throat	turn to **737**
A punch to the heart	turn to **454**
A kick to the solar plexus	turn to **42**

720

The ghost leaps high into the air with a boom like lightning rebounding off a tree. Jiro steps forward to interpose himself in front of the Lord Chancellor, but the ghost dispatches him with a hellfire bolt. You watch in horror as the smoking carcass falls to the ground at Kiyomori's feet.

'Time to die, chancellor,' cackles Akugenda's voice.

Kiyomori stares at the ghost. 'Do your worst.'

What will you do?

Run for it	turn to **362**
Leap in front of Kiyomori	turn to **40**
Drive the ghost off with prayer	turn to **61**

721

Takakura mentions that Kokoro loved to play the flute - especially one tune called 'The Vague Moon after the Rain'. This is enough for you to go on. You wander the outskirts of the city until the rain lets up and the full moon is unveiled. Then you hear the plaintive sound of a flute and, following it to its source, you find a small cottage with a green door.

Turn to **487**.

722

The newcomer is a tall gentleman whose silk robes hang around his spare frame like the wings of a bat. His eyes are narrow and deep-set and he seems ancient, but he has no trouble spotting you in the gloom.

'A stranger,' he says in a quiet, clear voice. 'Come forward, villain.'

As he speaks, the paper lantern that is hovering above his head rotates to throw a stabbing beam of light that picks you out in the darkness.

Run off	turn to **540**
Wait to see what happens	turn to **575**

723

She executes a sudden merciless attack, her pretty face transforming in an instant to a snarl of inhuman rage. But her fierce expression is soon wiped away when she sees the fake blade snap against the buckle of your belt.

Gaping in dismay, she takes a step backwards. 'I'm defeated!'

You give her a buccaneer's grin. 'Madam, I cheated.'

'It makes no difference.' She slumps in dejection. 'Father always tells us that trickery is half the battle.'

She pulls an **agate swan** pendant from around her neck and hands it to you. 'If you ever need to cross the bridge again, show this to whichever of my sisters is on duty. That way she'll know better than to tangle with you.'

Add the **agate swan** to your list of possessions and cross off the **paper sword**. Then turn to **448**.

724

The only sailors available for hire are the ones that are too old or too young to be worth pressing into service in the Moonrise navy. It will cost you 40 Shards to upgrade a poor crew to average quality, which is the best you will get hereabouts.

Once you've amended the Ship's Manifest (and crossed off the money) turn to **281**.

725

If you wish to become an initiate of the Sage of Peace, the monks will instruct you in the sacred doctrine. To comprehend this doctrine requires a SANCTITY roll of Difficulty 15. Success means you are made an initiate. The monks are open-minded and don't mind if you were already an initiate of another god; you can be both.

If you attempt the SANCTITY roll and fail it, the doctrine is so confusing that you must lose 1 from your SANCTITY score. (You can renounce initiate status freely at any time.)

Turn to **532**.

726

The mansion is heavily guarded. In their brocaded white tabards, the sentries resemble temple statues carved from blocks of pristine marble.

If you have the codeword *Frog* they recognize you as an ally of the clan and allow you to pass; turn to **467**. If you don't have the codeword *Frog* you are refused entrance and must turn back to **178**.

727

A comical little man leaps out at you brandishing a kitchen knife. As you watch him strike one absurd fencing pose after another, the main danger is that you might die laughing.

| Ignore him and walk off | turn to **316** |
| Fight him | turn to **490** |

728

You still have the other guards to deal with, but their shock at seeing Tadachika defeated buys you a few seconds. In a quick glance around the hall you count ten guards – too many to fight.

What now?

Pick up Tadachika's sword	turn to **83**
Run past the guards to the back of the villa	turn to **456**
Turn and flee back to the town	turn to **696**

729

The nearest soldier puts his hand on your arm, but you twist away and duck underneath the officer's horse. A hearty slap on the animal's rump sends it galloping off down the road. The soldiers take one look at their terrified officer as he vanishes in a cloud of dust. Forgetting all about you, they set off in pursuit.

You set out over open country since it won't be safe for you to use this stretch of road for a while. Turn to **704**.

730

Not only have you broken the man's taboo, but you have become ritually polluted into the bargain. Lose any blessings noted on your Adventure Sheet.

'Now I'll have to go to the shrine and be purified,' he snaps. 'Oh, why did you have to interfere?'

Turn to **79**.

731

The shrine stands beside a lake where willows dip their boughs in crystal water. Here you can pay your respects to the thousand gods of Akatsurai.

If you want to obtain a boon, leave a donation of 100 Shards and make a CHARISMA roll of Difficulty 18. You can reduce the Difficulty of the roll by 1 for each additional 100 shards that you offer up.

If you succeed in the CHARISMA roll, roll a die to see what the gods give you:

Score 1	Increase the COMBAT bonus of one weapon of +1
Score 2	Gain a blessing of Immunity to Disease/Poison
Score 3	Gain 1 Stamina point permanently
Score 4	Gain a blessing of Safety from Storms
Score 5	Change your profession to Priest
Score 6	The gods are annoyed; reduce your Rank by 1

When you are ready to resume your journey, turn to **147**.

732

You are in open country between the Urushi Mountains and the impenetrable forests of the Kwaidan range.

Go west to the coast	turn to **173**
Travel to Chambara	turn to **79**
Travel to Shingen	turn to **362**
Go north	turn to **631**
Go south	turn to **195**
Go further east	turn to **444**

733

You arrive at an inn nestling at the back of a broad bay. A couple of ships are anchored here. The crewmen of one, the *White Lady* out of Yellowport, are lolling supine on the veranda of the inn after spending the afternoon drinking bottles of rice wine.

'I like this place so much I don't think I'll ever leave!' declares one.

Stop at the inn	turn to **445**
Continue on your way	turn to **591**

734

Thin wailing ghosts rise with the ground mist at dusk. The spirits of miserly bandits, they are not interested in you so much as in any gold or silver you might be carrying. You must make a SANCTITY roll at a Difficulty of 17 to drive the ghosts off. If you fail, they seep into your backpack and devour all your money and any **silver nuggets** you are carrying. Now turn to **33**.

735

You arrive at the Chu River, a fast-flowing torrent flecked with white froth between banks of sharp black rock. Make a SCOUTING roll at Difficulty 13 if you try to cross, and if you fail the roll you must turn back after losing 1 Stamina point.

Turn back	turn to **97**
Get across	turn to **378**

736

It will not be easy to find the house where Kokoro has been taken. Fortunately, the rain soon lets up. You scour the suburbs all night long, stopping at each small house to examine the door.

Make a SCOUTING roll at a Difficulty of 17. You can add 2 to the dice roll if you possess a light source such as a **lantern** or **candle**.

Successful SCOUTING roll	turn to **487**
Failed SCOUTING roll	turn to **81**

737

It feels like jabbing your fingers against an iron bar. As you cringe in agony, Mister Dragon delivers a powerful blow that lays you out cold.

Turn to **63**.

738

'Your technique is magnificent,' remarks Kiyomori. 'A pity I must order your death.'

It certainly was a remarkable feat to overcome three skilled samurai like that. Roll two dice. If the total is higher than your Rank, you advance one Rank and gain 1-6 extra Stamina points permanently. Remember that going up in Rank also increases your Defence score by 1.

The rest of the chancellor's guards are already on their way – time to make a break for it. Turn to **577**.

739

The Sovereign is gravely ill. His doctors do not expect him to last the night. If you possess a **royal sceptre** and are prepared to offer it to save his life, turn to **65**. Otherwise, turn to **114**.

740

The giant is not used to drinking anything that actually tastes pleasant, let alone a drink with unusual properties. He quaffs it all down (cross the **faery mead** off your list of possessions) and is soon slumbering in his chair.

'It won't do any good,' says a thin gruff voice. 'He's such a light sleeper, he's bound to wake up as soon as you start nosing about.'

Startled, you look around to see a big scrawny raven glaring at you from a cage in the corner of the room.

'If you've got a length of rope I can tie him up,' it says. 'Otherwise I'd advise you to scarper.'

Give the raven some **rope** (if you have any)	turn to **513**
Just kill the giant while he's asleep	turn to **534**
Tiptoe out of the pagoda	turn to **501**

741

Darkness has begun to trickle between the boughs when you hear thudding footfalls.

A group of vampires in long black satin robes come crashing through the banks of ferns to seize you, bloodshot eyes gleaming from faces the colour of old ivory. Rigor mortis has made their legs so stiff that they have to move by hopping, but all the same they swiftly have you surrounded.

To break free requires a COMBAT or SANCTITY roll (your choice) at a Difficulty of 16, or you can choose to stand your ground and fight.

Successful roll	turn to **529**
Failed roll	turn to **459**
Stand and fight	turn to **46**

742

You might have expected unstinting gratitude for releasing him, but Morituri apparently refuses to be reasonable. You will have to fight here or else make a retreat to more favourable ground.

Dawatsu Morituri, COMBAT 15, Defence 25, Stamina 38

If you retreat, Morituri will get one free strike at you before you reach the open air. (If you do opt to do this, make a note of any wounds you have already inflicted on him before turning to **460**.)

Fight on and win	turn to **489**
Back out of the sepulchre	turn to **460**

743

You are reeling with exhaustion and almost snow-blind. The dragon's roar seems like peals of evil laughter resounding off the mountain peaks.

Dragon, COMBAT 13, Defence 25, Stamina 27

If you manage to defeat it, turn to **461** if you have the codeword *Farm* or to **488** if not.

744

The officer in charge of the armoury, Lord Saga of the Nine Lakes clan, does not even bother to ask if you are a warrior or a merchant.

'The time for such distinctions is past,' he says. 'All that matters now is to be ready for war.'

You soon find that the local arms and armour prices are severely inflated.

Armour	*To buy*	*To sell*
Leather (Defence +1)	100 Shards	90 Shards
Ring mail (Defence +2)	200 Shards	180 Shards
Chain mail (Defence +3)	400 Shards	350 Shards
Splint armour (Defence +4)	750 Shards	600 Shards
Plate armour (Defence +5)	–	1500 Shards

Weapons (sword, axe, etc)	*To buy*	*To sell*
Without COMBAT bonus	100 Shards	75 Shards
COMBAT bonus +1	500 Shards	350 Shards
COMBAT bonus +2	950 Shards	700 Shards

COMBAT bonus +3 — 1400 Shards

When you have finished your business here, turn to **178**.

745

The sea gleams like tarnished silver under a sky heavy with cloud. A faint drizzle, barely less fine than mist, mingles with the salt spray.

You are sailing the Ugetsu Straits that lies between Yodoshi, the main island of the Akatsurese chain, and the easternmost island, Toho.

Make for Port Kaiju	turn to **77**
Dock at Mukogawa	turn to **35**
Put in at Udai Island	turn to **209**
Go north	turn to **64**
Go south	turn to **641**

746

You strip your beaten opponent of her **splint armour (Defence +4)**, a **shortsword**, an **agate swan** pendant and an **iron fan**. You can also retrieve any weapon you gave her.

If you exchanged weapons before the duel	turn to **448**
If not	turn to **58**

747

It is a young man whose handsome face is set in a look of deep sorrow. He notices you without alarm. 'Ah, I thought the chancellor had sent away all my guards,' he says. 'But no, I see you are a stranger. What brings you to my palace?'

You are face to face with the Sovereign of Akatsurai. Turn to **37**.

748

The woman steps out from under a bridge. 'Didn't I tell you to deliver that?' she screams. She snatches the box from you and spits in your eye. By the time your vision clears, she has gone, taking the **lacquer box** with her.

Your eyes continue to sting for several days afterwards, and you never fully recover. Lose 1 Stamina point permanently, and then turn to **376**.

749

'Fair stands the wind for Yarimura!' cries the captain as you set sail. 'Sweeter to me than the taste of wine is the surge of the sea and the scent of brine!'

'You didn't know our skipper was a poet, did you?' asks the quartermaster. 'Er, did you pay the fee for your berth, by the way?'

Pay him if you haven't already, then roll two dice.

Score 2-10	You reach Yarimura safely	*The Plains of Howling Darkness* **280**
Score 11-12	The ship sinks	turn to **241**

750

'You've brought my children back to me!' weeps the man. 'How can I ever repay you?'

You wait a short while, but it seems the question was purely rhetorical. The fisherman takes his children home and you are left to resume your travels.

Turn to **514**.

751

By dint of intrigue, the artful Masayori has managed to raise himself to the position of minister of the interior. You run across him in the bark-roofed colonnade that leads from the outer palace to the rock garden.

'Ah, if it isn't our foreign friend,' he says in a tone like over-sugared sherbet.

You give the briefest of greetings and try to move past.

'A moment of your time, if you please. Lately the Sovereign's rest has been disturbed by an evil creature that descends by night to perch on the palace roof. Someone has to be found who can destroy this creature, and I took the liberty of putting your name forward.' He gives you a wide smile, reminiscent of a cat who has the key to the canary's cage.

Volunteer for the job	turn to **669**
Try to get out of it	turn to **384**

752

You retrieve your light source and rekindle it. There is no sign of your assailant, just a tiny broken clay figurine on the floor. You had better retrace your steps and either leave the tomb (turn to **583**) or try the other passage (turn to **604**).

753

In the topmost chamber you see a giant dozing in a chair. Treasure lies in heaps around his feet, but you must be careful not to wake him.

Make a THIEVERY roll at a Difficulty of 16 if you decide to risk it.

Successful THIEVERY roll	turn to **651**
Failed THIEVERY roll	turn to **534**
Back out and leave	turn to **501**

Adventure Sheet

NAME

PROFESSION

GOD

RANK

DEFENCE

ABILITY — **SCORE**

CHARISMA	
COMBAT	
MAGIC	
SANCTITY	
SCOUTING	
THIEVERY	

POSSESSIONS (maximum of 12)

STAMINA

| When unwounded | |
| Current: | |

RESURRECTION ARRANGEMENTS

MONEY

TITLES and HONOURS

BLESSINGS

Codewords

- ☐ Face
- ☐ Faded
- ☐ Farm
- ☐ Feral
- ☐ Fern
- ☐ Fire
- ☐ Fist
- ☐ Flag
- ☐ Fleet
- ☐ Flimsy
- ☐ Flood
- ☐ Flux
- ☐ Foment
- ☐ Fog
- ☐ Fortress
- ☐ Fossil
- ☐ Fracas
- ☐ Frame
- ☐ Fresco
- ☐ Fright
- ☐ Friz
- ☐ Frog
- ☐ Fruit
- ☐ Fuligin
- ☐ Fuchsia
- ☐ Fusty
- ☐ Future

Ship's Manifest

SHIP TYPE	NAME	CREW QUALITY	CARGO CAPACITY	CURRENT CARGO	WHERE DOCKED

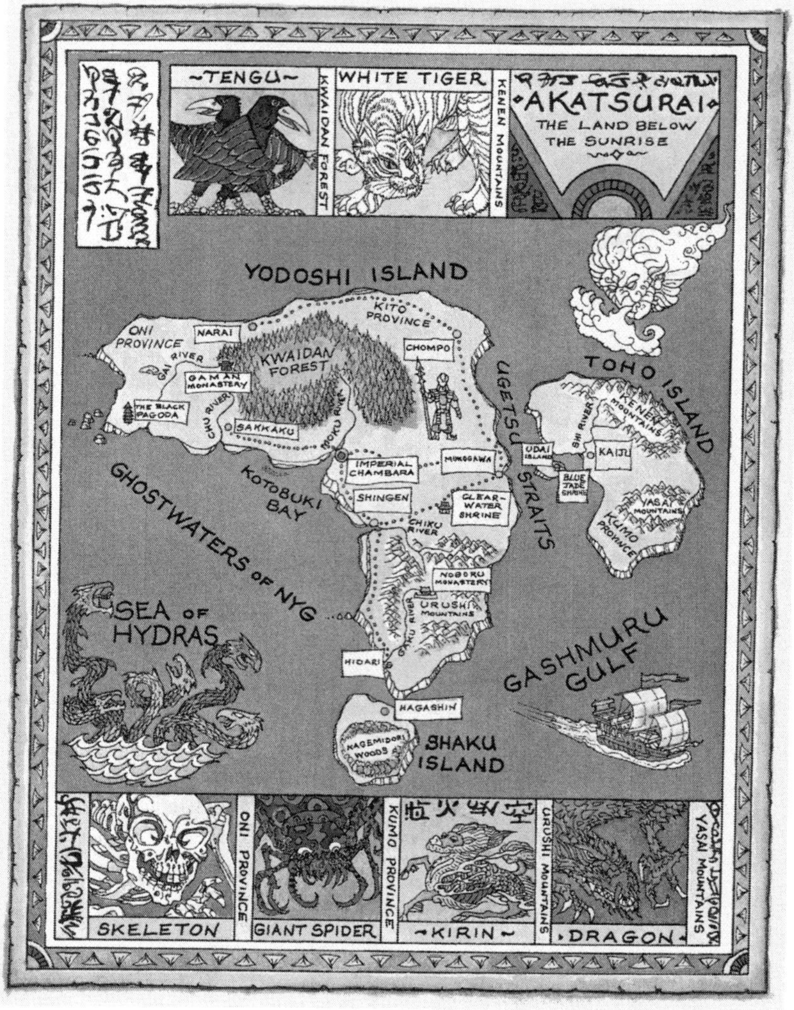
~TENGU~
WHITE TIGER
KWAIDAN FOREST
KENEN MOUNTAINS
AKATSURAI
THE LAND BELOW THE SUNRISE
YODOSHI ISLAND
KITO PROVINCE
ONI PROVINCE
NARAI
GAI RIVER
KWAIDAN FOREST
CHOMPO
GAMAN MONASTERY
THE BLACK PAGODA
CHU RIVER
SAKKAKU
MOKU RIVER
IMPERIAL CHAMBARA
MUKOGAWA
KOTOBUKI BAY
SHINGEN
CLEAR-WATER SHRINE
CHIKU RIVER
UGETSU STRAITS
TOHO ISLAND
KENEN MOUNTAINS
SHI RIVER
UDAI ISLAND
KAIJU
BLUE JADE SHRINE
YASAI MOUNTAINS
KUMO PROVINCE
GHOSTWATERS OF NYG
NOBORU MONASTERY
URUSHI MOUNTAINS
SAKU RIVER
SEA OF HYDRAS
HIDARI
GASHMURU GULF
HAGASHIN
HAGEMIDORI WOODS
SHAKU ISLAND
SKELETON
ONI PROVINCE
GIANT SPIDER
KUMO PROVINCE
KIRIN
URUSHI MOUNTAINS
DRAGON
YASAI MOUNTAINS

Starting characters

When starting Book Six *Lords of the Rising Sun*, you can create your own character as explained in the rules or you can pick one from the following pages. If you do that, transfer the details of the character you have chosen to the Adventure Sheet.

KINTU IRONHANDS

Rank: 6th
Profession: Warrior
Stamina: 27
Defence: 14
Money: 0 Shards

CHARISMA: 5
COMBAT: 8
MAGIC: 3
SANCTITY: 6
SCOUTING: 5
THIEVERY: 3

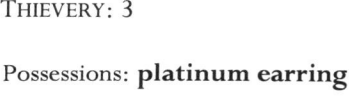

Possessions: **platinum earring**

Kintu believes weapons are for sissies and prefers to fight with his fists. People who have met Kintu describe him as constantly seething with proud anger, perhaps because he was unjustly exiled from his homeland. He has heard about the skilled martial artists of Akatsurai and intends to show them a thing or two.

ABRAXAS THE SEEKER

Rank: 6th
Profession: Priest
Stamina: 27
Defence: 10
Money: 0 Shards

CHARISMA: 6
COMBAT: 4
MAGIC: 5
SANCTITY: 8
SCOUTING: 6
THIEVERY: 2

Possessions: **platinum earring**

Although Abraxas has a strong spiritual sense, he questions whether the gods should be regarded as morally superior to mankind merely because they created the universe. His quest is for a religion that transcends man and the gods and instead aims for a single all-embracing truth. He believes he will find this in Akatsurai.

PANJANG OF THE EMERALD FLAME

Rank: 6th
Profession: Mage
Stamina: 27
Defence: 10
Money: 0 Shards

CHARISMA: 4
COMBAT: 4
MAGIC: 8
SANCTITY: 1
SCOUTING: 7
THIEVERY: 5

Possessions: **platinum earring**

A quietly competent young man, Panjang has dedicated himself to mastery of the mystic arts through a regime of fasting, meditation, and breathing exercises. He is intrigued by the mysteries of the Black Pagoda in Oni Province, but knows he must train hard before he will be ready to undertake the adventure.

ELEKTRA NEMORA

Rank: 6th
Profession: Troubadour
Stamina: 27
Defence: 11
Money: 0 Shards

CHARISMA: 8
COMBAT: 5
MAGIC: 5
SANCTITY: 5
SCOUTING: 4
THIEVERY: 6

Possessions: **platinum earring**

Elektra always has a sweet song on her lips to charm the people she meets. She believes all conflict is best settled by compromise, an attitude that makes her a natural diplomat and peacekeeper. As well as helping to calm the tense military situation in Akatsurai, she would like to play music at the court of the sovereign – a signal honour for a travelling minstrel.

SHIKIBU

Rank: 6th
Profession: Rogue
Stamina: 27
Defence: 12
Money: 0 Shards

CHARISMA: 7
COMBAT: 6
MAGIC: 6
SANCTITY: 2
SCOUTING: 4
THIEVERY: 8

Possessions: **platinum earring**

She's easy to miss, this slip of a girl clad all in black, with her voice like a wisp of silk. Then you miss your hoard of gold or silver too; when you look for Shikibu she's no longer there. She is determined to obtain the antique **golden katana** kept in the Imperial Palace in Chambara – and nothing will stop her.

ITHACUS

Rank: 6th
Profession: Wayfarer
Stamina: 27
Defence: 13
Money: 0 Shards

CHARISMA: 4
COMBAT: 7
MAGIC: 4
SANCTITY: 4
SCOUTING: 8
THIEVERY: 6

Possessions: **platinum earring**

A clever and resourceful survivor, Ithacus suffers from a restless nature that forces him to stay on the move. He can never hold on to treasure for very long because he is always planning and outfitting his next great expedition. His latest ambition is to scale the Kenen Mountains and see if the rumours of silver mines are true.

Printed in Great Britain
by Amazon.co.uk, Ltd.,
Marston Gate.